When

From the crinkled mind of Drake Vaughn

When the Devil Climbs

Copyright @ Drake Vaughn 2015

Moon Lily Press
1305 W. 7th St
Tempe, AZ 85281
query@kal-ba.com
www.cactusmoonpublications.com

Represented by: Melissa Carrigee; Loiacano Literary Agency
http://www.loiaconoliteraryagency.com/

Cover Design: J. Givner, Acapella Bookcover Design

ISBN 978-0692578780

Previous Novels by Drake Vaughn

The Zombie Generation

To Brad, for all your support through the good times and bad.
May your enthusiasm and pioneering spirit lead to great success.

Acknowledgments

I am indebted to the numerous people whose editorial input and support helped to transform this jumbled short story into a polished novel. First, a special thanks to Carole Cole, who organized the Writers' Workshop at the *World Horror Convention* in Portland, and to both Rain Graves and Carl Alves, who provided their professional critiques. Likewise, my utmost appreciation extends to Cher Eaves, the former editor of the *Tales to Terrify* podcast, who offered up her valuable time and input out of the kindness of her heart. I also can't forget all the beta readers from *Fictionpress* whose contributions are immeasurable: Frances Sebastian, Stephanie Kenific, Alexis Morgan, Wanda Lorelei O'Fallon, Drake Blaze, Lea Daniels, and proudnarutorfan1. Finally, I am eternally grateful to my agent, Melissa Carrigee, for her keen eye and editorial excellence, and Jeanie Loiacono, who assisted in finalizing this project. Thank you all!

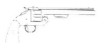 I heaved a deep breath and counted down from twenty, like the doc said I should anytime that evil hankering gored through me. On the other end of the call, Patti kept hollering on and on, so I wrenched the cell phone away from my ear. By the time my count reached zero, and I listened again, she still sounded peeved, but her words had lost a bit of their venom. Plus, my days of scrapping with Patti were long gone, so I held my tongue until her well could run dry.

"Okay," I said, as she paused for a breather. "If Tyler don't wish to talk, I won't force you to give him the phone."

"That's right," Patti almost shouted. "You're coming to visit on my terms and my terms alone."

"I can live with that, but can I at least have a brief chat with Tyler? Only if he wants to, of course."

"He can't talk now." Patti's tone sounded measured and succinct, similar to how one spoke when telling a stranger to skedaddle off your property. The evil hankering sparked anew and I kicked at the ground. The recent drought had scorched all but a few wispy strands of grass from the grubby patch in front of the bus station. As my foot dug into the parched earth, a burst of dust launched into the air.

Harley, seated on the curb beside me, fanned his face while spitting a cough. He shot me a hairy eyeball, forced another hack, and then lit up a smoke. I chuckled at this absurdity.

"You think that's funny?" Patti continued.

"Nope. That ain't what tickled me." I returned the stink eye to Harley, but he'd already turned his attention from me, slumping against the curb for a nap.

"Can I please speak to my son?"

"What you got to say that can't wait until Monday? Hell, it ain't like you two been overly chatty for many years."

"I aim to fix that." I kicked again, but this time the dust had enough common sense to remain fastened to the ground.

"I said I'd give you a chance, and unlike your lies, my word is sacred." Patti would've never lipped off like that when we were together, but again, maybe if she had, she wouldn't now be bunked up with that blonde-haired dunce Frazer. Tyler even called him "Dad," while I was just plain-old "Russ."

Who am I kidding? I would've done it all the same. Addiction bitched one like that.

"Thank you. I sure appreciate it," I said. "Can I tell Tyler how excited I am to see him before he splits for school?"

"He's already there." Patti snickered. "You should've called two hours ago."

I'd plum forgot about the time difference between California and Kansas. I fiddled at the frayed strap of my watch, which held about as tight as a wet sniffle to the end of a runny nose. I kept the cheap plastic watch for one reason, since Tyler chose it for me when he was four. At the time, the sparkling electronic screen had mesmerized him, but now, I couldn't look at the cruddy watch with its cracks and layer of grime without scowling.

"Make sure you have the correct time, since I won't be waiting for long on Monday," Patti continued.

"I'll be there. Right at 7:04." According to the schedule, that was the time the Greyhound would arrive in my former home of Gelder, Kansas. She'd have no problem finding the bus, since it was the only one that passed through that dinky town just twenty miles north of the Oklahoma border.

My journey, set for tomorrow morning, began here in Cuadrante, a slightly larger town situated in California's San Joaquin Valley. Though, for whatever Cuadrante offered in ways of modern conveniences, the stench expunged any and all benefits. I grew up acquainted with the peculiarities of farmlands, but nothing in Kansas could hold a candle to the overwhelming stench of manure needed to fuel California's fruitful agricultural needs. The odor wafted across the entire landscape as if God himself took a dump with every sunrise.

I couldn't wait to escape, and if all went right, four bus lines and fifty-two hours later, I'd wake up Monday morning to witness my son's beaming face for the first time in almost a decade. He was fourteen years old now, almost a man. I grinned.

"You promise?" Patti asked.

"I promise." My voice cracked. "This means the world to me and I can't wait to see you both."

"Hey, you need a tissue?" Harley sat up and wiped his sweat-drenched forehead. "Or maybe a tampon?" He poked his tongue through his outstretched fingers in a vulgar gesture.

"This is a private call." I kicked a mound of dust in his direction.

Harley staggered up, not taking the time to brush off the dirt clinging to him. He stretched his long twiggy arms, yawned, and I whiffed the familiar odor of his previous night's binge. He tugged on his oversized T-shirt, untucking a small portion that had jammed into the waistline of his torn blue-jeans. His only attempt to appear more proper was by spinning his baseball cap so the bill was face-forward. Not that our job required a dress code. None of us were that lucky.

"Private time's over. The wetback's here." Harley motioned toward Victor, our stout and muscular Mexican coworker now exiting from an arriving bus.

Victor took wide, rapid steps as he approached, swinging his arms out like he was carrying dumbbells. He sported the same get-up he had the previous month, a short-sleeved flannel shirt and baggy khaki pants. The typical cholo-style fueled Harley's racist comments, but I just ignored him. No matter how obnoxious, I figured it best to avoid ruffling feathers, doubly so in a crew of ex-convicts.

I told Patti I'd ring her tomorrow once I was on the road. She eased up a little, even wishing me a safe trip. Those were about the kindest words she'd uttered to me in many years. I jammed the phone into my pocked and greeted Victor as he strode up, using his respectful proper name as I always did.

Harley, on the other hand, dropped to his knees and prayed to the sky. He chanted something supposed to sound Latin, but came out like a toddler trying to recite Shakespeare. Victor and I didn't as much as smile, but Harley persisted.

"Ipso, facto, pharaoh, sparrow, my main bro in the big sombrero, Jesus, amen," he chanted, crossed himself, and stared up at Victor. "What? I thought you of all people would appreciate a prayer circle before work."

"Is no joke," Victor replied. He crossed himself, peered up, and mouthed a silent prayer.

"Yeah, this isn't a joke either. Licensed or not, you're chauffeur for the day." Harley flung a set of car keys at Victor, which bounced to his side and skidded across the chalky ground. Victor snarled.

"What? I thought you guys enjoyed baseball," Harley quipped. "Though, if you prefer el football, I can kick-"

"Slake's here," I interrupted as the company pickup truck entered the parking lot. The truck was unmistakable, not only from the pounding clatter heard from blocks away, but from the giant logo plastered to its side. The *Soaring Banners* poster displayed two giant eagles swooping through the sky barely obscuring the mismatching color of the doors from the main cabin.

Our boss, Slake, a chubby, middle-aged black man, sat in the driver's seat clutching the top of the steering wheel with an impeccable posture, almost like he believed this dilapidated ride was really a golden chariot. He slammed the pickup to a sudden halt, stroked his bushy goatee with one hand and motioned at Harley with the other.

"What did I do now?" Harley grumbled, before yelling "shotgun" as he staggered over to the pickup.

Slake said something to Harley, but I couldn't hear the words over the whirling clank of the engine. When it became apparent they were only discussing the details of this morning's job, rather than their typical bickering, I turned around. I caught Victor as he bent over to fetch the keys, and though the sight lasted for a flash, I got a good peek. Tucked into the small of his back was a gun.

The piece was dinky, likely a .22, but any weapon on a job spelled instant shit-canning. Guys had gotten bounced for bringing pocket-knives nevermind guns. And with that big-F for felony on his record, there was no way he had a license for it. One slip of the tongue and he'd be slammed back into a cage faster than it took to skim one of Soaring Banner's billboards.

I turned back toward Slake and Harley, but they were preoccupied with each other, failing to notice what I'd just seen. I took a step toward the pickup, paused, and glanced back at Victor. He noticed my look, but stood disinterested, oblivious or unconcerned at my discovery. I couldn't tell which.

Since Victor was a trainee, I didn't know him any better than a speckle on a cow's ass, but I reckoned he did not differ from the rest of us and needed the job. Make no mistake, hanging billboards ain't the most revered line of work, but again, us ex-convicts ain't the most revered folk neither.

Half of me wanted to sprint over to Slake and spill the beans. I'd reformed a bit over the years. Everything from quitting the sauce to being regular at church, even been keeping my cussing to a minimum, but I'd never played the snitch. I've lived under the philosophy that a man's got the freedom to hang his own signs and anyone who paints over it, is only asking to have his front teeth knocked in.

I took another peek at Victor, who yawned and scratched at his chin. I stepped closer toward the pickup and paused, picturing Tyler waiting for me at that bus station. One more shift to endure until my two-week vacation, was I ready to tussle with Victor? Maybe I hadn't seen right. Maybe I'd fallen into Harley's racist world and mustered up a reason to hate on him. That had to be it.

Harley grabbed my shoulder, and I lurched around. He jerked back like I would smack him. I realized I was holding up my arm. I dropped it to my side and exhaled. How long had I been standing there? I couldn't recall. My mind had fixated, spinning around and around. I hadn't zoned like that in many years. At least back then with the drugs, there'd been a reason.

"I need some coffee," I muttered.

"You need to drive." Harley chuckled and handed me a set of keys. They were for the cargo van, the same ones he'd pitched at Victor. I glanced where Victor had been standing, but the lot outside the bus station was empty. I turned toward Slake and the pickup, but he too was gone.

"Slake insisted Victor ride with him. Some shit about giving final instructions before sending him up today. What nonsense. If this job needed instructions, they wouldn't have us doing it." Harley chuckled again, and I followed him across the parking lot.

5

"You seem frazzled," he continued. "You know I was only messing with you earlier. No worries about getting emotional. I don't know how I'd act if a woman wouldn't let me see my boy. Probably strangle the bitch." Harley grinned as he made a choking motion.

"No, it ain't her fault," I replied. "Just karma I guess."

"That's nonsense. Karma don't exist. If it did, I sure wouldn't be stuck at this shitty job."

I nodded, and spotted the cargo van on the far side of the lot. Similar to the pickup truck, a poster with the Soaring Banner's logo was glued to the side, just above a large dent. I climbed into the driver's seat and unlocked the door for Harley.

"You really don't believe in karma?" I asked, while cranking the stuttering engine to life. It usually took a few tries to catch, but this time, the ignition sparked right away.

"The only mystical thing I've ever encountered is how every time I flip to the same movie on cable, it's always playing the exact same scene." Harley kicked his feet onto the dash and slouched into the seat.

"Sometimes I wonder." I flicked the turn signal and headed toward Highway 99.

"No wondering about it," Harley replied. "Karma doesn't exist, just rackets. Either you're in on the take or you're one of the suckers they prey upon. It's all tribal. Don't believe for one second that those Wall Street sharks are any less of a gang than the Brand or the Ride. Shit, at least prison gangs don't bullshit about their rackets. You're either in the tribe or the tribe is trying to get in you. That's the entire history of humanity in a nutshell."

"I never took you for a historian," I said.

"And I never took you for no fool." Harley punched into the air. "Rackets, the whole damn world's a racket. Hell, take this for example. While on parole, I got a ticket for an open container. One damn beer on my walk home from this mess of a job, but being I was a dangerous criminal mastermind, the state forced me to wear an ankle bracelet, and then they sent me a bill for it. When I refused to pay, they added penalties and late fees. Imagine that, on our salary. As if they're forcing us to steal to avoid going back to prison."

"But you can afford cable?" I asked, turning up the freeway's onramp. The cargo van shuttered, same as it did every time I pushed over forty mph, but at least it wasn't raining. On those days, we were lucky to even reach that speed.

"Who said jack-shit about paying for cable? You're missing the point," Harley continued. "No karma could justify taking away a son. I never had a dad and life sure as shit didn't make up for it by doing me any favors."

"It's not the lot in life that determines a man, but how he deals with it." That was one of Doc's favorite quotes. He sure had a ton of them. Most weren't worth a lick, but I pretended to believe. Sometimes pretending was about the best life had to offer. And anything was better than believing those evil hankerings.

"Don't get me wrong," Harley continued. "I don't want a pity party, but I just can't buy that there's any cosmic reason for preventing a kid from seeing his dad. Not unless you've killed someone else's kid. And I know you haven't done that, since I've seen your jacket and-"

"You have?" I interrupted. I had no idea our prison records were floating around the office for anyone to peep.

"Damn straight. Bad enough I'm stuck with a bunch a criminals, but I'm sure as shit not working with any cho-mo's." Cho-mo was prison slang for a pedophile, and though I'd had suspicions about guys I've worked with throughout the years, I never knew for sure.

"Linda keeps me informed," Harley continued. "She has a thing for me. I even let her blow me once in the photocopier room."

"You're fuller of shit than that pasture." I pointed out the window at a particularly stinky field of rye. "You had me until the Linda part."

"Okay, you got me. All that stuff is online nowadays. Don't think I haven't looked you up. But that's how I know, you don't deserve to be bitched like this. Fuck karma." Harley tapped me on the shoulder, flashing a sympathetic smile.

"I guess," I replied, and turned my attention back to the crowded highway.

He was correct about my prison record. Hell, maybe even correct about karma. Though he was mistaken about one thing, I had

7

killed a child. A couple if one wanted to get technical about it. And I wished that was the worst I'd done.

Friday 8:26 A.M.

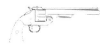Harley was passed-out cold. The cargo van reeked of booze from his snoring gasps, so I cracked the window. The thunderous noise of the highway filled the cab, but the hangover must've worked Harley over good, since he failed to stir as the cold air whipped through the cab. He didn't even react when his cell phone buzzed its vibrating ringer.

I almost reached to silence it, since the way it bucked across the armrest was distracting, but held back. Better for the cell to bounce onto the floor than deal with Harley. Anytime he came to work hung-over, which was quite often, a quarrel always trailed right behind like a busted taillight.

Just as Harley's phone settled, mine bellowed its electronic chime. I hated the chirping noise, but never changed the ringer, fearing if it was less jarring I might miss one of Tyler's rare calls. Plus, the phone was one of those cheap pre-paid ones, so there weren't a whole heap of musical options.

Someday, I'd save up and buy one of those fancy mini-computer phones and set it to play Kenny Roger's, Through the Years. Patti chose that song for our wedding and I wouldn't be surprised if Tyler had been conceived to it. That would sure be swell, but for now, I couldn't justify wasting what little cash I had on trivial things like a jukebox for my pocket.

I swerved a bit, but managed to remain in my lane as I hit the answer button. I hated chatting at the wheel, since nothing was more obnoxious than a daredevil whipping through traffic with a robot glued to his ear. When I was a long-haul trucker, I'd holler a warning on the CB to box-in these menaces, but those days of squabble-seeking were long over.

As the phone connected, Slake's gruff voice motor-boated on the other end. He didn't even start with as much as a "hello" before the berating began. He demanded to know why Harley hadn't answered. I told him "cause this is my phone," but the joke crashed, landing on an icy silence, and he insisted I pass the cell to Harley. Even though I was at the wheel, I replied that Harley was busy driving and I could relay any relevant info. He chewed on this for a long moment like a stale piece of gum. After a second, Slake relented, and told me the exit for Big Bertha was closed. That was the nickname for this morning's massive billboard job-schedule. He sounded affronted as if the sole purpose for the closure was to rile him up. But again, that was typical Slake. I bet if he scored a date with a supermodel, when she cleared only half of her dinner plate, he'd bicker with the restaurant over paying the full bill.

Before I could interrupt and suggest we take the service road south of the proceeding exit, Slake beat me to the punch, proposing the same thing, yet somehow managing to turn it into an argument. Likewise, he insisted on texting a map of the new route, even though I'd driven up and down that service road since before Big Bertha was even constructed. I relented though and told him to send it to Harley's phone, since I didn't want the extra texting charges.

A minute later, Harley's phone buzzed again, but neither one of us gave it a second glance. When I exited Highway 99, the off-ramp spun around into a choppy dirt road. Harley sprang up in his seat, bounding to attention. He glanced out the window with a curious stare, and I said "detour" before he could ask.

"Not a good one," Harley replied as we pulled up to the T-intersection of the service road. A police cruiser sat parked at the crossing, blocking all traffic. The blue and red beams of the light bar zigzagged atop the cruiser, their brightness dampened in the gleam of the morning sun.

The company pickup truck flanked the cruiser, with both Slake and Victor on the dirt road beside it. An officer stood with his arms crossed, nodding as Slake talked. From the way Slake swung his arms around like a bat, I figured the only way he was going to drive down that service road was in the back of the cruiser.

To the officer's credit, he must've sized up Slake same as we did, as a cell warrior, mouthy and volatile when safely locked up, but if that door should crack, he'd zip-it real quick. The officer continued to nod at every insult, waiting patiently for Slake's steam to evaporate. I parked and glared out the window, anticipating I'd be the next on Slake's list of chew toys.

"I can't comprehend how an entire road can be closed and you won't give me a reason," Slake yelled. "This isn't a dictatorship. I have a right to know."

"Will he give it a rest?" Harley rubbed his eyes. "Some of us are trying to nap."

"I want your badge number and the name of your superior officer," Slake continued. "I'm not leaving until I find out what's going on."

"Seriously? What's his deal?" Harley straightened and punched at the dash.

"We have a job to do. Unlike you, we can't just sit around inconveniencing people for a living. Look, I have a crew who depend..." Slake motioned toward us.

"Oh no, he's not dragging me into his nonsense." Harley yanked at the door. Before I could reach to stop him, he lunged out. I followed as Harley stomped toward the others.

"You don't belong here," Harley shouted, while pointing at Victor. "Go back to the pickup."

Victor strode off without protest as Harley whirled his outstretched finger toward Slake. A peculiar expression splashed over Slake, one I'd never witnessed before, half confusion, half seething anticipation. His face crunched as he turned around.

"And youuuu..." Harley stretched the word. "I don't know. What were we talking about?"

"Do you have something serious to say?" Slake asked. He tapped his side with an open palm, waiting for an answer. Harley turned to the officer and squared his shoulders.

"You know anyone I can talk to about a speeding ticket-"

"Unbelievable," Slake interrupted. "Don't pay him any mind. Time for the adults to talk, so turn around and go back."

"It's time all of you returned to your vehicles," the officer chimed in. He uncrossed his arms and placed his hands onto his utility belt. Not quite on his gun, but close enough for me to step back. Slake likewise shuffled to the side. Harley remained cemented in place.

11

"Yeah, of course," Harley said. "Just back up your cruiser and we'll be on our way."

"I'm not one of your taco jockeys. You don't give the orders. Understand?" This time the officer pawed his gun. Harley beamed, grinning a full mouth of stained yellow teeth.

"Yes, sir. Orders received." Harley shot the officer a salute.

"Move along." The officer returned the salute, chuckled, and motioned for us to leave.

"That's our answer." Harley winked at Slake. "By the way, officer, is the trouble with the road north or south of here?"

"North, but the whole area's closed." The officer gestured, but I spotted no sign of construction or anything other than the barren dirt road.

"That's good," Harley replied. "We're heading south to swap out the sign on that billboard, so we'll avoid the trouble." Harley motioned at Big Bertha. The outline of its towering frame peeked in the horizon. I sometimes forgot the billboard's massive size and wouldn't have guessed we could spot it from this distance. Though, outside of the heat, the morning was spectacular, not a cloud in the sky to obscure the visibility.

"That's why we need to drive that way," Slake chimed in.

"The officer said the road's closed, so the road's closed," Harley replied. "I know a detour. Follow me."

Harley turned, and crunched off toward the cargo van with hurried steps. A trail of dust spouted behind him, and I heard Slake mutter something undecipherable. I didn't wait for a translation and trotted after Harley.

The van was already rolling backward as I jumped into the passenger-seat. Harley spun the wheel and his grin hiked high across his face. He waved at the officer, who gestured a two-finger salute in return.

"Who does he think he is?" As Harley asked the question, his lips failed to inch away from their smirking position, even though the indignation in his tone was palpable.

"No!" I protested, but Harley's hands clutched the wheel tighter as he spun it around. Instead of turning back toward the highway, he swung the van in a full circle, so we were facing the officer again.

Harley slammed the gas. The van squealed, gunning toward the cruiser. The officer stood frozen, even his jovial expression remained plastered to his face. Just before colliding, Harley cranked the wheel and lurched onto the shoulder. The van shuttered as we squeezed onto a weedy patch of grass between the road and a tattered fence. The wooden beams blurred as they zipped by, inches away. I bounced in the seat, clutching the armrest to brace myself. The van tipped onto two wheels as bucking back onto the service road.

Harley whooped as the wheels bounced down with a grinding squeal. The engine screeched as if in agony, but Harley didn't ease up any on the gas. I stared out the side-view mirror, but couldn't spot anything behind us through the hazy cloud of dust. I managed an exhale and pawed at my seatbelt. My hands shook while locking it in place.

"That will teach him for being racist toward our crew." Harley beamed as he rapped his fingers against the steering wheel. "Only I get to do that."

Friday 8:39 A.M.

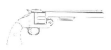 Unwilling to glance behind us a second time, I kept my eyes locked onto Big Bertha, figuring a blaring siren would be a clear enough signal of any pursuit. So far, I heard nothing other than the crunch of the dirt road as we sped closer to the billboard. Big Bertha began as only an unfocused outline, but after a minute, it sprang into view like one of those time-lapse videos of a plant sprouting. Even after all these years, I still marveled at the way it floated over the surrounding farmlands like a glistening magic carpet.

The billboard spawned over eighty feet into the air, by far the tallest in our region. The reason for its massive height was due to some local regulations requiring it to be recessed quite a distance from the highway. I could never understand why, since the only land between it and the highway was a lot full of weedy shrubs. This jungle was so thick and overgrown that at the base of the unipole (which was the name for the vertical steel pole connecting the platform to the ground) it completely obscured the highway.

Seeing that today was Victor's first time climbing, Big Bertha was chosen to break him in. Soaring Banners did that for all the newbies, figuring if they could handle its towering summit, then all the other billboards would be a cinch in comparison. I was sure grateful Big Bertha wasn't yet a blueprint when I started, otherwise, court ordered or not, I might not have been able to handle the job.

Don't mistake that for being nostalgic, since those days were pretty rotten as well. Nobody had any training or safety lessons, instead they just plopped a hardhat on you and said "Good Luck!" before scooting you on your merry way. This changed a couple years back when a fellow named Richard Lamar fell forty feet to his death during his first week. Since then, OSHA had been sledgehammering our asses in place, so it was all by the books now.

"I didn't think Slake had it in him," Harley said, while glaring into the side-view mirror. He chuckled and slapped the steering wheel. "I can't wait for him to hate on me, especially after I saved us a half-hour detour."

"I'm more worried about the cop," I said.

"Why? He's not there," Harley replied.

Curiosity beat out my stiff-neck lock on Big Bertha, so I swallowed and rubbed my hands together, forcing myself to peek into the mirror. Harley was correct. The pickup with Slake and Victor were the only ones behind us. They were quite a distance back, since Harley hadn't eased one bit on the gas, but the dust had cleared enough to spot nobody in pursuit behind them.

"He might be calling for backup." I stared some more, but spotted nothing other than the empty dirt road. Even the cruiser's flashing light bar had bleached away into the burnt dust-brown landscape.

"Get real. He doesn't want the trouble. I could tell that when he allowed Slake to lip off for so long." Harley exhaled a heaving gasp, so I knew he was a bit less flippant about the possibility of a police chase than his nonplussed voice let on.

"I guess," I replied, still uncertain the entire affair was settled. Cops aren't known for their ability to dismiss a slight, and running a blockade was a damn big slight. The dead-eyed man who'd followed me sure waited a long while before pouncing, so one could never be certain. On the other hand, someone sent this officer to patrol an empty dirt road, so maybe Harley was onto something.

That certainly seemed the case as we parked in a dirt lot beside Big Bertha, no trouble in sight. That was discounting Slake. Harley was right about that too, since Slake whizzed past at a breakneck speed, which was unusual considering he never so much as tempted the speed limit. As he hurtled past, missing us by inches, Harley joked that the cargo van did need a second dent to match the first, but I didn't laugh.

Slake ground the pickup to a halt about fifty feet away, turning around so he was facing toward us. Harley shot him a wave, which went unreturned. Slake scowled an unblinking gaze, his eyes bulging like he was exhaling through them. Harley yawned, but knew better than to break off this stare-down. I was thankful he didn't, since Slake appeared ready to charge toward us like a tank.

This standoff lasted for over a minute, until Slake stroked his long goatee. He must've muttered something to Victor because a moment later Victor exited the pickup. He crossed the dirt lot with hurried steps, and stopped outside of Harley's window. It remained rolled-up as Harley continued to stare straight ahead. Victor knocked once, which prompted Harley to light a cigarette. He cracked the window just enough for the smoke to ripple out.

"Slake say—" Victor began.

"A bacon, egg, and cheese sandwich on a Kaiser roll," Harley interrupted. "And make sure when you order the coffee, they leave some room at the top to add cream. I can't stand it when it overflows."

"He want you to know if you pull another stunt—"

"That was no stunt. That was the real deal, chalupa." Harley took another drag from his cigarette. The window bawled a rasping creek as he rolled down the remaining portion. He exhaled a mouthful of musty smoke, tinged with a boozy aftertaste. If it bothered Victor, he failed to show it, and instead leaned closer. With one hand, he grabbed the window frame, while the other reached toward his back. Seeing this, and remembering the gun, I lurched up in my seat.

"My ticker's not good enough to eat that crap," I said. Both Harley and Victor spun in my direction, shooting identical stink-eyes. I continued anyway. "Get me a yogurt and whole wheat toast. Low-fat yogurt if they have it. Better yet, that Greek kind."

"Yeah, I'm sure you love the Greek," Harley quipped, causing even Victor to laugh at the obvious sex joke. I was just grateful Victor's arm had fallen to his side.

"What do you care what I eat?" I asked. My diet had been one of the numerous parts of my life needing tinkering once I was released. So I'd swapped out fried foods and cheese for goopy plates of brown rice and vegetables. I found pushing away from the table was the best form of exercise, and the more I exercised, the more those evil hankerings stayed in check.

"Shit, I'd rather die than eat that," Harley replied, turning again toward Victor. "Make sure to add some special sauce to Russ' food. Needs that extra protein."

"I give your food a special sauce." Victor spat a loogie to the side, but Harley only chuckled.

"Go on now, chop-chop," Harley continued. "Best be quick or we'll sic la migra on your ass."

Victor turned to leave, but Harley yelled out to stop him.

"Get me a yogurt and whole wheat toast as well." Harley shot me a wink. "Might help with this headache."

As Victor strode back over to the pickup, Slake remained propped in place. Hell, Big Bertha appeared to have more sway than his stiff posture. He only broke his transfixed stare after a brief conversation with Victor, and even then, his movements were slow and deliberate. Most days, when handing over the funds for breakfast, he flipped the bills down like he was betting on a cockfight, but now, he peeled each one in a plodding bank teller-like motion.

Victor nodded, collected the money from Slake, and swapped places with him in the driver's seat. The pickup lurched backward as Victor sped off for the breakfast run. Slake stood for a moment in the dirt lot, peered in either direction, and started toward us in a measured pace. The fever splashed across his constricted face made me wish I was the one heading out for the breakfast run.

"We should meet him halfway," I muttered.

Harley flicked the remainder of his cigarette out the window, and kicked his feet up onto the dash. I yanked on the door handle twice before realizing the lock was engaged. Slake was about ten feet from the van by the time I raced out. He stopped as I intercepted his path, but eyed Harley like a cat on the prowl.

"We working the steps today, Slake? If we are to live, we have to be free of anger," I quoted from the Big Book. Slake sneered, gritting his teeth. I knew that expression well, having worn it most of my life like an old pair of favorite sneakers. I'd been trying to support Slake ever since his return from rehab, parroting all the pithy quotes I could recall from *Alcoholics Anonymous* and the good old Doc.

"I don't need any of your A.A. crap right now," Slake answered. "What I need is five minutes alone with that clown."

"I ain't stopping you," I said. "But remember, you can walk away."

"You know I can't." Slake stepped to my side.

"Okay," I replied, gesturing for him to continue. "I know I can't control others, only how I feel about them."

Slake spun back around. "Cut that Zen shit like you have the whole world figured out. Best examine your life before lipping off advice about mine. Just because you can't be a daddy to your son, doesn't mean you can pull that father knows best crap with me."

This time counting down didn't work. I zapped into a flutter of motion, not realizing I'd raised my arm until Harley grabbed me from behind. Unbeknownst to me, he'd crept up on us. He wrapped his arm around my waist, bear hugging me in place. My feet kicked as he raised me into the air.

"I think you're onto something with this diet. You barely weigh a thing." Harley released his grasp, and I plopped onto the ground. He kept one hand on my waist in case I should buck up a second time, but the moment had passed. I cursed for allowing Slake to nail through me like that. The stress of the upcoming trip must've rawed me more than I understood. I closed my eyes and began the countdown.

Slake tore into Harley good, hollering this manner of insult or that. Unlike me, Harley grinned the entire time, which helped crank up Slake's fury. He yelled so much, I almost failed to notice when some spit shot out and clung to his goatee like a long piece of string. When I did spot it, I couldn't help but grin. Slake's steam eventually petered out and his tirade ended with a typical, "Get to work!"

"I'm not doing a thing until the wetback arrives with the grub," Harley replied, baiting Slake for another round.

"His name is Victor," Slake shouted back. "Cut the racist shit. One more word and I'm sending you back to the office and you can spend the next week discussing tolerance and PC crap with Linda."

"Sounds like a promotion," Harley quipped. "But check the time, we're not on the clock yet."

I glanced at my watch, noting we had exactly two minutes until nine. Slake threw his hands into the air.

"See that?" he asked, pointing north. "We have a storm rolling in. Can we just get this done before it arrives?"

I stared in the direction where he was pointing and spotted a haze cresting in the horizon. It floated just above the tree-line, muddied and appearing like smog. I glanced to either side, noting no other clouds. Odd. When a storm or fog rolled in, it typically spanned the entire landscape, but this cloud appeared only in one section, past a nectarine orchard.

"That's no storm," Harley said. "Looks like smoke."

"No, that's dust," I added, noting the haze's murky brown color. "Maybe that cop called backup and they're kicking it up while driving here."

"The service road's over there." Slake pointed to the left of the dusty haze. The sky above the road sparkled blue, lacking a single blemish. The haze spread out, spanning a distance much wider than the road.

"Dollar to none, that's the reason why the road was closed," Harley said. "Probably shut down the area for some so-called training exercises, which in reality consists of cops riding around shooting guns from ATVs."

"Bastards," Slake cursed. "That sure looks like it. Imagine closing down an entire road just so they could horse around."

"There are sure worse ways to spend a Friday at work, such as hanging billboards," Harley replied.

"I don't hear any gunshots," I added.

"Doesn't matter," Slake said. "They don't answer to me, but you two do, so get to work!"

"Yes, sir." Harley reached over to fist-bump Slake, but was left hanging. Slake stormed off to do whatever Slake did, mostly calling folks on his cell. Harley shrugged, and headed toward the rear of the cargo van. He tugged on the ladder, and I trooped over to assist him.

We carried the ladder toward the base of the unipole, where it attached to one welded into the side. Most billboards were designed so their ladders ended about twenty feet from the ground, a deterrent to any kids or miscreants who desired to climb up. Not that this stopped everyone, since I'd discovered my fair share of beer bottles, condoms, and cigarette butts while on various jobs. Once, I even had to call the fire department on a belligerent drunk who'd refused to climb down.

"Hey, thanks for having my back," I said, as we clipped our ladder into the one attached to the unipole. "Slake really got to me with that kid comment."

"Don't worry about it," Harley replied. "Us gringos got to stick together in case shit wilds out. If you hadn't noticed, El Mariachi has been packing heat all week long."

"What?" I asked, pretending I hadn't spotted Victor's gun at the bus station.

"Don't get steamed, I brought protection." Harley raised his t-shirt and showed a Sig P290 tucked into his belt. Small, but the 9mm delivered a mammoth punch. Harley smirked as he ran his fingers over the gun's slick black side.

"Maybe we should give Slake a heads up about Victor," I suggested.

"You can't be serious. Tell that rat and you might as well plaster it across the damn billboard. No, people like you and me know how to handle our business." Harley placed his arm around my shoulder. "I trust you can hold your mud."

That was prison slang for not snitching. I nodded, and Harley clutched me tighter. I peered at the ground, kicked at a few pebbles, and struggled to find the right words. Harley's racist coalition provided no comfort and went against all my beliefs, but I remained unwilling to bring the situation to a head. I peeked down at my watch, counting off the remaining hours until the end of this cluster-fuck of a day.

"Time to get to work," I replied.

Friday 9:32 A.M.

 Slake tapped his watch with an irregular beat. He grunted and glared over at Harley. I chewed the final crumbs of my whole-wheat toast, pretending to be oblivious of the time. Harley barely cracked his yogurt and, instead of eating, he used his spoon to pantomime a riotous tale he'd heard from a cellmate. He pointed the spoon into the air and hollered "Stick 'Em Up!"

"So as the tellers were filling his bag with cash," Harley continued. "A woman in the corner stood up. My cellmate yelled at her to drop back onto her fat ass, but this set her off real good. She screamed that he was the reason for her fat ass, which he didn't quite understand."

"Okay, enough monkey-mouthing. Time to get to work," Slake interrupted the story. Harley dipped his spoon into the yogurt, swallowed a gulping bite, and continued.

"Then it hit him. This broad did know him and must've recognized his voice. He recalled crashing at her place a few years back and bouncing after hearing about a bun in her oven. Knock it and rocket was far wiser than paycheck docking it."

I chuckled at the expression, while Slake kept rapping at his watch. Victor stood with his arms crossed, glancing up at Big Bertha every minute or so. He appeared disinterested in Harley's story, but at the same time, from his edgy stare, I figured he wasn't itching to climb anytime soon.

"Of course, he claimed she had the wrong guy, but this crazy bitch insisted he raise his mask to prove it. He refused, so she stormed over, screaming how she had to take double-shifts at the Golden Corral to make ends meet. As soon as the teller handed over the bag, he tossed her a wad of bills, just to get her to shut up."

"Now!" Slake insisted.

"And get this." Harley rolled his eyes. "She then thanked him for the money, said she missed him, and asked if he wanted to meet up for drinks sometime. And the fool agreed. The idiot scribbled his phone number onto one of the bills."

"What a romantic," I quipped. Slake, less amused, kicked up a cloud of dust. Victor wheezed and covered his mouth with a napkin.

"I was just saying what this yogurt needed was some dirt," Harley added. "Can't make it taste any worse."

"Break's over." Slake motioned to kick a second time.

"You have to give us time to finish," Harley protested. He waved his half-eaten yogurt as proof of this assertion, but he was the only one still working on breakfast.

"Call your union rep." Slake sneered. "Oh, that's right. I'm the one who makes the calls. So get your ass in gear or you'll have plenty of time to eat while wearing peels."

The idea of going back to prison must've struck Victor hard, since he bounced to attention like being probed during a strip search. Harley simply grinned since his parole days were long over. At worst, he'd be fired to a seat on his couch. Not bad, if he really had cable.

"I haven't got to the moral yet." Harley gulped the yogurt like he was guzzling a drink.

"What's that?" I asked.

"True love conquers all?" Victor guessed.

"Are you kidding, chalupa?" Harley replied. "True love doesn't even cover the electric bill."

"No parole for the stolen hearts?" I added my own guess.

"Geez, enough with the interruptions," Harley said. "Anyhow, I don't tell stories with morals. So as I was saying—"

"That's it." Slake snatched out his cell phone. "I'm calling some parole officers if you all don't follow me."

Victor trailed like a shadow as Slake stomped toward the cargo van. Harley rolled his eyes and tossed the empty yogurt container on the ground. Without even peering back, Slake yelled "and pick up after yourself!" Harley shot me a dumbfounded glance, as if he believed Slake had eyes in the back of his head. I returned the look, but considering the cluttered state Harley kept the cargo van, it wasn't much of a guess for Slake.

"What's his deal?" Harley asked, as we paced a few yards behind the others. "Guess he hasn't had his morning pick-me-up yet. Good to the first drop." He sniffed and rubbed his nose.

"Not funny," I replied, but smiled at Harley's drug reference.

"At least when Slake was a cokehead, he had a reason for being an anal-retentive dick. It's always the ones who've fucked up their lives the most who pretend their shit don't stink after finally learning to wipe their ass." Harley heaved a deep yawn, and though he'd had breakfast and coffee, his breath still reeked of booze.

"I don't think you should be the one to judge." I waved the stench from my nose. Harley stretched his arms while walking and even his pits smelled like a distillery.

"Got a mint or something?" he asked.

"Won't do no good. You've got the sweat-stench. Must've been saucing pretty hard."

"Early start to the weekend," Harley said, sniffing at his armpit. "You're messing with me. I took a shower."

"Won't help the sweat-stench. The alcohol oozes through the pores. You can't do nothing about the smell."

"Then why'd you bring it up?" Harley lit a cigarette and waved it attempting to mask the odor.

As we approached the cargo van, Harley tossed away the cigarette and slapped Victor across the back. "Been thirty days. Time to whip off that training bra."

"Get your hands off me," Victor replied, shrugging away.

"What's the deal? This should be a cinch compared to scaling that border fence." As Harley dropped his arm, his hand came dangerously close to touching the gun tucked into Victor's belt.

"You want me to show you the deal, mamón?" Victor stepped back and squared his feet.

"Mamón." Harley chuckled while saying the word. "I like that one, mamón. Easier than yesterday's jibber-jabber. What was it? Poncho Rastafarian or something?"

"Pinche racista," Victor replied. "It mean fucking racist."

"That's enough, you two," Slake commanded. He yanked a toolbox from the rear of the van and dropped it beside them with a tinny clunk.

"That's why I love this job. So multicultural," Harley replied. "I learn something new every day."

"I'll learn you, if you don't cut that shit out," Slake said. "Take those."

"Come on. He hasn't taught me how to say your breath reeks of Tapatío and moldy tacos yet." Harley grinned, but when Slake spun around, Harley hoisted the toolbox into the air.

"Maybe when I do enough blow to pop my brain like a zit, I can win carte blanche on being an asshole," Harley muttered, as he strode off toward the unipole.

When Victor returned from the breakfast run, he parked in the same spot Slake had parked for our faux-Mexican standoff; probably because he considered that the norm. It was a bit of a hike to the unipole, but after all the morning's drama, it came as a relief to haul the tools over in silence. Being so recessed from the highway, I didn't fret about leaving the van unlocked. We'd see anyone coming for miles. Plus, considering Soaring Banners employees, if anything grew legs and went missing, it will likely be an inside job.

We arrived at Big Bertha's base and I peered up the towering column. I hated training days, since listening to Slake ramble about the differences between saddle beams and purlins was worse than waiting around in a holding pod to be processed. At least there you could take a seat. Swapping out a billboard usually took around an hour at most, but with Slake's drilling instructions, the time could be triple that.

There was one perk to training-days and the sole reason anyone signed up for them. That was scoring Ground Man. While everyone else climbed up top, the Ground Man stayed with the cargo van, mostly napping the day away. It was like winning the lotto and I can't say I wasn't a tad jealous when Harley netted the Ground Man, but from the way he kept mouthing off, I doubted he keep the position for long.

Slake's training began by passing around hardhats. I plopped mine on with no second thoughts, but Harley just tossed his from hand to hand. Probably figured he didn't need one because he would spend most of the day conked out inside the van. When Slake glared over, Harley tipped his baseball cap as if that was an appropriate substitution. Slake yanked the cap from Harley's head.

"Hey, give that back," he protested.

"I'm not getting written up for something so stupid," Slake said. "Any more lip and Russ will take over for Ground Man."

"Fine," Harley relented. "At least be careful with my hat. It's vintage."

"Terry's Hardware?" Slake read the logo printed on the hat.

"I picked it up at a second-hand shop for a quarter, so like I said, it's vintage."

Slake shook his head and flipped the hat upside-down. "Deposit all cell phones, smokes, dip, loose change, whatever. Empty your pockets, gentlemen."

"You joking?" I asked.

"Yeah, are you the TSA now?" Harley added.

"New policy. There's been complaints about guys making calls while up on the deck. Today there will be no distractions, period. Don't make me ask twice." Slake dug into his pocket, being the first to deposit a cell phone into the hat.

"I have a kid—" I began.

"Safety is the highest priority," Slake interrupted. "Best empty your pockets, or I'll grab that phone and make a call to the office."

That jolted Victor into action and he placed a cell along with a crumpled pack of gum into the hat. The one item I wished he'd removed, remained firmly wedged to his back. I stood with my hands locked behind me. Not that I expected Tyler to call, but if he did, I wouldn't miss it for this nonsense.

Slake exhaled, easing his tone. "Harley will be down here in case of any emergencies. I don't make the rules. Please, can we just get through today without any more gruff?"

"Fine," I replied. It would only be for a couple hours and Tyler wasn't set to get out of school until three, one our time, so I placed my phone into the hat along with a crinkled receipt for last night's dinner at Denny's.

"I almost forgot." Harley tossed an unopened condom into the hat. "Or you guys can take it up with you if you feel the urge to join the mile-high club. Like Slake said, safety first."

"Take your damn vintage hat." Slake shoved it at Harley. Harley shuffled through the contents and removed Slake's cell. He pretended to press the buttons like he was snooping, but when Slake didn't pay him any mind, he lost interest and dropped the hat next to the tools. He then grabbed for a safety harness.

"Might want this for when you fall." Harley shoved the safety harness to Victor, but when Victor spun and jerked up his arms, Harley wrenched back. "Jumpy, I see. Well, put that on outside your clothes, that way when you shit yourself, the mexcrement doesn't get all over."

"No worries, bolillo. I aim for you." Victor yanked the safety harness from Harley, and blew a raspberry.

"That's enough, chuckleheads," Slake interrupted. "Russ, go climb up and secure the lines."

I tossed on a safety harness, tightening it around my waist. The lanyard dangled down my back and I clipped the latch to the end onto the safety line. That way if I fell, the lanyard would break my momentum. Likewise, there was a rope catch, designed so the safety line would only run in one direction. To go down, I had to raise a small release on the side of the catch.

The rungs baked my fingers as I climbed, already sizzling from the dry morning heat. Some fellas wore gloves, but my calloused hands had worn-in years ago, so I hardly noticed. Plus, considering Soaring Banners' track record, I knew better than to place my trust into the equipment. That be about as silly as using my tattered wristwatch to rappel down.

The wind whipped like a lasso, offering a modicum of relief from the heat as I reached the top. Climbing was always easier than the descent, and even considering Big Bertha's height, I managed to arrive at the deck in next to no time. The safety harness had two carabineers, that way I was never dangling free while switching safety lines. I clipped into the line attached to the deck before releasing the one on the ladder. Once my feet planted firmly onto the metallic beams, I gave both lines a firm tug. They snapped into place like rubber bands, stiff and secure.

The wind shrieked a pitter-patter of gusting exhales, suffocating any other sound. So instead of shouting down the all-clear, I flashed Slake a thumbs up. He waved a confirmation, before assisting Victor onto the ladder. Victor gazed up at me as he clung like a barnacle to the rungs. He appeared to mutter a prayer, releasing his grasp for a moment to cross himself before climbing.

He moved at a slow and measured pace, unlike most of the newbies who pretended they had it conquered on day one. Harley shouted something I couldn't decipher, but when he rattled the ladder while holding it, I knew he was taunting Victor. Slake followed Victor up the ladder and booted Harley's hands with a firm kick while ascending. That put an instant halt to the shenanigans.

Big Bertha comprised of three platforms, one in front of the sign (the outer-deck) and two in the rear. The ladder on the column fed into the two rear decks, and I stood on the bottom one, called the lower deck. The one at the top rear of the sign was the upper-deck.

I scanned the platform, noting a thick layer of bird droppings scattered across it. This was hardly unusual, some billboards were so revolting that bird shit crusted them like a covering of snow. I remembered Big Bertha being tall enough to deter most birds, so I peered around searching for a nest to explain the mess. That was when I spotted the dust. I'd almost forgotten all about it.

I'd expected the cloud to have smothered out by now, yet it persisted, tipping above an almond grove to the northeast. As it zigzagged along, I realized we were correct in our earlier assessment. This was not weather, but something zipping across the fields, kicking up dirt in its wake. I couldn't understand. I would've been able to spot a car, even from this distance. To span such a wide girth, it would've had to been an entire motorcade, yet I saw only dust.

I tracked north up the service road, able to spot the police cruiser we'd raced past earlier. It was a bit blurry, but the shadows provided enough of an outline to distinguish it. Hell, I could even make out the faint trace of the officer propped against its side. I knew I should've found relief seeing him parked there, but just recalling the incident made my heart flutter. I grabbed the edge of the railing and leaned out for a better glance.

Whatever was kicking up the dust was moving west, straight toward the service road. If it broke from the almond grove, I'd have a clean view, mystery solved. I watched as the brown dust sprang over the treetops, thinning into an unfocused haze a moment later. It reminded me of an old-timey train spewing up its exhaust.

The police officer must've sensed the dust was moving in his direction, since he jerked upright and flung open the cruiser's door. The flashing light-bar switched off, allowing for a better glance. He held something in his right hand, a walkie-talkie from the look of it, but I couldn't be sure. He crossed into the middle of the service road as the dust rolled closer.

The bushes at the side of the road swayed, but this could've been on account of the gusting wind. I was about to chalk it up to just that when a pudgy animal darted through the shrubbery out onto the street. The officer straightened and waved his arms. The animal galloped on stout legs, wiggling its rear like a pendulum. Its head was stained black with floppy ears and a dark streak running down its portly rear. If it'd been all pink, I might've identified it immediately. It was only after the silly thing trampled past the officer's side, I recognized it as a pig.

The officer remained cemented in place as the pig continued to dash down the service road. A dozen more pigs darted out from the brush trailing the first. A thick smattering of dust spewed up from their trampling hooves, obscuring the officer as they darted to either side of him. The wind smoothed, easing its howling whispers, but the silence added to the peculiarity of the scene unfolding below. A steamy line of sweat exploded across my brow and I whisked it away with the rear of my hand. When I peered again, the officer had disappeared.

My eyes locked onto the cruiser, wondering if he'd dashed inside to avoid the stampede. The doors were closed and it appeared empty, so that didn't seem correct. Plus, I'd glanced away for just a second and would've spotted him running; even through the dusty haze. More pigs exploded from the almond grove, all of them following the others in an endless flood. At the spot where the officer had been standing, a group assembled. They lined around in a circle, nose to nose, picking at the ground.

I blinked. No way. I could see enough through the shadows to recognize them as domesticated pigs, not a trampling horde of wild boar. Most were stout, barely a few feet long, and not capable of taking down a grown man. Yet, it seemed far too coincidental that the group should assemble at that exact spot. They flung down their snouts, slashing the dirt like a saw.

A bird chirped right beside me, shattering the eerie silence. I yelped, lurching back from the railing. A flutter of wings pattered into the air, almost instantly muted by a breezy gust. I turned toward the bird, but only spotted a wispy shadow flying away. When I spun back toward the pigs, the circle had broken. They were running south down the service road.

Friday 9:57 A.M.

I bolted across the deck, my hurried legs clanging metallic thuds with every step. As Slake demonstrated to Victor the proper technique for clipping into the platform, he yanked at the safety line. The lanyard attached to my harness bucked, and my left leg stumbled. I pawed at the handrail, catching my balance before toppling all the way over.

Both Victor and Slake glared up at me. Victor appeared concerned, as if I might just crash down, ejecting us all over the edge. Slake smirked. Neither reached out to help me.

"And that's why we never rush while up on the deck," Slake said. The haughty expression remained plastered to his face, shuddering any concern for my safety to stress the point. I almost zipped back that it'd been his fault for pulling on the line in the first place, but instead motioned toward the galloping pigs.

They were swarming down the service road, aligned in rows like the twitching segments of a millipede. Only the misaligned portions were in front where a couple pigs would dart off to the side similar to an exploring antenna. The trail of dust thickened now they were on the road, hiding those in the rear and obscuring their numbers. If I'd had to guess, I would've said there were more than fifty of them suckers.

Slake shrugged and continued lecturing on the dangers of hastiness. I pointed again, but this time, he ignored me, as if spotting a trampling horde of pigs was part of the daily routine. Victor, taking Slake's cue, glanced briefly before zeroing in to the safety lesson. From the way he clenched the railing, I believe he spooked more over my stumble than any wild animals.

Slake switched topics, showing Victor how to raise the supplies. He had three ropes attached to his harness: one for the tools, another for the fiberglass rods, and the final one attached to the vinyl banner. The tool bag consisted mostly of ratchet straps, tie downs, and the occasional hammer or screwdriver. Slake threaded the rope attached to the tool bag first since it was the heaviest and tugged. The bag raised a couple feet.

Slake released the rope and the safety catch locked. The tool bag remained dangling mid-air. As he handed the rope to Victor, I interrupted again, pointing toward the police cruiser. The pigs had cleared from that portion of the road and dark blotches marked the spot where the officer had stood. I couldn't tell for certain from this distance, but the more I stared, the more I became convinced those were bloods stains from a brutal attack.

"Yes, I see," Slake replied, motioning for Victor to continue. Victor tugged, the safety catch popped, and the tool bag lurched up. The pulley rattled as he heaved, rocketing the tools up like a high-speed elevator. The line jerked, but held in place. From the way Slake bit his lips together and tilted his head, it was obvious he lacked patience for any more of my interruptions.

"No, look." I continued to gesture toward the cruiser and that dark stain spread across the service road. Slake craned his neck, but instead of looking down, he glared right at me.

"I said, 'I see the drift'." He pounded at the railing to emphasize his point.

"Drift? No, over there." I lowered my arm, pointing right at the service road. Was he blind? Why in the world was he focusing on some drift, or wind, or whatever?

"A herd of pigs is called a drift," Slake replied. "I worked one summer at a swine farm. Sometimes a drift escapes and needs to be rounded up. Not all that uncommon."

"That's one helluva drift," I replied. The pigs continued to race closer, moving at a breakneck pace I wouldn't have imagined possible. I estimated they'd pass the billboard within minutes.

"Yes, muchos cerdos," Victor added. His voice cracked as he pulled, but the tremble reflected fear over any exhaustion. His breathing hadn't increased at all while raising the tool bag and the only indication of any exertion were the bright blue veins bulging out from his muscular biceps.

"Whatever the size, it's not our concern." Slake leaned over and grabbed the tool bag. He plopped it onto deck with a clunky thud, and proceeded to thread the rope attached to the fiberglass rods through the pulley. He yanked with a series of exasperated breaths, and though paunchy compared to Victor, he managed to raise the rods at a similar speed.

"Slake, I think those pigs attacked that officer."

"Well, they can't harm you up here." Slake chuckled, while raising the rods the rest of the way. He deposited them to the side and exhaled a gasping breath.

"I'm serious. He was right next to his car, the pigs rushed up, and I can't see him no more." I rubbed my eyes to emphasize the point.

"And that's a bad thing? Just be thankful he didn't chase after us this morning and slap on the bracelets." Slake clinked his wrists together.

"Look. The road's stain with blood. How do you explain that?"

Slake leaned over the deck's railing, placing his open palm over his eyes to shade the morning glare. He pivoted around like a periscope, taking it all in. The roar of a motorcycle's engine broke through the howling wind and increased as it zipped down the highway.

"You really think that's blood?" Slake asked. "I can't make out anything other than shadows."

"I'm sure that's blood," I replied. "But I don't see a corpse."

"What do you see?" Slake asked Victor.

"Nada," he replied. Unlike Slake, he didn't dare lean over the edge. He could only look down for a second or two.

"I could drive up the road and check," I suggested after an extended pause. That caught Slake's attention and his head jerked up like he'd stuck his finger into an electrical socket.

"Oh, I get your game. Forget it. There's been enough fooling around this morning. We're here to do a job and a few stupid pigs aren't going to work as a distraction. Nobody's going anywhere." Slake stomped to emphasize the point.

"How about Harley?" I persisted. "Shouldn't we give him a heads up?"

"I hardly think he's in any danger except for some nightmares." Slake motioned at the cargo van. Inside, Harley lay sprawled out, his twiggy legs kicked up onto the open window frame. Clearly, he'd gotten a head start on his nap-filled day as Ground Man.

"No, the real danger are those." Slake pointed in the opposite direction, toward the far side of the deck. A set of high-voltage wires ran from treetop poles, situated beside the billboard. Most zoning regulations allocated for only a sliver of space to hang billboards, and more often than not, this coincided with the same spot used for wires. This was handy for illuminating the signs at night, less so for anyone who didn't want to be charbroiled.

In this matter, Slake was correct. Besides falling, juice was the second most dangerous part of the job. Quite a few fellas had been zapped into a pine box after ignoring nearby lines, and it didn't help matters that a unipole was basically the world's largest ground. Most guys don't realize electricity can jump, and it can hurtle like a damn Olympic athlete, sometimes ten feet or more.

"Always know the location of any nearby power lines before starting," Slake continued. "Less than a year ago, we lost a guy who failed to heed this warning. Zapped him right over the edge."

I might've felt the need to correct Slake, if my attention wasn't so focused on that empty police cruiser. Sure, our coworker, Tad Ferrell, was electrocuted, but it had nothing to do with high-voltage lines. He'd been mucking about with the lights on the outer-deck since Soaring Banners had been too cheap to hire a real electrician. Some fool had forgotten to turn off the power and the lack of a failsafe switch had sealed Tad's fate.

As for zapping him over the edge, truth was, when juice hit, you blasted nowhere. Instead, your body would seize, paralyzing you in place. The worst part was how they found Tad with his eyes pried open, unable to blink. Imagine that, forced to stare as his blood boiled from the inside and his skin browned like a pig roasting on a spit. The only real lesson learned was once you smell charred human flesh, you don't never forget it.

"Snap out of it," Slake said, tapping me on the shoulder. "Your vacation doesn't start until the end of the day. Until then, you're mine. So if you don't start pulling your weight, this job won't be here when you get back." As if to emphasize a literal interpretation of his point, Slake handed me a rope and motioned to pull.

I sighed and took it. The rope sagged in my palm, heavier than usual attached to the vinyl banner with the billboard's advertisement printed across it. The weight wasn't surprising considering Big

Bertha was about double the size of a typical billboard and the banners had to be special ordered. For this one, Harley and I had to drive forty miles into the boondocks to a printer we'd never used before.

The advertisement was for a family-owned auto repair shop a few exits north of here. A picture displayed an elderly man holding up a boy, both grinning as they stared into the cracked hood of a '62 Buick. The tagline at the bottom read: *From Our Grandfather's Socket Wrench to You.* I thought it was cute, but Harley said the old man's quirky smile looked like he wanted to give the kid more than a socket wrench.

Recalling Harley's quip, I almost lost my grip while chuckling, but luckily, the bundle steadied mid-air. I took another breath and ignoring the sweat airbrushing down my back, I humped it the rest of the way. I was panting by the time Victor assisted me with hauling it onto the deck.

We unfurled the banner, revealing a few wavy strands of the old man's hair at the topmost portion of the ad. Not only did Victor remain silent, but he showed no expression as we worked. Way different than his first day. I recalled how he'd been shocked to discover we used ratchet straps to hang the sign, rather than an adhesive. A lot of guys came to the job thinking we glued one sign atop another like garage-sale posters across a telephone pole. I don't know why, maybe they saw that on a cartoon or something.

Some even came to the job thinking we used paper banners. A silly belief considering what rain would do to both paper and glue. Most all billboards used vinyl, since it was lightweight, flexible, and durable enough to resist all the elements.

When we finished spreading the banner from one side of the deck to the other, Slake raised the end and demonstrated how to insert the fiberglass rods for added stability. Having endured to this spiel countless times, I peeked back toward the 'drift' of pigs, a huge misnomer if I'd ever heard one.

Far from 'drifting', they moved in a haphazard line, galloping at varied speeds depending where I looked. Some bounced into others while dashing ahead, while others just strolled in the rear. The most peculiar part was how the stragglers would fly into a sudden frenzy as though struck by an inspiration. And then, just as odd, they'd settle once again. Forget drifting, a more apt description would be pandemonium.

Slake, observing my wandering gaze, poked me with one of the fiberglass rods. "Notice the flexibility and how easy it is to lose control. Of course, it doesn't conduct as well as metal, but you sure wouldn't want to lose your balance and hit one of those power lines. Remember, safety first."

I scowled. What really came first was the tax write-off Soaring Banners got for hiring us. Nobody cared a lick about anything else. As long as there were prisons, there'd always be replacements. The only thing the company minded was the hassle of training them.

"Isn't that correct, Russ?" Slake asked, obviously noting my spiteful expression. I nodded, repeating his "Safety First" mantra, though another poke from that pole and I might zap him worse than any high-voltage wires.

Slake must've had a lick of sense inside that cement skull of his, since he drew back a step, and placed the fiberglass pole across the deck's railing. Though his mouth kept rambling, chugging some nonsense about banner dimensions as if Victor was studying for a big test and needed to recall that a 30-sheet was the standard size. His voice grated over my internal countdown and those evil hankerings bubbled like tar inside me.

"I'm heading up," I said, starting across the deck.

"Go ahead," Slake said, as if needing to provide some retroactive permission, but by that time, I'd already reached the ladder and clipped into the safety line.

I calmed a tad as I climbed out onto the upper-deck. The lower one was just twenty or so feet below, but the howling wind hushed Slake's prattling. I stared out into the expansive farmlands, noting how the flush greenery spread all the way to the mountainside like a toasty rug. For a moment, while taking it all in, I almost forgot all about that cop, those pigs, and even my upcoming trip to see Tyler. That was the majesty of heights, they blurred all life's minor problems into a unified beauty. That was also what made them so dangerous.

Slake's chirping voice snapped me from the trance. I couldn't make out the exact words, but from the way he flapped his arms, I knew he was signaling for me to unhitch the old banner. I was just about to do exactly that when I noticed the cargo van's door had cracked open. Harley was standing outside, puffing long drags from a cigarette. He noticed my gaze, grinned, and flipped me the bird.

I scanned the area toward the service road. The pigs in front had passed the small curving intersection to Big Bertha's parking lot, continuing down toward a section partitioned by chain-link fences on either side. From their zippy pace, I figured the others would likewise follow suit and almost turned without giving a second glance.

Then one pig scrambled across the road, veering in different directions, and twisted toward the parking lot. A gray one with dark blotches on either side as if someone had tattooed wings across its hindquarters. The animal must've spotted Harley, since it slowed and swung its head from side to side, fanning the air with an oversized snout. It skidded to a halt about thirty feet from Harley, kicking up a billowing haze.

Harley chucked his cigarette butt and raised his chin. He tucked his thumbs into his belt, leaning his arms back into a V. The pig took a single step closer. Harley stomped and the pig scurried back. A high-pitched trill shot out and it took me a second to realize Harley was whistling. The pig swung back around and raised its snout. It huffed and a lime-green ooze dribbled from its nostrils.

Harley whistled again, this time crouching as he did so. The pig lowered its head and trotted closer. Harley reached out and patted its head. The animal nuzzled to Harley, rubbing against his jeans. It arched its neck and Harley scratched it. The pig flopped onto the ground, rolling over exposing its belly. Harley stroked his fingers across the pink underside, tickling it. The pig twitched, digging at the air with its hooves.

Harley continued to stroke the pig. Its hooves whirled faster, until one nicked the ground, showering up a handful of dust. Harley inhaled a mouthful of the muck and coughed. The pig spooked, squealing as it sprang back to its feet. Harley remained crouched, but the animal trampled away as if hit. Harley stood and held out his hand. The pig spun around and galloped back toward the road. As it raced away, Harley whistled again. In return, the beast yowled an agonizing noise, sounding as if it was on fire. Harley shrugged as it rounded the corner.

What he couldn't see was the line of pigs that crashed to a halt on the service road. Almost as if in unison, a dozen pigs raised their snouts toward their wailing companion. One broke from the frozen trance and crashed straight into the chain-link fence, soon followed by dozens of others. The pigs who'd passed the intersection, circled back toward the group gnawing at the fence. They shoved their writhing bodies against it, slamming together until a portion tore free.

Then off they galloped across a field of wheat, bowling through like a bullet. I tightened my grip on the railing and shouted a warning. They were rushing straight toward Harley.

Friday 10:11 A.M.

 I swung my arm, signaling toward the charging pigs. The gesture caught Harley's attention, but instead of turning around, he grinned and parroted the motion, whirling his arm like a baseball pitcher. I hollered a warning, but doubt he heard anything through the snarling wind, since his antics continued now pretending to swing a bat. Only when a single pig darted in from a neighboring field did he take pause.

The pig was lean and trampled on wiry legs. Unlike the first, its skin was smooth and unblemished. A bit of dirt crusted its hindquarters, likely the result of kicking up all that dust. As it charged straight toward Harley, it jerked its head from side to side in a spastic motion, which contrasted the syncopated gallop of its hooves.

Harley crouched and motioned for the pig to approach, as if wanting to pet it same as the other. The pig needed no luring to continue, since it sped up with every stride. Similar to the other animal, a lime-green ooze rocketed from its snout, trailing a film of mucus across the ground.

Harley remained cemented in place as the pig trampled closer. Right before colliding, it veered away. Harley didn't so much as flinch as it brushed past his side. His eyes followed the pig as it continued across the lot, so he failed to note a dozen more emerging from the fields. Even more trampled in from the road. A line of three broke ahead of the others and as they passed the pickup truck, they lowered their heads in unison, locking onto Harley as he remained stooped beside the cargo van.

"Harley, watch out!" I yelled.

At that very moment, one pig roared a high-pitched squeal, similar to the sound of shrieking tires. I don't know which caught Harley's attention, but something did, since he spun around and spotted the three charging beasts. He scrunched his face and kicked back his chin. The swine stormed closer, picking up speed. Harley stomped, kicking up a smattering of dust.

The pig to Harley's left spooked and darted to the side, but the other two drove ahead. Harley whistled and stomped again. A layer of fine dust spread across the lot, the result of both Harley and the pigs. I hollered again, this time insisting he run, but Harley steadied in place, bracing for the charge.

This time, he was the one to flinch as the animals bolted up. He lunged to the side just as the first one trampled within arm's reach, but wasn't quick enough to avoid the other. The pig walloped into Harley's leg, causing him to stagger and trip against the side of the cargo van. He found his footing with a hot-coal-like prance.

Instead of springing into the cargo van, Harley stood frozen as a dozen more pigs raced up. I couldn't blame him for being awed by the sight, since I too could not peer away. The pigs flooded in from every direction, not just circling closer, but arranging into lines as if in formation. Their squeals pounded the air, overpowering the wind, until they merged into a single gnashing pulse. Harley returned a guttural roar of his own, arching his back while stomping his feet. My stomach wrenched as he darted straight into the stampede.

Pigs broke to either side as he ran, parting like waves across a ship's bow. He plowed ahead until reaching an empty portion of the parking lot where he skidded to a halt. He whooped and threw up his hands in victory over this game of chicken. One pig spun around, but instead of charging back, it hoisted its snout and revealed a set of sharp grinding teeth. I thought I was seeing things, but Harley must've noticed also since his hollering cut short.

The animal clenched a pair of rangy lips, drooling a thin piece of translucent spittle. It lowered a phlegm-coated snout and clawed at the grubby dirt. Another trotted next to it. Both leered at him with polished black eyes. Harley plunged in their direction, but the pigs simply watched as he approached, never once breaking their unblinking stare.

Harley was almost upon them when he must've realized they would not budge, so he juked, darting away. The pigs sprang in unison, galloping after him. As he sprinted, more pigs joined the pursuit as if lured magnet-like until over two dozen were nipping at Harley's heels.

He bolted back toward the cargo van, but when one of the beasts lunged into his path, he had to career deeper into the lot. When another pig blocked this route, Harley reeled, staggering in yet another direction. He swung his head, scanning for any break. At every turn, the masses of shrieking potbellies surrounded him, twitching corkscrew tails, and crunching snouts. He spun once again, but this time tripped.

I gasped as the closest pig pounced. It dropped its head, grinding its snout to the ground. Harley scrambled across the dirt, attempting to regain his footing. He launched onto one leg and staggered upright, but not in enough time to dodge. The beast rammed his knee, toppling him over. He kicked, rocketing the squealing pig a few feet back. The triumph was short-lived, since another pig struck, wheeling Harley across the dirt.

Crack. I instantly recognized the sound. A gunshot. The pig closest to Harley darted backwards, paused, and shook its head like it was wheezing. The group circled around him wrenched a few feet back. A couple even scurried off altogether, disappearing into the fields. Most remained, holding in an unsteady waggle just out of reach. None dared charge as their companion writhed and spat a throaty hiss.

Harley rose to his feet, clutching the gun out in front of him. The injured pig stomped closer as if deciding to make a final assault. Harley aimed, readying another shot, but the animal flopped onto its side and settled into a motionless heap.

Harley spun, searching for a gap within the swarm. There was none. Harley stomped and hollered for the pigs to skedaddle, but they remained fixed. He beat two hurried steps at a nearby pig, but it responded with a heedful shuffle closer, not away. Harley blasted another shot. The bullet shattered into the nearest pig, sprinkling a pink mist. The animals scrambled further back, forming a narrow hole. Harley raced into it.

He'd managed to sprint a couple yards before the pigs exploded from their paralyzed trance. He must've been injured during the commotion because he ran with a limp, dragging his right foot. His pace quickened as a torrent of pigs sprang after him. Though, unlike before, not all of the pigs joined in the pursuit. Dozens remained where he'd been standing and pounced onto their fallen kin with drooling snouts. They cleaved away chunks of meat from the two carcasses, devouring the gooey flesh in a saw-like blur.

Harley hadn't made it halfway to the van by the time the creatures reduced their fallen companions to a heap of scarlet-stained bones. Not a single ounce of flesh escaped their gnawing teeth. If they'd done that to one of their own, I gulped at what they could do to Harley. So far, even with the limp, he'd had no trouble dodging the few who'd darted into his path. Still, in his injured state, the others had no issues catching up.

As they drew closer, Harley peeked over his shoulder and fired off a shot. The bullet ricocheted across the dirt lot in a line of powdery grit missing the pigs. Now considering the difficulty of a rearview shot while sprinting, I doubt his aim was for anything more than a good fright. However, not a single pig detoured.

Harley turned once again as the closest pursuer nudged into his kicking boot. He fired another shot. The bullet dynamited into one pursuer, catching it in the hind leg. The animal careened onto its belly and squealed once before two others dove onto it. Harley smirked at this unbelievable shot, reveling in the moment. But in this brief victory, he failed to spot another two pigs darting in from ahead.

They crisscrossed his path, blocking him from either direction. He didn't have time to dodge, so he jabbed his good leg into the dirt and sprang. One pig, trailing behind, dove with a snapping jaw but missed by a breath. The jump was solid, soaring and high, appearing to have to plenty of space. I clenched the railing, worried more over his landing, since a single misstep on that injured ankle could spell disaster.

I slapped my mouth as a pig skyrocketed up. Impossible. No way. Such a height seemed inconceivable on those stubby legs, but it smashed into Harley mid-air.

He toppled onto the ground with the beast wrapped around his waist. He somersaulted over it. The pig squealed underneath his crushing weight. Another vaulted onto the rolling pair. The collision jarred Harley free. He scrambled back to his feet, but before he could find his balance, one barreled into his knee. He spun with the blow, bouncing across the dirt, and somehow sprang up before another had time to strike. Dust showered like a coating of snow, muddling my sight, but I could see blood spilling down his shirt where the pigs had walloped him.

Harley broke into a sprint, but his right arm dangled limp as he ran. I feared he'd dislocated it. Worse, I realized he was no longer holding the gun. Either blinded by dust or disorientated from the fall, he darted in another direction, heading away from the cargo van. I hoped he would go retrieve the gun, but when he veered in yet another direction, I knew he'd lost his bearings.

I dropped to my knees, yelling "Over Here!" while pounding on the deck, hoping the noise might assist him. The truth is I could no longer stand there and just watch him being attacked. Slake must've felt the same, since he joined in, hollering from lower deck. A metallic clank added to the chorus, the result of either Slake or Victor striking the platform with a hammer. My only tool was a ratchet strap, so I beat the railing with my fists.

Harley must've heard, since he whirled around and dashed toward the unipole. A pig darted up, breaking in front. He motioned as if still holding the gun. The animal screeched and tore off to the side. In any other scenario, I might've chuckled at such antics. Instead, I smacked the railing until I could no longer feel my hands.

As Harley drew closer, I realized with all his injuries, he would need help, so I raced across the deck. My numb fingers quaked as I unlatched the carbineer and attempted to clip into the ladder's line, but my hands refused to steady as if connected to someone else's body. I inhaled, counted down from five, and forced myself to concentrate. As soon as I reached zero, I clicked the metallic snap, hooking right onto the line.

Hand after hand, step after step, breath after breath, I descended. As if in a trance, I blocked all the screeching noises, beaming my entire focus onto each individual rung. I hadn't realized I'd passed the lower deck until I heard the hammering ring from above. I almost paused, wondering if I should climb up and fetch the others, but I was certain if I stopped, I wouldn't start again.

As I drew closer to the ground, I reached a cloud of dust, making my eyes water followed with a hacking cough. I steadied enough to regain my breath, but found moving to be impossible. I yelled for Harley, not because I could offer any help still being so far up, but hoping that the sound of my own voice would rekindle my will to continue. To my surprise, Harley hollered a sharp reply.

"Help me!" His cry emerged from right below, but when I peered, I caught only blurry shadows. The dust thickened the air like a moss, and I heaved shallow breaths. To be honest, my gasping had more to do with nerves than any dust.

"Find the ladder!" I rapped against Big Bertha's giant metal column. A tinny clink echoed out, but the reverberating uproar on the ground consumed it.

"Fucking pigs ate my...my thumb," Harley stuttered. Even through the clamor, the words dropped like icicles in my ear.

"As long as you got legs, you can climb." A cold reply, but this was what popped into my head. "You see the ladder?"

Harley grunted what sounded like an affirmative reply, though it might've just been panting. I spotted his lanky body for the first time, galloping through the murky haze. Gloomy shadows from the pigs fluttered behind him like a writhing tail. I almost cheered as he emerged at the base, but when he clasped the rungs, a nauseous wave bubbled in my throat.

Blood surged from the end of his right hand and dribbled down his raised arm like a can of spilled paint. All that was left of his index finger consisted of chalky gray bone attached to a slushy mound of muscles. What little remained of the flesh chewed into a moist mound. No sign of any thumb.

"Climb!" That was my intention, but the word that emerged from my wavering lips sound more like "Lime!" or "Lined!" Not as if Harley needed any prompting as he plopped onto the lowest rung. He winced and cried out a curse as he clutched what little remained of his hand around the ladder. He raised his other foot, steadying to climb when a pig charged in from his left.

Harley shrieked as the creature smashed into his leg. His unsteady grasp shook free and he fell. Somehow he managed to kick out while dropping, and clobbered the pig right in the snout. It squealed a nasally howl before scurrying off. Dozens of others lurking within the shadows instantly echoed the howl.

"Get up, dammit!" I yelled.

Harley reached with his mutilated hand, waving it around in a circle. The sight sparked my frozen legs into motion. The unipole appeared endless as I scrambled down the rungs. Harley floundered closer. As he struggled to climb, the ladder rattled against the clips attaching it to the pole.

The noise piqued the interest of a colossal pig emerging from the shadows. Its bulging gut was so massive that it scraped the ground while dashing closer, but this failed to slow its approach. Triangular ears flopped over its eyes like blinders on a racehorse, yet its focus remained focused onto Harley. A seeping crust of snot coated its snout like a layer of wet varnish. I yelled a warning, but Harley could barely hold himself upright against the ladder, forget dodging.

I hadn't even reached the point where the ladder connected to the unipole when the pig smashed into Harley. His feeble grasp released and he collapsed. The animal straddled his crumpled body, raising its filmy snout in a trouncing squeal. Harley twitched underneath the pig's bulk, breaking one arm free. He slapped its side, but the creature didn't hesitate mashing its snout into Harley's face.

His frail scream, both tormented and oddly muted, was so unnerving that I lost my balance. Before the safety could catch, I tightened my grasp on the rungs and swung like a trapeze artist. The commotion caught the beast's attention, since it glared up with tense, brittle eyes. Under this sinister gaze, I felt like a juicy piece of fruit dangling from a tree.

In this brief distraction, Harley bucked, flipping the pig over. He launched at it, but it scrambled back, dodging the blow. Instead of charging a second time, Harley staggered toward the ladder. He scrambled up as if gravity was working in reverse.

"Is it bad?" He pressed his palm to his cheek where the pig had attacked him.

"Keep climbing!" I insisted, even though he'd cleared the range where the pig could reach him. Plus, I couldn't answer his question. His injury wasn't bad. No, it was horrible.

His ear was severed off and bits of hair poked out from rubber-band-like tendons where it should've been. His cheek was worse. A gaping hole exposed the pureed flesh of his gum along with a couple crooked teeth. Blood spurted in hiccups, dribbling down his chin. He mashed his hand against the wound attempting to plug the geyser, but this only changed the geyser into a powerful, streaming hose.

Unable to endure any more of the grisly sight, I returned to climbing. When Harley screamed again, I feared I was too late and he'd lost his grip. I peeked, realizing the opposite was true, he'd actually hoisted himself up another couple steps. I did my best to ignore the gaping wound in his cheek. At least the spigot of blood had lessened, transformed into a dribble, but I still couldn't look for long before feeling dizzy.

On the ground, a dozen or so pigs had gathered around the ladder. Some pawed the ground, licking the spots where Harley had bled, while others stood motionless, staring up with empty expressions. One raced back and forth, veering only to avoid a collision with the ladder.

"You did it!" I hollered, but Harley displayed an expression as vacant as the pigs. He exhaled in rapid pants and clutched the ladder in a life-preserver grasp. I grabbed his wrist. He broke from his daze and smiled.

"I wa…want bacon for dinner. Lots of fa…fucking bacon."

"Sure thing, but let's get you patched up first."

I released my grasp in order to unclip one carabineer. Harley wasn't wearing a harness, so I scanned his blood-drenched clothes, wondering if a belt loop might do the trick. He was in no shape to climb, not that we needed to go anywhere, but a break from those barbaric pigs up on the deck would do everyone some good. At the very least, if he passed out from shock being attached to the line would prevent a fall.

"Ha, bacon." Harley chuckled in frenzied bursts. A frothy red foam dribbled from the corner of his mouth. He seized a couple times, swaying on the ladder.

"Hold still," I said, needing him to settle. If I could secure him, then Slake could pass down a harness from the deck and we could haul him up.

I was about to tell Harley the plan when everything became still. Somehow, as if receiving a transmitted signal, every last pig settled into a frozen stance. The sudden shift to silence was almost more unnerving than their squealing stampede. Both Harley and I glared down in astonishment.

Then, as if given another signal, the pigs broke into a mad dash, charging straight toward the ladder. In a blinding speed, they bashed together like a blender. The ladder bucked, shivering against the support pole. Harley wrapped his arms around the rungs in a bear-like hug. I reached to secure him, but swiped only air. The rungs had been right there, just inches below.

"Russ, no!" Harley cried. "Help, I don't want to—"

"Hold on!" I yelled.

The ground underneath moved with writhing bodies. An ocean of green-colored snouts swayed like seaweed in the tide. But this wasn't the worst sight. That honor went to the ladder, which had jerked free from the column and was floating straight up. Harley bobbed at the top like a sailor clinging to a mast.

I kicked, attempting to jam the ladder back in place. The top rung slid across my heel. I shoved, waiting to hear the distinct double-click of the ladder's snaps engaging. They didn't. Harley screamed as the ladder sprang perpendicular to the ground. He reached out, swiping for my ankle. No luck. Too far. The ladder stood upright for a long moment, almost as if it would hold in that teetering position forever.

When the ladder wrenched again, it fell, sending Harley into the buzzing horde where he instantly submerged. He didn't scream or make a noise of any kind. The only sound was the chomping of the pigs. Hell, a scream would've been preferable.

I curled my head into my chest and hung. My entire body pulsed and I couldn't stop shaking. If the safety latch hadn't been holding the majority of my weight, I would've joined Harley in that maniacal squirming pit. It wasn't until I felt a tap and spotted Slake, that I mustered the courage to move. He grabbed my shoulder and hoisted me back onto the rungs. The pigs sized us up the entire time with those glassy pitch-black eyes.

Friday 11:28 A.M.

The Phillips-head screwdriver plummeted like a missile; guided by its plastic grip toward a rabble of pigs congregated at the base of Big Bertha. The blunt end hit right on target, smashing against the head of the largest pig and pin-wheeling down its back. The animal wheezed, shambled a couple steps, and pivoted in our direction. A trickle of blood dribbled down its rear, but rather than storming off, it shook a couple of times as if unhitching an invisible harness, and settled back onto the ground. The others around it hadn't even glanced over.

Slake thumped a fist against the railing and cursed. I noticed his hand continuing to shake. Slake quickly folded his arms behind him. Why he felt it necessary to hide this anxiety was beyond me, since after Harley's vicious goring, I doubted any of us could settle in for quite some time. Perhaps never. Only an hour had passed and my heart was still thrashing.

Slake cursed again while kicking the toolbox over. Only a plastic flashlight rolled onto the deck. He'd flung the other tools in a blitzkrieg barrage, attempting to run off the pigs. With exception of the screwdriver, none had drawn blood, and in Slake's maniac fury, most had missed their intended targets altogether, tumbling across the ground in feeble clonks. Not only had this failed to scatter the pigs, but most didn't take the energy to dodge, as if knowing this shower of tools offered no threat.

"Stop staring or they'll never leave," Slake said, while hurling the flashlight over the edge.

"Sure," I replied, though from the way the pigs remained cemented in place, I knew staring wouldn't make a lick of difference.

When the flashlight likewise failed to elicit any reaction, Slake dropped to his knees and slumped against the railing. Victor, who'd already taken a seat, peeked over and shook his head, before folding his hands across his lap and closing his eyes. I doubted he'd be able to nap, figuring this was his way of processing things. I wished to join in whatever spell had overtaken him, but my fidgeting nerves refused to settle. Instead, I paced across the deck, my mind spinning but not really thinking about anything at all.

Outside of the two dozen pigs amassed at the base, triple that amount circled the perimeter in a skulking parade. Every ten minutes or so, they'd explode into a stampeding flutter, darting in one direction or the other, then a calm would follow as they returned to their prowling. I don't know what set them off, perhaps a flock of birds or a car growling down the freeway. Whatever caused them to charge, or attack in the first place, remained a mystery.

Stranger yet, they'd remained placid when we'd climbed onto the outer-deck right after the attack, attempting to signal anyone driving down Highway 99. We'd jumped, clapped, and hollered, making a big ruckus; not a single driver slowed. Any other time, attracting attention wouldn't be a problem, since most billboards were so close to the freeway that the cars sounded like rockets launching right underneath. Big Bertha, recessed so far in the distance, must've made us appear like ants.

To counter this, we'd yanked the banner halfway down, hoping that might spark some attention. It flapped a bit in the wind, mirroring our frantic waving, but the only result had been to turn our faces red.

"We just have to wait," Slake said, answering the unspoken question pounding through all our minds.

I peered over the edge and immediately regretted doing so as I locked onto the overturned ladder. About a foot from its end, the ground stained a dark crimson. Harley's ribcage poked up from the soiled spot, picked to the bone. Flies buzzed around it as a couple pigs poked their snouts in search of another gooey morsel.

Just beyond that, another two pigs batted his blue jeans between each other, which was about the only part of Harley's wardrobe not shredded into cotton-ball sized pieces. At least they'd stopped pawing at his skull, which had been likewise scoured clean except for three tangles of hair. Both eyeballs were missing, which made it appear less human, less real, and I was thankful for that.

As for his other bones, some of the pigs ground them between their teeth, gripping them as if they were trophies. Every so often, a skirmish would erupt between the animals and a new victor would claim control. But mostly, after gnawing the bones down to a pale gray chew-toy, the pigs left them alone.

My attention drifted toward the cargo van, parked around forty or fifty feet away, an insurmountable distance through the throngs. The rusty pickup truck was even further than that. Some of the pigs had dropped for a mid-morning nap, but enough remained awake to prevent any lingering ideas of escape. Plus, there was that twenty-foot drop from the edge of the ladder onto the solid ground.

"I told you not to look," Slake said.

I stopped pacing and took a seat beside him. The view in the other direction wasn't much better, since I could see the police cruiser along with the discolored portion of the service road. After Harley, I was now certain this stain was all that remained of the officer. I stared at the service road, following it north, but failed to spot any vehicles or other reinforcements. Whomever or whatever was pursuing this drift, Slake's word for the pigs, had either lost the trail or suffered a worse fate.

"You said you worked at a swine farm, right? You ever hear of anything like this?" I asked.

Slake shook his head as he wiped a thick layer of sweat from his brow.

"What about that green snot? Is that a type of rabies?"

"I never heard anything like this, but again, I only worked for one summer when I was a teenager. That was a long time ago, still, I doubt pigs change. Once a couple break off, the rest of the drift will follow. There's not that many."

"Ninety-two," Victor interrupted, breaking from his monk-like trance. He remained fixed, not moving as he spoke, but I did notice his fingers curled around the railing, clutching it like he might accidentally fall off.

"What's that?" Slake asked, rubbing his forehead and straightening a bit.

"Maybe I count wrong," Victor replied. "I think is ninety-two."

"Wow, almost a hundred of those green-snotted freaks. Hope whoever comes to rescue us brings plenty of Kleenex." I chuckled, but then caught myself and cut the laughter short.

"The number doesn't matter. We'll wait them out." Slake settled against the railing, but I suspected that was for show, since his shoulders remained rigid.

"No. The pigs no leave. Never." Victor shook his head.

"Don't be silly." Slake stood and stretched his arms wide. "All this idle waiting isn't healthy. You get too much into your head and become paranoid. We should finish swapping out the signs, so we can get out of here as soon as the pigs scatter."

Neither Victor nor I moved as Slake crossed the deck. Work was about the last thing on my mind and damned if he would get another minute of my time after what had happened to Harley. I'd rather jump into that swarm than worry over this stupid billboard. Slake persisted, motioning for us to follow.

"When the devil climbs, never shall he return." Victor gestured an upside-down V with his fingers; an inversion of the devil's horns I knew from teenage rock concerts. Of course, that was always an expression of superficial adolescent rebellion, but Victor was quite serious, since he followed this gesture by bowing his head and crossing himself.

"Did you just call me the devil?" Slake spun around, shooting an incensed stare. Victor rose and returned the hairy eyeball with crossed arms.

"What I say is pray to the devil and he shall rise. But curse him and he no fall. For when the devil climbs, never shall he return."

"What are you talking about?" Slake tilted his head in a befuddled look.

"My mother say this when…" Victor paused, taking a deep breath before continuing. "I no comprendo then, but now I do. We climb. We no leave. Never." Victor motioned at the sky as if this somehow clarified his point. Slake glanced at me as if I had a clue, but I just shrugged.

"That's a real nice quote and I'm sure you can pass it down to your own children someday, but right now, I need you to focus. Not up there, not down there, but right here." Slake pointed at his face. "See, I'm the one in charge."

"What I see is the eyes of the pigs. Black. Evil. The eyes of el Diablo."

"What I see is a half-hung billboard." To emphasize the point, Slake smacked the rear panel as if attempting to dislodge a sticky piano key.

"The tail of the devil is forked and never-ending."

"So is my cock," Slake snapped. He took a deep breath and continued in a calmer tone. "That's quite enough about the devil. We need to keep our heads until help arrives. Maybe nobody stopped, but there's a good chance someone on the highway saw us and called the police."

"I call already if someone no take my phone," Victor snapped back.

"Enough, otherwise my first call will be to a parole officer once we get down. What we have here is some run-of-the-mill rabid pigs. That's what Russ said, and I tend to agree with him."

Hearing my name, I stiffened and turned away. I'd only asked Slake about rabies on consideration of his former work experience, far from any declaration of fact. Honestly, I had no idea. It was odd how there wasn't any white foamy drool or muscle spasms normally associated with rabies. Green snot was a peculiar detail I'm certain would've stuck in my head, but I'd never heard of anything like that. But, again, it was a clear indication this was a disease of some sort.

"Isn't that right, Russ?" Slake pestered, waiting for an answer.

I nodded just to get him off my back. The last thing I want is to be dragged into their bickering nonsense. I sure hope it was rabies, since that made sense. One thing about Harley's death… it made no sense. I couldn't comprehend it, even though I'd seen every gory detail with my own eyes. Sure, rabies it was. And if Slake had that right, maybe he is correct about help being on the way as well.

"Is no rabies," Victor countered. "Is curse. A curse of the devil."

"I said zip-it with that devil talk." Slake stormed across the deck. "We don't need any of that. Understand?"

"We need a priest." Victor uncrossed his arms, tilted his head, and leaned toward Slake. A massive vein throbbed across his neck, seeming to burst from his skin. His eyebrows lowered as he stilled into a statue-tight pose.

I shuffled away, knowing tempers tended to heat-up with the thermostat. It'd been in the low-nineties all week long, which wasn't altogether intolerable as long as we had work, but standing around waiting for help was bound to set something off. I just didn't expect it to be this quick after Harley's death. The entire argument seemed downright disrespectful. Not that I'd jump in to tell those two that.

"What we need is animal control." Slake poked a bony finger into Victor's shoulder. "Because uncivilized beasts need to be caged."

Victor slapped Slake's hand to the side. Slake jerked forward, shoving his elbow into Victor's stomach. A gasping exhale shot out as Victor whirled back, staggering to catch his breath. Slake beat another step closer, curling his fists into tight, sweaty knots. The deck thumped as Victor sprang onto the balls of his feet, raising his arms. Slake swung first, but Victor dodged, spinning a step back. Slake toppled into the railing. Victor hovered over him, but waited to strike.

I couldn't understand his hesitation, but then I heard it. *Country music?* It sounded like a song. I squinted, scanning for the source. I spotted nothing on the deck, but the faint melody became clearer as Slake and Victor settled. It was coming from somewhere below.

"His phone," Slake gasped. "That's the ringtone for Harley's phone."

We all rushed to the railing. The pigs must've likewise noticed the song, since they circled around the remains of Harley's blue jeans. They crowded together, pressing toward his jeans as if lured by a magical amulet. The closest ones lowered their snouts to the dirt, sniffing in frenzied bursts while the ones in the rear jammed closer, vaulting onto the backs of the animals in front at times.

Just as the mob appeared ready to strike, the song cut off mid-note. The pigs lost interest as quickly as it'd been piqued, most scurried away, returning to their naps. A couple kicked at the blue jeans, shooting the shredded fabric across the dirt. The jeans bounced against the unipole and settled into a heap. I squinted, noting the slight bulge. Somehow the phone had remained lodged inside the front pocket. I doubted it would survive a second scuffle.

"We need to get that fucking phone," Slake said, beating me to the punch.

Friday 12:06 P.M.

 I watched in silence as Slake poked feebly at Harley's jeans with a fiberglass pole, failing time after time to snag them. He stood on the bottommost rung, but even this short distance proved to be too unwieldy. What made the fiberglass ideal for hanging banners, its weightlessness and flexibility proved useless for hitching the jeans. Every time he snagged the tattered denim, the pole teetered and bent then the jeans would slide back onto the grimy dirt.

Worse, the slightest flutter of movement would alert the pigs so they barreled in as soon as Slake motioned toward the jeans. To counter this, he had to jab rapidly, causing the thin pole to wobble and bounce out of control. During one ferocious attack on the pole, he lost his grip, catching it seconds before it dropped forever out of reach. As for poking the pigs away, it proved to be as good of a weapon as a wet piece of spaghetti.

Slake's impatience grew with every failure until the point he was whipping the pole so fast it hummed while slicing through the air. That was when his foot slipped. The safety caught, leaving him dangling. He shoved the pole into the ground to regain his balance, but instead, the pole flexed like a straw and snapped up, toppling him into the side of the ladder. The animals swarmed, almost smirking as they brayed a mocking chorus at his misfortune. Slake cursed and flung the pole away. None of the pigs scattered as it plunked onto the cracked earth.

He returned to the deck, dancing a klutzy step while tripping over an uneven beam. Neither Victor nor I said a word as he snatched another pole. He turned as if to descend again, but instead, he sighed and dropped the pole. It hopped across the railing threatening to roll over the side. Slake made no motion to stop it, instead he patted his lower back, kneeled over, and groaned. The pole wobbled at the edge, but steadied without falling.

"Maybe we can attach a hook to the end," I suggested.

"*Hook*? I forgot to bring my fucking tackle box," Slake snapped, still doubled-over. From the forceful zeal of his tone, I figured this for a performance over any permanent injury. When a short tumble had busted my back, laying me out for two weeks, the only sound I could muster was a muffled whisper. Though, perhaps that had been on account of the pain medication.

"A carabineer might work," I replied.

"Fine, brainiac. How do we attach it to the pole?" Slake groaned as if this suggestion hurt him worse than the injury. He slapped his lower back to emphasize the point, like we weren't already aware.

In the middle of his theatrics, the country song played, this time cut short abruptly after a few notes. That was enough to spin Slake into a hysteria of roaring profanities. Thankfully, the pigs weren't as riled and left the jeans alone. I wondered how many more phone calls the jeans could endure until they, along with the cell, were shredded to pieces.

"This is what we're going to do," Slake said, after his rancor tuckered out. "The pole is too unstable from the end of the ladder. We have to get closer. If we can cut half the distance, we might get enough stability-"

"Wait," I interrupted. "You want to hang there, free floating? Remember how those pigs can jump? You're willing to do that?"

"I can't do anything with my back shot. One of you two will have to go."

"No way. I'm not going anywhere near those things." I shook my head and stared over at Victor.

"Phone do not matter," he replied. "We never leave."

"You afraid?" I hoped the insult would spark Victor to action, but the only sign he'd even heard me came from a slightly raised eyebrow. I waited for a response, but he didn't so much as chew his lip while mulling over the decision.

"I do it," he said, after a long pause. Even then, the reply held about as much enthusiasm as a disgruntled husband forced to take out the garbage.

"No, Victor stays here," Slake said.

"Is it your back that's shot or your head?" I snapped. "Out of all of us, he's the fittest."

"Think about it, Russ. Can you hold Victor's weight? With this injury, I sure can't. Of course, we could lower him, but raising the line could be an issue. And if things go south, we'd be pressed to do so in a hurry. You that strong?"

"I can't. Not after Harley." I crossed my arms. Sure, steadying Victor's bulk would be an issue, but it was also our only asset. And he could hang all day until help arrived as long as we snagged that phone. Hell, with those muscles, he could climb the rope himself. I could barely do a single pull-up.

"Fine. I don't blame you." Slake sat, spreading his legs across the length of the deck. He braced his feet against the railing and bent toward his toes, gasping as he stretched.

"Don't pin this on me," I said, but refrained from flinging the blame back at Slake. Really, it wasn't anyone's fault. Nobody other than those damn porkers.

"It's probably best we don't try anything stupid," Slake said. "It's like being lost; we wait in place until help arrives."

"Help no come," Victor muttered.

Slake paused his stretching and rolled his eyes. "Somebody is on the other end of those calls. Since Harley failed to answer, it's only a matter of time until they investigate his disappearance. I bet it's the office. Trust me, they don't like losing track of us. So we wait until they come. Or, maybe if we wait long enough, the pigs might leave on their own."

Slake rubbed his temples before closing his eyes. I was just about to join him in a nap when a thought struck. This was Friday, and unless Mr. Murray, the illustrious owner of Soaring Banners was in the office, which was less than one percent of the time, most everyone ducked out for the afternoon. I checked the time and swallowed hard. Most Fridays, Linda, the office coordinator never checked back in after lunch. It was about the only perk of this rotten job.

"I'll do it." I reached for the pole and stood.

Slake bounced to his feet, bad back aside. From the way he sprang up mid-slumber, I wondered if this was all part of some reverse-psychology ploy. Even so, if I'd been played, I didn't want to know, since a single ounce of hesitation would easily derail this rash decision. Without peeking down, I clipped into the ladder's line.

Before I had time to reconsider, I found myself on the bottommost rung. I didn't know how long I'd been standing there, since it was as if a murky haze had dropped like a curtain. I didn't recall the descent, not the sizzling touch of the rungs, not the escalating noise of the grunting pigs, not even my unsteady foothold. For the second time that morning, I'd dropped into a blank zone of nothingness.

My heart shot into my throat as the world snapped into brilliant focus. I scanned the horde spread across the lot, noting most of the pigs were snoozing, laying snout-to-snout. This position struck me as odd, considering how their neon-green mucus slopped together into gooey pools. I didn't ponder this for long, since I was more concerned with those who remained wide awake. A dozen or two trampled around the outer perimeter, and a couple noted my presence, but most continued on, oblivious to my arrival.

Slake yelled down from the deck and I shot him a thumbs-up, but 'thumbs-up' was the exact opposite of the feelings slamming over me. The rope attached to my harness drooped as Victor threaded a bit of slack into the line. I kicked out, freeing my feet, but kept a firm grip on the rungs. The line snapped taut. As my feet dangled, I released my grasp and lowered into the air. The free-floating sensation was all too familiar, and I shivered, cursing myself for agreeing to such a stupid idea.

As I held hovering in place, Slake lowered a pole tied to another line. It whizzed down at an elevator-like speed, and I feared it might just crash past me, so I reached out as if expecting to catch a fly ball. Slake must've sensed my anxiety, since the rope slowed to a crawl. By the time (seemingly forever) the damn pole reached me, a handful of pigs took notice of my presence.

Thankfully, none of them launched, remaining firmly fixed to the ground, but as they lurched closer, nudging through the sleeping throngs, a crowd gathered. I did my best to remain focused on Harley's blue jeans and that phone, but when my eyes did drift, I noticed a swarm of snouts aimed like canons waiting to ignite.

I untied the fiberglass pole, swinging it like a baton, as Slake hauled the rope back onto the deck. Even if he hadn't been faking his bad back, two sets of hands were certainly better, so I waited for him to finish before motioning at the safety catch. Slake grabbed the line and nodded back. I clutched the rope in one hand, the pole in the other, but releasing the catch in this awkward floating position proved to be too cumbersome, so I released my hold on the rope.

I blinked, doing my best to ignore the ocean of pigs glaring up. With a solid grasp, I yanked at the catch. A tinny clink shot out as the gears freed. I closed my eyes, swinging horizontally. When I looked again, I half-expected to see the ground racing up. I pressed my hand to my heart realizing I had remained locked in place.

My head flung up as I lurched a foot lower. The safety harness tore up my back, wrenching the fabric into my crotch. I groaned, but before I could yell up to the two to lower me at a slower pace, the line jerked and I dropped another foot. As I hung with my limbs akimbo, I wondered if this was how spiders felt descending on their prey. When the line jerked a third time, I started to feel less like a spider and more like fishing tackle.

Inch after inch, I descended toward the ground. Reaching the halfway mark, around ten feet above the huddled pigs, I bucked to a halt. Victor stood at the deck's edge, clasping the rope in both hands. Even from this distance, I could spot the veins pulsing from his biceps, but his hands remained in a cement-like steady grip.

Outside of the dozen or so pigs gathered to watch my descent, most remained asleep. Their combined snoring puttered against my eardrums so loudly I could feel the vibrations across my chest. A group of three snoozed inches from Harley's jeans, their snouts pressed so close together I wondered if that green snot worked as some type of glue. And every time the trio exhaled, always in-sync, the puddle of mucus between them bubbled into a blistering foam.

I raised the pole, shoving it toward the jeans. The fiberglass bent into a curved U the further I reached, but considering my proximity to the pigs, I didn't dare signal to be lowered any more. I jammed the end into the jean's waistline and steadied the wobbly grip. The pole bowed as I lofted the jeans an inch into the air, but held.

A pig on the perimeter howled and stormed closer. I wrenched in the harness, almost losing my grip. The jeans plopped back onto the ground. The charging pig reached a crowded portion of its snoozing brethren and crashed to a halt. A mountain of grainy dust spewed up as it squealed a second time. The pigs near the edge wrestled awake, glaring at the interloper. The animal continued to huff, swinging back and forth as if having to pee. One of the others lowered its head and rushed at it. Both dashed off toward the fields.

I froze, fearing their attention would spin around in my direction, but after a moment, the pigs dropped back into their slumbering positions. I counted to ten before raising the pole for another pass. I poked the end into the huddled fabric, and to my astonishment, without even aiming, I hitched one of the belt loops. As I raised the pole, the tattered jeans hoisted into the air.

Either Slake or Victor, I couldn't tell who, yelped in delight as I hauled the jeans closer. The belt-loop slid down the pole, crawling toward my grasp like an overeager toddler. I raised the pole even higher, increasing the speed. But before I could grab it, the belt loop tore free. I swiped for the jeans mid-air. Success. The denim folded into my hand like a warm glove. I almost whooped, then realized I was holding the jeans upside-down. The cell teetered at the pocket's edge for a long agonizing moment, then fell.

It dropped onto one of the snoozing pigs, slamming against its head, bounced twice down its back, and skidded across the ground. The beast lurched to attention, waggling as if on fire. Another pig screeched and bashed into the first. They wheeled around, colliding with a third. A chain reaction exploded as pig after pig jolted into a giant writhing pit.

The line attached to my harness bucked and I rocketed into the air. My arms slung around as if attached to a spring and I couldn't distinguish which direction was up. My eyes rolled back and I feared I was crashing toward the earth. The rope snagged taut and I continued to spin like a top. Reaching out, I latched onto a hard piece of metal. I don't know why I thought this was the phone at first, since it was hot to the touch, but I did. When my equilibrium settled, I realized I was clinging to one of the ladder rungs.

I peered down, staggered by the height. Indeed, instead of falling, I'd been raised almost a third of the way up. Slake yelled something, but my muddled head couldn't decipher the words. I scanned the ground. No trace of the jeans, the pole I'd been holding, nor the phone. Only hoof after hoof stampeding through puddles of that cursed green snot.

Friday 1:18 P.M.

The outer-deck pealed a string of discordant beats as Slake stomped from end to end. He rubbed his temples and clenched his teeth while marching as if grinding an invisible piece of bark. His face glowed a mud-colored rust as a giant vein throbbed across his forehead. When reaching one end, he never hesitated in whirling around for another pass. Every so often, he would pause though, mostly to glare over the railing and immediately follow with blistering profanities.

I sat slumped at the corner where the inner deck curved around toward the outer platform, the only portion offering a sliver of shade. Even this brought little relief since the midday sun was brutal and unending in its pounding blows. The lack of water just worsened the effect of the scorching heat.

I kept glancing at the cargo van, imagining I could see through the rust-coated door where our electric-blue water cooler relaxed nestled in the rear. I ran my tongue across the roof of my mouth, amazed how it'd already transformed into a sandpaper-like grit. I told myself to stop staring, but lacking anything else to occupy my mind, my eyes kept darting down.

The only one who appeared immune to the ravages of the heat was Victor, who sat beside me with his legs sprawled out as if sunbathing on a beach. His head tilted against the railing, hands folded behind it with eyes closed. He puttered shallow breaths, the only indication of any discomfort, but also appeared to have a slight grin.

Slake glared over as he approached with a thudding stomp. This time, instead of his typical exhale-curse-pivot dance, he hovered over Victor like a blimp. When Victor failed to peer up, Slake rapped the railing with a tinny beat. Victor cracked his eyes, took a cursory glance at the boss's distended jaw, and chuckled.

"You think this is a joke?" Slake smacked the railing with a reverberating *whack*.

"You no care what I think," Victor muttered, closing his eyes again.

"Stand up," Slake ordered. He nudged his foot into Victor's thigh. Victor nodded and rose to his feet. He yawned and stretched his meaty biceps like a peacock. Slake swung his arms against his torso in a sideways V. Victor tilted his head and extended into a broad stance.

I likewise stood, but shuffled back from the two, withdrawing from the fragment of shade. Not that this made a lick of difference, since the temperature in the direct sun was only a nick hotter. I inhaled a mouthful of scorching vapor and wondered if a person could boil from the inside.

"Good," Slake said, pressing a step closer. "I need you to listen and listen good."

"I listen," Victor muttered. "But whether good or no depend on what you say."

"Temper that 'tude," Slake replied. "It's your fault Russ dropped the cell. If you hadn't yanked on the line, we'd be out of this mess by now."

I took another step back, turning my focus toward the pigs. Those slimy bastards hadn't moved a single inch, which was fine by me, since I hoped that when help finally arrived, they'd slaughter every single last one of them.

"Maybe we do not need the phone if some bobo no take the others," Victor replied.

"If you're going to insult me, do it in English," Slake snapped. "And stop mean-mugging. You better change your attitude quick because I'm not one to forget. If not, you best be prepared for extra dates with your parole officer, dozens of random inspections, and constant piss-tests. So understand, if you so much as fart from now on when I say you can't, I'll make sure you'll be spending the next month picking up used condoms on the side of the freeway."

"Si, you do that. Say I naughty. Act like a mommy. Give me spanking." Victor turned and stuck out his ass. I watched from the corner of my eye, grateful Victor swung back around before Slake could take him up on the offer. Or worse, spot the gun sticking out from the small of his back.

Slake craned his neck and even though they were again face-to-face, he raised a flat hand as if he might take a whack at Victor's rear. Victor stepped closer, smirking with one corner of his mouth. Slake reconsidered and dropped his arm.

"Go ahead, enjoy yourself now. Chucklehead it all up. I'll be the one laughing later."

"You no understand," Victor replied, shaking his head. "We are trapped. No escape. Never."

"You better hope we never escape, since this, right here, right now, is the best your life is ever going to be."

Victor cracked his mouth to reply, but then, it just hung open as if at a loss for words. He held frozen for a long moment with this peculiar expression plastered to his face. Slake leaned in like Victor was speaking, but I didn't hear anything other than the baying wind.

"You have something to say?" Slake poked Victor's shoulder.

"You right," Victor answered. "Now is the very best. Later, not so good. So I will enjoy the day."

He began to sit, but as he turned, Slake grabbed his arm.

"We're not through here. Actions have consequences. You jerked the line and that caused Russ to drop the phone. That means it's your responsibility to climb down and fetch it."

"You go fetch." Victor proceeded to take a seat. "Now, I rest."

"I'm not asking." Slake yanked Victor to his feet. They stood chest to chest, pressed together like a Band-Aid.

"I no fight you again," Victor said, stepping back. "Russ drop the phone, not me."

He glanced over in my direction and I peered down. From the way Victor wrinkled his forehead, I knew he seen me glancing over. Both of us knew he was telling the truth. The phone hadn't fallen because of an unsteady line. It was due to my haste, my fumbling hands; but I just stood there, arms crossed.

"No excuses," Slake said. "We're getting that phone. I'll start by distracting the pigs with a pole. Once the ground is clear, you'll drop and retrieve it."

"Is crazy," Victor replied. "You no can stop the pigs with pole. Nothing stop the pigs. We sit. We wait. We relax."

"Fuck that. We're getting that phone. You got a better idea?"

"My idea is sit." Victor wrenched away from Slake's grip and flexed his bulging arm in case Slake got any hot ideas about grabbing him a second time.

"You want to sit?" Slake asked. "Is that what you want? As I'm trying to do everything to solve this mess, your decision is just to sit?"

"Yes, I sit."

"Fine, take a fucking seat." Slake lunged forward and shoved Victor. I doubt Victor expected the blow, since he lost his footing mid-squat and tumbled across the deck. He extended his arm in a last-ditch attempt to dampen the fall, but his hand collided with a loose beam. The jagged metal edge tore across Victor's palm. He yelped, crashed onto his side, and clutched his fist as blood oozed between his fingers.

Slake's mouth dropped, revealing he hadn't anticipated the forcefulness of the blow. He staggered a step back and bowed his head. I brushed past toward Victor who panted and clutched the injured hand to his stomach. From the way he steadied his breathing and straightened as I approached, I think he was wary that I might double up on Slake's attack.

I raised my palms in a peaceful gesture, but he didn't break from this guarded posture. Even as I removed my t-shirt and passed it over, telling him to use it as a bandage, he remained cautious. Swiping the shirt and backing away quick like a squirrel snagging a peanut from a stranger. It didn't help matters that Slake was hovering beside me and kept leaning closer in order to assess Victor, so I nudged him back.

"Fine," he said, thankfully stepping away. "I'll go to the outer-deck and try again to flag someone down. When you two are done moping around, feel free to join me in solving this mess."

"You do that," I replied.

Slake strutted off without further protest, but as he rounded the corner, he cursed while meat-hooking the sign with both arms. In any other circumstance, I would've at least cracked a smile at this outburst, but his refusal to settle even after Victor's injury had me worried. For someone who rambled on and on about consequences, he sure didn't seem all too concerned over his own. To be honest, I enjoyed the cell-warrior Slake far better than this newfound beast.

"Keep pressure on it," I said, glaring at the make-shift bandage wrapped around Victor's hand. Blood seeped through the thin cotton of the t-shirt with amazing speed, but appeared to have stopped for the moment. I guess I should've been concerned over Victor's huffing and pained expression, but really, I was fuming at Slake. I'd really liked that t-shirt. Not to mention, it'd been my sole protection from the sun.

Victor motioned to sit. I plopped beside him, doing my best to forget about that shirt, trying to remind myself I should really care about my co-worker's well-being instead. For some reason the shirt continued to irk me, but I knew enough to fake it, so I kicked out and leaned deep into the railing. The sun-scorched bars sizzled my bare back.

"I bet it won't even leave a scar," I said, trying to muster up any conversation as a distraction. When Victor failed to reply, I decided a question might loosen him up, so I asked if he thought that green snot was a type of rabies.

Again, no reply. Victor's gaze remained locked on the horizon as if in a trance. I didn't blame him. Ever since witnessing Harley's death, all my sensations had dimmed. Oddly, I found I was more pissed over that silly shirt than seeing Harley shredded to pieces. Every so often a wave of emotions would flood over me, but mostly I felt a whole heap of zilch. I almost envied Slake's wild frenzy, since at least that was something.

As I licked my cracked lips, I realized I did feel something. A sensation I couldn't ignore – thirst. I looked again toward the cargo van, imagining how I'd rip open that cooler hidden inside. I could almost feel the crinkled plastic of a water bottle wobbling in my hands. Its ridged cap spinning between my fingers. The slight swish the water made while raising toward my itchy mouth. I closed my eyes, hoping to shake the feeling.

God, if I didn't know better, I'd say this thirst was worse than those evil hankerings. They cemented to me in the same way, clawing my every thought. I started to count down.

"No rabies," Victor replied, pulling me from this daze. I was so spun around I'd almost forgotten about the question. How long ago had that been? Had we been sitting here in silence for only a minute? Or had it been longer? I couldn't tell.

"How do you know for certain it ain't rabies?" I asked, sitting up. I heard Slake stomping across the outer-deck, so perhaps it hadn't been that long.

"I know," Victor replied. He leaned back as if any further discussion would be futile.

"I guess," I relented. "But if it's not rabies, it must be some other disease, right? I've never heard anything about pigs acting like this. Even boars in the wild would've spooked off. It's almost like they know we're up here. But that's crazy."

"No, is the truth." Victor folded his arms. "They know."

"I tend to agree with you," I replied, acknowledging what I'd been thinking all morning. "Still, it don't make a lick of sense. Why would they act like this? Slake thinks they came from a swine farm, so maybe it's due to a steroid or a drug they pumped into them. Imagine that, zombie pigs created while man searches for a better tasting bacon."

Victor shook his head.

"Yeah, I guess you can't make a better tasting bacon." I chuckled. "Whatever it is, I hope the drug wears off soon. Or all those bastards drop dead choking on their own snot."

"They no die." Victor paused, peering up. I was about to say something when he continued. "We die."

"Don't say that," I replied. "Remember how being inside felt like it was gonna last forever? But then, one day, it ended. This is like that. In a few hours, our mugs are gonna be plastered all over the TV like we're famous. Shit, one day, we'll all sit down for a drink and have a big laugh. Until then, could you ease up a bit with the despair-talk? All it does is rile up Slake."

"Slake controls Slake, not me." Victor pointed at his injured hand as if it proved he held no responsibility. I nodded, though I disagreed.

"He shouldn't have pushed you, but let's try to keep our tempers sorted until we get down. No reason for any more injuries. You can at least agree on that?" I asked, thinking about that piece tucked into his back.

"We all are injured. Only choice is make peace or not before we die." Victor waved his bandaged hand in a cross.

"Hey, I'm not saying you can't believe in whatever you want, but let's keep it to ourselves."

"Like you do when Slake say I am reason for dropping the phone?"

Victor's words stung. Of course, he had every right to be irked after taking the blame for my butterfingers, but for a man who said he desired peace, he was sure running his mouth as if arming up for battle.

"Does the reason why the phone dropped really matter?" I shot back. To my surprise, Victor nodded in agreement.

"No, what matter is you say the truth. Maybe truth hurts, but is where there is peace. Your peace not in Slake. Not in me. Is in you." Victor pointed at my heart. "Until you understand, until you say the truth, no peace."

"Fine. I dropped the phone."

"No. The phone do not matter. What is truth?" Victor tapped at my chest.

"I told you it was my fault the phone fell. What do you want?"

"The truth." Victor continued to tap at my chest, this time with increasing vigor. I brushed his hand away.

"Enough. Give it rest." I stood. The heat had crisped all but my final nerve and the last thing I need was to be baited into a fight, especially with an armed man twice my size.

"Yes, you run. Run from the truth." From the grin unfolding across Victor's face like a carpet, I realized my frustration was only fueling his twisted amusement. I'd seen enough of these religious converts to know their game wasn't a search for morality, but rather control.

"Yeah, I'm gonna find my peace elsewhere." I crossed the deck.

"The truth is the pigs are demons," Victor yelled, but I ignored him while clipping into the column's safety line. I peered toward the upper-deck, knowing it offered not a lick of shade, but started up the rungs anyhow.

"The demons no die," Victor continued. "They trap and they eat. They eat the body. They eat the truth. They eat all."

I said nothing as Victor continued to rant about demons or some shit. As I reached the upper-deck, Harley's cell began to play that same blasted country song. The pigs burst to life as the ringtone chimed, but I couldn't bring myself to look at the ruckus. By the time I'd crossed the upper-deck, taking a seat at the end, the song had stopped, but the pigs continued to squeal and stomp.

Demons or not, Victor had been correct about one thing, those foul creatures weren't leaving until they'd eaten it all.

Friday 4:53 P.M.

The ladder jangled as Slake climbed onto the upper-deck. He stomped twice gaining a foothold and muttered a string of undecipherable words resembling a radio tuned between stations. I peeked, saw the pigs hadn't left, and snapped my eyes shut before Slake could realize I was awake. Not that I'd been able to doze in the muggy afternoon sun, but sitting with my eyes closed was better than the alternative.

Slake stopped beside me and tapped the railing, an obvious attempt to rouse me from this faux-slumber. If he had any real news, such as the arrival of a rescue, he wouldn't hesitate telling me, so I chalked this intrusion up to boredom. I had no interest in engaging and still felt peeved over his tussle with Victor. Since sacrificing my t-shirt for a bandage left my entire upper torso to crisp like a charred jalapeno.

"You should know a second wave of pigs has arrived," he said. When I failed to reply, he repeated himself louder.

"What's that?" I muttered, unable to dodge any longer. I stretched and heaved a deep yawn.

"Now there's over a hundred." Slake didn't glance in my direction while speaking, instead he stared over the edge in a hypnotic gaze. His fingers scraped the railing, peeling a loose piece of paint.

"Is that so?" I hugged my legs while resting my chin onto my knees. I ached while shifting up, and even after settling, the throbbing failed to cease. I swished my tongue around, searching for any moisture, but only a gummy wad of spit remained. I wiped my forehead and it surprised me to discover, it too was dry; the sweat replaced with a mild headache. I felt like a discarded sponge that had been discover behind a sink, blistered and shriveled to half its original size.

"From that dust, I believe there's more." Slake pointed across the fields, but I lacked the will to confirm the sight. Not that it mattered. Add a hundred, or a thousand, the pigs already gathered below were more than enough to thwart any lingering notions of escape.

"Ain't that something" As I spoke, a chorus squeals erupted along with the rumble of trampling hooves. I flinched and unable to help myself, watched as another dozen pigs trotted in from a neighboring field. The others rushed to greet the newcomers, some nuzzling snouts, others bashing heads in displays of dominance. A couple newcomers spooked, galloping a trail of dust as they disappeared back into the fields, but most remained.

"Can I run something by you?" Slake asked, but continued before I could reply. "At first, when nobody stopped, I thought I was crazy. All that jumping and waving, yet not a single person slowed. Sure, we're a bit far, but that half-hanging banner is clear as day."

"Maybe they mistook you for one of them viral campaigns like those fellows who prance around on street corners dressed as lady liberty while advertising insurance. Everyone sees them, but nobody ever really looks."

"At first, I thought it could be coincidental." Slake exhaled and turned toward me. "Then a police truck arrived."

"Wait, what?" I scrambled to my feet.

"It's almost five." Slake tapped his wristwatch as if I'd asked the time. "I doubt the office lost track of us, but if everyone ducked out early, it could be a possibility. Linda does-"

"What was that about a police truck?" I interrupted.

"I was getting to that." Slake motioned at the police cruiser parked up the service road. "Even if our absence was overlooked, which I doubt, there's no way that's going unnoticed. Police tend to take care of their own."

"They sure do." I stared at the police cruiser, trying to distinguish any differences from this morning. It appeared exactly the same. And the one change I did desire, for that bloody stain smeared across the road to disappear, had only grown clearer now that the sun had shifted west. Every time I glanced at that cursed blotch, I was reminded of Harley's death. I rubbed my jaw, which was sore from scrunching into a frown. I took a breath, attempting to relax, but whenever I didn't concentrate on doing so, the scowl returned.

"When I spotted the police truck, I figured they were coming to investigate." Slake puffed a half-laugh, half-sigh. "I cheered as they pulled up to the service exit, lights flashing. Then, well, I can't believe it."

"What?" I almost screamed.

"Those bastards only put up a barricade."

I craned over the billboard and peered at the highway. Indeed, a bright blue police barricade blocked the exit for the service road. Cars continued to zip past, oblivious to the horrors just a short hop beyond. I winced, feeling dizzy and out of breath. My legs wobbled and I clutched the railing for balance.

"Where did they g-go?" I stuttered.

"Hell if I know." Slake chuckled again as if I'd asked the most ridiculous question in the world. "After they assembled the barricade, they just drove off. Not even a single peek toward the service road. They continued on as if this were an everyday construction project."

"You can't be serious." I shrank onto the deck, my legs folding underneath me like melting cheese. I waited for Slake to say he was only riling me up before help arrived. But from the way his head bowed and his lips pressed together as if glued, I realized he was telling the truth. Slake was many things, but a bull-shitter wasn't one of them.

"I thought you should know," he replied, barely speaking the words.

"Do you think they'll return?"

"What I think is this is a quarantine," Slake said, peeling at the loose paint of the railing once again.

"That's great news," I beamed. "Bring on those guys in biohazard suits and lock me up in a bubble. Anything is better than this."

"You remember how I worked at a swine farm? Well, once we had a viral outbreak that caused all the pigs to have a nasty case of the runs. Filth was everywhere, like a volcanic explosion. According to the regulations, we were supposed to halt production and wait for a containment crew. But nothing changed outside of some extra hosing off. When I asked a coworker, he told me the primary rule: AKIL."

"A kill?"

"No, it's an acronym. AKIL, *Always Keep It Local.*" Slake pointed toward the barricade, but I lacked the will to look a second time. "Do you think if the CDC was involved the only backup would be a lone truck putting up roadblocks?" he continued. "No, they'd shut down this entire damn highway. I bet whoever owns the plant where this all started has a connection with the local police. Maybe some people driving did spot us and dialed 911, but the calls were rerouted."

"Maybe," I replied, though Slake's theory was kind of a stretch. Covering up the death of a police officer sure seemed far more involved than a call from a chummy business owner. Plus, the highway recessed quite a distance, so being missed by overly distracted drivers wasn't altogether out of the question.

"What we need is for someone to pull over, but damn if I haven't tried everything." Slake slunk his head, shaking it like a child who'd been caught pilfering a candy bar.

"We could try dropping the banner and putting up our own sign," I suggested.

"Unless you want to spell out *HELP* in your own blood, I'm not sure what we'd use as paint," Slake countered. "And once the sun sets, nobody will be able to see even that."

A sharp pain splintered down my side with the mention of sunset. Even though hours had passed without help, I hadn't considered the possibility of an overnight stay. Odd, I'd spent the majority of the afternoon wishing for the blazing rays to disappear, but now, faced with this new reality, I wanted it to remain light forever.

"What about dropping the banner?" I asked. "That might work as a distraction. Maybe scare off enough pigs to make a break for the van."

Slake chortled as if I'd suggested we jump over the edge and try to fly away.

"I already tried that with the new sign. Not only didn't the pigs scare off, but they rushed in and tore the vinyl apart as if I was dumping food into a trough."

"You did that by yourself?" I yelled.

"Hey, you don't get to judge. Last I checked, your biggest decision was where to nap. Somebody has to be in charge. Do you have a problem with that?"

I shook my head, noting he did have a point about the nap. It didn't surprise me that the pigs had shredded the banner to pieces. If they weren't spooked by sharp tools whizzing in the air, a giant piece of fluttering vinyl was bound to fail.

"Here's what I think," Slake continued. "The police must know we're stuck, so either they're too busy rounding up the pigs or they're bent on letting the quarantine run its course. And considering I haven't spotted anyone chasing the pigs, my guess is it's the latter."

"Do you think we're infected?"

"I think whoever is in charge believes we might be and has decided to wait it out to be certain. Or worse, they are trying to cover-up the incident and figure we're expendable. Easier to explain some worksite 'accident' than those creatures down there. Cut a check and wash their hands." Slake pantomimed peeling money from a wad.

"You can't be serious," I replied. "Nobody's going to leave us up here to starve."

"No, we'll die from dehydration long before we starve." Slake glared at me as if I'd somehow missed this obvious point. "Bet those bastards are doing a cost-benefit analysis as we speak. Cheaper to write off four ex-cons than close an entire factory."

"If I had to guess, I'd say I'm worth at least a car. Maybe a used one if it was foreign." I returned the stare as if he was the one misunderstanding the point.

"You done?" Slake snapped. "Focus. We have to settle this before dark or we'll be out of options."

"The lights," I gasped. "You're forgetting about them. They'll switch on after sunset."

"I didn't forget anything. The lights don't matter, not unless you know how to signal for help in shadow puppet."

"That's not what I'm getting at." I scowled, though the idea of flapping a giant silhouette of a bird was quite amusing. "We need someone to come and investigate, but with the roadblock, I doubt any random driver is going to do that. But a utility crew wouldn't hesitate if there was a power outage."

"Yeah, they'd have to come." Slake clapped his hands and grinned.

"So how do we short them?" I motioned toward the high-voltage lines. Slake's smile faded as we both realized most of the tools were flung over the edge.

"The poles?" Slake said this as if asking a question, but scurried off before I had a chance to reply. I chewed my lip, not having the faintest clue how to short power lines. Sure, I'd been told fiberglass isn't supposed to conduct electricity, but the idea of poking around to find out for certain struck me as a good way to end up charbroiled. Sensing no other option, I followed Slake down.

As I climbed onto the lower deck, I peeked over at Victor, who sat sprawled on the far end. He returned the glance with a flick of his bandaged hand, spotted with patches of dried blood. I waved back, motioning for him to follow, but he didn't inch from his slouched position.

"Here," Slake said, handing me one of the poles. He clutched another as if expecting to tangle the lines like we were poking rice with giant chopsticks.

"Slake, you really think this is such a hot idea?" I held mine vertically, similar to a pole-vaulter balancing before a leap, but kept a safe distance.

"You got another?" He dangled his wobbly pole, poking closer to the lines.

"How 'bout this?" I flung my pole. It swooped onto the wires. I wrenched, fearing any contact might rocket out a fireball, but instead, the pole danced a jiggling bounce, seesawing across the lines for a moment, before plummeting. No fireball. Not even a single spark.

"Good job. Now we have even less." Slake pointed at the remaining poles. "Take another. We have to crisscross the lines."

I took a second pole, my hands shaking. Slake leaned over the railing, prodding closer. The carbineer attached to his safety harness jerked taut, reaching the end of its give. He clasped a rock-solid grip, suspending his pole directly above the lines. He motioned for me to approach. I took a wavering step closer.

"I'll come in from the top, while you swing yours up. We'll press the wires together on the count of three."

"Maybe we should try tangling them again without holding on," I suggested. "Or toss the banner over them."

"Shut up and concentrate. I don't know how long I can hold in this position."

I raised my arms, dipping the pole over the edge. I glanced down, noting an audience of a dozen or so pigs glaring up. Their black, beady eyes followed me, appearing eager for any mishaps that might send me plummeting over the side. The rigid safety line attached to the harness did little to ease my nerves. The pole teetered in my outstretched arms as I angled up, mirroring Slake's position. The poles slanted into a sideways V.

"One," Slake began to count.

A pig trampled below, bashing into another like a bucking bronco. Both squealed a high-pitched trill, punching their snouts together. A third darted in, joining the ruckus, and I glanced down. It was only for a moment, but this break in concentration was enough to loosen my grip. Maybe this was my unconscious will, maybe not, but my hands fumbled across the smooth surface of the pole. It whirled free, plunging from my grasp, and I held only air.

"Are you kidding?" Slake yelled. Before I could apologize, he hurled his pole at the wires. Similar to my first attempt, it stuck between them, hovering like a tightrope walker, before tumbling without a spark.

Bam. A booming crack reverberated like a sledgehammer. From the pain rocking my skull, my first notion was I'd been punched, but then I smelled the familiar odor of a gunshot. Slake gasped, freezing in place, while I spun toward the noise. Victor stood right behind us, his bandaged hand clutching the gun. He arched up his chin as a second shot boomed.

I spun back in time to witness a shower of white sparks glinting through the air. The source was the transformer attached to the utility pole. A syrupy cloud of gray smoke billowed out as the power lines buzzed a husky noise. The air pulsed and fluttered in a tornado-like swoop. The humming noise peeked into a piercing crescendo, then stilled. I caught a single breath before another explosion barreled out.

The transformer on the neighboring pole likewise exploded, but Victor hadn't fired at it. How had it ignited? I barely had time to ponder this new blast when a third transformer detonated. Then another after that. I lost count as the eruptions filed down the line of succeeding poles, shorting transformer after transformer in a machine-gun like burst. Each one bellowing an eruption of sparks before the pulse zipped down the line to the next.

The transformer closest to the billboard hissed again as another blast chimed through the soupy smoke. One of the power lines split from the box and swooped down, trailing a yellow band behind it like a sparkler. The wire flopped across the ground, bounding as if alive, until it smacked into one of the pigs. The creature managed a single high-pitched wheeze, more of a cough than a squeal, before freezing in place. A draft of burnt flesh wafted up, sour and pungent, not like any pork I'd ever smelled, but not altogether unpleasant either.

The wire cracked one final hum as the pig shivered and toppled onto its side. The surrounding pigs lurched back and settled into a hushed perimeter, as if they could sense the danger of rushing in to devour their electrified companion.

The air calmed as the static hum of the power lines faded into nothingness. Though there had been periods of uneasy quiet throughout the afternoon, this silence was mammoth, almost like being wrapped inside a giant cotton ball. I hadn't even considered all the background noise emanating from the wires. Now that it'd disappeared, a nervy coolness slipped over me.

"That did it!" Slake was the first to break the silence. He released a giant whoop, hollering like we'd all just hit the lotto. He didn't even appear to register that Victor was holding a gun as he grabbed him in a bear-like hug. He turned and high-fived me, certain help would be arriving soon. I yelped and returned the gesture, confident in his enthusiasm.

Victor, on the other hand, shrugged and pursed his lips into a half-frown. He spoke in a hoarse tone.

"Power no matter. The only visitor coming is Death. Light or dark, Death look with burning eyes and see all. Now we sit and make peace before too late."

"Yeah, now we wait," Slake replied, shooting me a glance. We both backed away from Victor, who remained at the edge, still pawing the gun.

Friday 5:55 P.M.

 As soon as we were out of Victor's earshot, Slake grabbed my arm and tugged me close. "Okay, what the fuck was that?"

I shrugged while glancing back toward Victor. Slake didn't need to worry about being overheard, since from Victor's glued-shut eyes, I doubted he had any interest in our conversation. He'd resumed his meditative position, kicking his feet out and leaning into the railing as if it was a pillow.

"*Death looks with burning eyes,*" Slake spouted, adding his own eye-roll. "Give me a break. If he meant to say he's going to hell, I might just help him achieve that goal." Slake shoved his hands out into the air.

"Chalk it up to being lost in translation," I replied. "Don't pay him no mind. There's been enough death for one day."

I peeked toward the highway. No sign of any repair crew. Outside the blur of a couple red tail-lights receding into the distance, the road was mostly empty. It was a bit peculiar for a Friday afternoon commute, but not unprecedented on this stretch of 99, considering we were in the deepest reaches of farm country.

I hoped this thought would be reassuring, but it had the opposite effect. It made no sense. Why build Big Bertha in such a remote location? I wondered if this was some delusional engineer's scheme to build the world's tallest billboard. Perhaps the owners of these vacant fields were the only ones crazy enough to take him up on the offer.

"First Harley, now him," Slake said. "Am I the only one who missed the memo stating today was bring your gun to work day?"

I chuckled, not because I found the joke particularly funny, but I was thankful for any break in my paranoid thoughts. Being stuck allowed for too much time inside my head. That always led to bad places, to those evil hankerings. I wouldn't have minded if Victor was right and the devil did arrive, if only to break the monotony.

"I'm serious," Slake continued. "Don't get me wrong, I'm thankful we were able to blast that transformer, but I can't let this pass. Once we get down, I'll have to file a report."

"Yeah, I guess," I replied, but Slake must've sensed my lack of conviction, since he grabbed my arm.

"No guessing about it. This is dangerous shit. Bad enough he's a hundred percent cray-cray, but he's armed. With all that death talk, we need to keep our distance until help arrives."

"Sure." I nodded and Slake released his grasp.

"We're all ex-cons, how did he even get a gun?"

"This is America," I replied.

"You don't have one, do you?"

"I wish. Hell, even a slingshot would be nice." I mimicked shooting pellets at the pigs.

"How could I've missed this? I've never considered the possibility someone could be stupid enough to bring a gun."

"Don't beat yourself up," I replied. "We've worked with a lot of cretins throughout the years, so it was purely a matter of time. Sorry it was today of all days." I raised my hand, considering a reassuring tap on his shoulder, but when Slake appeared ready to grab me a second time, I reconsidered.

"What are you sorry about?" Slake must've noticed my hesitation, since he leaned closer. "You knew, didn't you?"

"Of course not," I said, a little too on the defensive.

"You certain?" Slake crossed his arms, tilted his head, and chewed on his lip. "You didn't seem all that surprised when he started shooting."

"I've seen worse." At least that much was true.

"Honest?" Slake asked. "You had no idea?"

"No idea," I repeated.

"Why do you think he has it?"

"Self-protection, I guess." From my own experience, I knew there were numerous reasons for possessing illegal firearms, and not a single one was good. Best to remain in the dark. It kept matters simple that way.

"What if he's suicidal?" Slake continued. "That would explain his odd obsession with the devil and death."

"Yeah, maybe," I replied, but out of all the possibilities, suicide had never crossed my mind. I don't know why, since Slake did have a point about that devil talk, but somehow Victor had never struck me as the suicidal type. It wasn't like he was positive about life, but he wasn't depressed either.

"If he wants to off himself, that's one thing. But damn if I'm gonna let him do it on my watch." Slake pressed close, whispering into my ear. "We're taking that gun."

"Don't bother," I whispered back. "He's not suicidal."

"That wasn't what I was thinking." Slake exhaled as if this was precisely what he was thinking.

"It's only a .22. You'd never hit anything from this distance," I guessed, hoping to derail any more of his crazy schemes before they left the station.

I was far from a gun expert, but knew enough that hitting one pig on the ground would be near impossible, forget raising attention on the highway. Even if the tiny cartridge could travel that far, there were too many variables to consider, the wind, the height, the fact the target would be moving. No, it'd be a waste of bullets.

"Wouldn't you like to be one of those commuters? Driving home right now to a cool apartment and a fridge full of food?"

I nodded and spotted a motorcycle as it raced down the highway at a breakneck speed. From this height, I felt like I could reach out and snatch it up like a toy, while at the same time it felt as far away as the moon.

"That gun is the answer. Our only hope for getting home tonight," Slake continued to whisper.

"What about the electric crew?" I peeked toward Victor to see if he was listening, but his eyes remained closed.

"I hope they come, but hoping is far from being certain. And now that it's past five, they might just put off repairing the wires until Monday. Do you want to spend all weekend up here on a hope?" Slake motioned at Victor. "With him?"

"Slake, we can't do this. He's crazy as fuck," I replied.

"Which is all the more reason we can't allow him to keep it. I'm not risking my safety on a hope. What's certain is that without that gun, there's no escape."

"Maybe," I replied, still doubtful the two of us had any chance of overpowering Victor.

"You willing to risk missing your trip on a maybe? Risk ever seeing your son again?" Slake's words stung, though he had a point. If my ass wasn't plastered to that bus seat tomorrow, I doubt Patti would give me another opportunity. However, getting shot would likewise reduce my chances of ever seeing Tyler again to zero.

"Let's just wait and see if that electric crew arrives," I replied.

"In another hour it'll be dark." Slake pointed at the shadows creeping over the mountaintops as if I'd been unaware of the impending nightfall. "Listen, if not for you, do it for Harley."

"What does Harley have to do with anything?"

"Think about it. Victor had a gun the entire time. If he'd wanted, he could've popped off a few shots to scare the pigs back. Harley might be alive if he hadn't just watched. He could've changed things, but he didn't. That places Harley's death right on his shoulders."

"You don't know that," I replied, but I couldn't help but recall how that pig straddled Harley and tore off a chunk of his cheek. If anything could've saved him, a warning shot would've done the trick. In fact, Harley appeared to have the pigs beat until his gun ran out of bullets. Perhaps Slake was onto something. I felt a volcano of anger bubbling inside and began the countdown.

Twenty. Exhale, just like the doc said to. Nineteen...

"Think about it, Russ. He was up here this entire time and never once mentioned the fact he had a fucking gun. Lied to us and is preventing our escape. He wants to keep us here."

Eighteen. Exhale. Seventeen. In and out. Easy.

"Not acting is sometimes worse than doing the wrong thing. You know I'm telling the truth. Do you want your son to know you didn't do everything you could to see him?"

"Even if we got the gun," I blurted, a little too loud and paused to see if Victor heard. He hadn't so I continued in a whisper. "Even if, that clip likely holds ten rounds, so subtract two for the transformer and that leaves eight bullets. There's over a hundred pigs. At best, you scatter half then it's a long dash to the van."

"We have to try. I can't take it myself. He's too big. You know that."

"That's right, he's too big. How we gonna roll him over? It's impossible-" I paused. Harley's cell chimed that wretched country song and we both leered down.

"Forget the van." Slake grinned. "All we need is that damn phone."

I nodded in agreement. The blasted thing was almost touching the base of the unipole. Two, maybe three shots would be enough to scatter the pigs in order to snatch it.

"Remember, Victor's the reason you dropped the phone in the first place. Now he's the solution whether he likes it or not."

Slake's words reverberated a certain confidence I couldn't shake. I almost forgot that fumbling the phone had been my fault, but when this irksome reality surfaced, it only made me more determined to remedy the problem. Yes, I had another chance and I vowed not to muck it up.

"Okay," I agreed. "But how do we do it? Not like there's any place to hide. He'll see us coming."

"Not in the dark. We wait until after sunset. Plus, that gives some time to see if the electric crew is really on the way. If not, I have to know that you're all in."

"A thousand percent," I replied.

Friday 7:48 P.M.

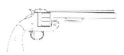 It took far more wrangling than expected, but we unhitched the outer-deck's safety line. I wound the polyester rope into a fireman's coil, leaving the end dangling for a quick release. With the final rays of sunlight vaporizing behind the mountains, I couldn't afford any delay while unfurling the rope in the dark. Slake secured the other end to the railing with a clove hitch, and with a flick of his wrist, signaled to proceed.

I slunk across the deck, stopping within arm's reach of Victor. His eyes closed, legs sprawled, and he puttered throaty snores, but I was paranoid this outward show of sleep was merely a ruse.

Inching a step closer, I raised the rope. As if confirming my worst fears, his breathing settled and I froze. If he was lying on his back then tying him down would be a cinch. As long as his back remained pressed to the railing, we'd need at least two ropes; one across his chest, another securing his legs. And considering his bulky size, even this might not be enough.

Slake tugged, confirming the rope was taut, and motioned to continue. I stepped over Victor, but my eyes remained locked on his face, anticipating any sudden arousal. Though his breathing fluctuated, wavering between shallow huffs and a deep wheeze, his blank expression never altered as I kneeled beside him. The rope hovered inches above him as I looped it to the railing with a slip knot. One yank and the line would snap, fastening across his chest. It dangled in the air, wagging like a dog's tail, erratic and waiting to bite.

I uncoiled a bit more, causing the rope to tighten and press against his chest. Victor didn't flinch, so I motioned for Slake to approach. He crossed the deck on tippy-toes, almost in a comical gait, but I forced down any amusement and instead scowled at this ridiculous prance. Clearly, Slake had no experience sneaking around, since the worst possible way to appear nondescript was by trying to appear nondescript.

I handed the rope to Slake, whose hand shook while taking it. I could almost tap the rhythm of his jittery vibrations floating in the air. Victor must've likewise sensed them, since his eyes popped open. Slake gasped, fumbling the rope, but thankfully held on. Victor craned his neck and glared up.

"No news," I whispered in a calm tone. "Go back to sleep."

Victor nodded once and closed his eyes. I slipped a couple steps back and eyed the rope. It was within arm's reach if Victor should bolt back to life. One tug and it'd snap across his chest like a rubber band. But I waited. Slake glared over, lingering for some signal, but when I motioned for him to back away, he stood locked in place. Even the startled expression remained plastered to his face.

It was only when Victor stretched, cracking his elbow with a snap that Slake bounded into action. He whirled around, almost crashing into the railing. His hands quivered as he looped the rope around the bars. So focused on the knot he failed to notice Victor shifting.

Victor brushed against the slack line and the coarse fibers of the rope must've prickled his skin, since he scratched at his bicep, flexing it like a bow. He opened his eyes, zeroing in on the rope.

"Now," I yelled.

I dove for the rope. My fingers wrapped around it and I yanked. The rope plucked taut. Victor wheeled forward, bucking like a bull freeing itself from a lasso. The rope tore across my palm, skinning away a layer of raw flesh. I recoiled, losing my grasp.

Slake swiped for the other end as Victor hurled the rope away. Slake lunged over Victor, rope in hand, and tumbled beside me. He yanked and the rope snapped across Victor's thigh. Victor yelped, crashing down. He attempted to stand again, but when he shoved with his injured hand, he seized over in pain. The rope slithered in front of me and I grabbed for it.

Victor was still seizing as I yanked. The rope whizzed across his neck, flinging his head back in a gasping choke. Victor punted his legs and a thin line of spittle drooled from the corner of his mouth. He clawed at the rope, wrenching from side to side clearly suffocating, and as much as I wanted that gun, I couldn't kill for it.

I'd made that promise. Too many deaths chained to my ankle already. Damn. I released my grasp.

The rope slackened and Victor wheezed. He spun onto his side, legs still locked by Slake's rope. I swiped for the gun, but Victor lurched back up. He braced his elbows against the deck and with a mammoth jab, pried his legs free. Slake tumbled back, losing his grip. I still held my rope, which had fallen from Victor's neck down to his chest, and gave a final heave. Victor countered, tugging forward, and the rope wrenched free. I staggered back and Victor charged straight at me.

There was nowhere to dodge. I spun around, pressing against the railing and as we collided, Victor shoved me into the rigid bars. His meaty fists walloped my shoulder, pounding me into a wet tissue. My legs buckled, collapsing underneath me. I should've tumbled, but remained suspended. In fact, I did the opposite and lurched into the air. It wasn't until I gasped and failed to catch a breath when I realized he was clutching my neck.

I struggled to form a single word, but barely an agonizing gurgle emerged. My feet dangled, dancing across an invisible platform. My hands scrabbled across his tree-trunk of an arm, which held me suspended in this choking grasp. I dug my nails into his bicep, but it was as futile as scratching my name in dry cement. My eyes fluttered and I found a slight reassurance they were still under my control. The world faded, in and out; either from my blinking or lack of breath. I couldn't tell which.

Something thudded against my chest and knocked my vision into a dull blur. My first thought was Victor was punching me, but the blow radiated over my entire body. A sliver of air burst into my lungs and I gasped for more. A vibrant flash of light flooded over as I rolled through a billowing white cloud.

As the color settled into a hazy gray, I realized I'd been flopped across the deck. I inhaled another mouthful and spun over onto my back. Slake crouched at my side, his knees buckled as if waiting to pounce. Wondering why he was in this awkward position, I spotted Victor. He was aiming the gun straight at us.

"Easy...now," Slake said, drawing out every syllable. "Let's...put...the...gun...down...and...talk."

"Time for talk is over." Victor focused his aim on Slake. I wanted to find relief in this, but my gulping inhales quickened. From what I'd gathered, Slake must've knocked into us, toppling me free from Victor's grasp. At the same time, this allowed Victor time to remove the gun and corner us.

"Hold on," Slake said, speeding up his words. "Don't let this misunderstanding do things that can't be undone."

"The rope is no misunderstanding." Victor kicked the loose rope away as he stepped closer.

"Look, the lights didn't come on," Slake said, motioning up at the billboard. "That means someone will soon be on the way. If you do this, you'll go straight back to prison."

"Nobody will come." Victor chewed his lip while speaking. "I understand now. You are the devil. And you come for me."

"No, no," Slake repeated, motioning for Victor to lower his aim. "Please don't do this. I'm not the devil, I'm not."

"Victor," I wheezed, squeezing the word from my sore lungs. "We just wanted the gun. That's all."

"The gun?" Victor asked, as if he didn't realize he was holding one.

"Those pigs are the devils, not us. We wanted the gun to escape and were afraid you wouldn't give it up."

"So you try to kill me?" Victor swung his aim from Slake, focusing it on me. I took a deep breath and continued.

"No. We didn't mean to hurt you, only tie you up. It was when you moved the rope caught your neck, but that wasn't the plan. We were afraid you wouldn't want to leave. That's the honest truth." I crossed myself, swearing to the Almighty.

"Yes. That's all we wanted, the gun. I promise," Slake added, likewise crossing himself.

"Sorry I forgot to put it in the hat." Victor grinned for a moment, then his face dropped into a scowl. "You want the gun?"

"It's okay," Slake replied. "You can keep it."

"You say you want it, no?" Victor jammed the muzzled against Slake's forehead. Slake lowered his eyes. "This is what you say."

"Victor, don't," I yelled.

"You want it?" Victor asked. "Yes or no?"

"Yes," Slake replied, closing his eyes.

"Take it."

I figured Victor wanted Slake to swipe for the gun before blasting him, so I adverted my eyes. It wasn't until I heard the clonk of metal on metal that I peered over. Victor had dropped the gun.

"Is no use anyhow. Fate is sealed." Victor turned his back and strode across the deck.

Slake snatched the gun. He didn't aim at Victor, but held it close enough should Victor change his mind. Victor grabbed the ladder, but turned back before climbing.

"All you needed was to ask," he said. "All clear now. I must climb all the way up before falling."

"You do that," Slake replied, squeezing the gun tighter. After Victor disappeared onto the upper-deck, he finally let his shoulders slump and exhaled.

"Did that really just happen?" he asked.

"I guess that could've gone better," I replied. "You okay?"

Slake leaned forward and groaned, as if my question had reawakened his injury. I crossed my arms and stared over the edge. Our fight hadn't gone unnoticed by the pigs, who were galloping around the unipole in a frenzy.

"Once they settle, we grab that phone. You ready?" I asked.

"This has to be all you," Slake replied, continuing to groan while patting his back.

"Okay then." I could've argued, especially since my entire body was throbbing after that chokehold, but kept my annoyance with Slake's theatrics to myself. I'd already settled on the idea I'd be the one who'd take the plunge and didn't see the need for aggravating an already prickly situation.

I coiled the extra rope, ignoring the searing pain radiating down my neck. Even before the chokehold, my throat was parched, but now it felt like I'd swallowed a hot coal. I gulped a deep breath, knowing whatever pain couldn't compare to how I'd feel if we didn't escape this jinxed billboard soon.

Slake stood near the edge, arms crossed, staring down at those vile creatures. I tapped his shoulder.

"Well, come on." I motioned toward the ladder. "I have a bus to catch."

Friday 8:29 P.M.

 A tug whipped across my exposed back and I clamped my fists. I was hanging onto a piece of metal, one of the ladder's rungs. Unlike during the day, it was frigid to the touch. I kicked to steady myself, but swatted open air. My grip tightened and I attempted to distinguish anything through the murky nebulous floating all around. My left foot connected with something solid, metal from the feel, so I scrabbled across the smooth surface, but discovered no foothold.

I blinked and the unipole came into focus in front of me. Okay, at least that much was clear, but why no rungs? I peered down and almost lost my fragile clutch. I was at the ladder's end, hanging twenty feet above the ground, and the snoozing pigs. Not wishing to rouse them while in this precarious spot, I froze, allowing my legs to dangle. I took a breath and heaved myself up, rung after rung, until my feet firmly planted back on the ladder.

"Really, again?" Slake's voice was a whisper, so when I spotted him hovering right above, I was taken aback. He was grabbing the ladder with one hand, my safety line with the other. "How many times are we going to do this?"

How many times? His question made no sense. How long had I been hanging here? I didn't recall climbing onto the ladder. One moment, I'd been up on the deck after our confrontation with Victor, and now, I was here.

"Hey, you okay?" When I failed to respond again, he tugged and a knock shot across my harness. I realized this to be what jerked me to attention in the first place.

"Yeah, stop that," I answered a tad louder than I'd wanted. A couple pigs stirred, but soon settled.

"Then stop horsing around," he replied, giving my safety line another yank.

"You want to swap positions?" I wrenched at the rope. He released his hold, splayed out his palm, and shot me an icy glare.

"Sure, whenever you're ready," he said, after exhaling through clenched teeth. "Let's just try to get this done before sunrise." He pawed at a bundle of fiberglass poles he must've brought down with him, removing one. He descended a few more rungs until his feet were right above my head.

"The phone is there." He pointed toward a spot on the ground a couple yards from the base of the unipole.

"I know," I snapped, though I didn't. I needed another moment to gather my thoughts before proceeding and wanted to ask precisely how long I'd been hanging here, but decided the answer didn't matter. I did my best to shove this momentary lapse from my mind, chalking it up to the toll of this shitty day, compounded by barely sleeping this entire week. I'd experienced brief spells similar to this during my dark days and found with some rest, all soon returned to normal.

"Okay," I said, after counting down and steadying my pounding pulse. Slake handed me a pole and the fiberglass bowed as I stretched it toward the ground. The pigs rustled a bit as I steadied the edge of the pole against the phone. Before the first one could trample in to knock the pole away, I shoved.

The phone slid a foot closer. Another few swipes and it would be directly underneath. Once there, all I'd need was a momentary distraction in order to drop down and grab it. I'd almost achieved that the first time around and that was without the gun. Now we had it, scaring the pigs back should be a cinch. At least, that was what I told myself while the pigs awakened.

By the fourth whack, the phone slid into place directly underneath my dangling legs. As long as it wasn't playing that country ringtone, the pigs gave it no regard and lost interest entirely as I raised the pole back to Slake. If only their locked gaze on me could easily be dismissed. Instead, the pigs circled underneath, eyes focused up, steady and waiting.

"Now hand over the gun," I said, not wishing to delay any further.

"Don't you have it?" Slake's chin kicked up and he almost lost his grip. He steadied and tapped his waist, motioning for me to do the same. I had no recollection of him handing the gun over, but when I reached down, I discovered it in the hem of my pants.

"Just testing to see if you're awake," I said, sliding the .22 into my palm.

"I am," Slake replied. "Are you?"

"I can't wait to blast away a few of these porky fucks and get the hell out of here."

Slake nodded and swung the pole he was holding. He waved it around a little while hollering for the pigs, before jamming it into the ground as far as he could reach. A couple of the pigs bashed through the crowd toward it taking the bait, but most remained rigid, glaring up at me. I released my grasp and the safety caught, holding me dangling in place.

I clutched the gun while the rope settled into a calm sway. Forget a warning shot, I locked my aim onto an overly aggressive pig near the center of the pit. The creature must've sensed my gaze, since it bucked, displaying a set of gnashing teeth, before dipping behind another pig. I attempted to track it within the horde, but soon lost sight. My sight shifted onto another, but it too disappeared within the vortex. I decided to descend a measure to ensure my aim.

The catch whizzed as I dropped over half the distance to the ground. Dozens of upturned snouts raised in my direction, throbbing a feverish rhythm. I exhaled a strangled breath while hanging only a couple feet above their pirouetting bodies and gyrating teeth. I rubbed the ridged handle of the gun, taking aim, but still unable to focus enough to zero in on any one pig.

"Incoming," Slake yelled. I jerked toward a flutter to my left. A pig throttled through the air, soaring as if in flight. Without aiming, I blasted off a shot. The bullet whizzed past the pig, missing it completely, striking a weedy patch just beyond the group circled below.

I dodged the best I could, yanking up my legs. The pig chomped at me, but caught only the air and tumbled back to the ground. It landed with a springy thud, squealed, and plowed through the others, clearing a space like an unfurling roll of carpet. The gunshot likewise worked to scatter the crowd as brief pockets of space rippled out. I swung my aim toward the phone, but didn't need to fire again, since the area had cleared enough to descend. I hit the catch and dropped.

My first thought after striking the dirt was an odd curiosity on the firmness of my foothold, as if the day spent up on the deck had warped my memory of how it felt to stand on solid ground. I shook off the feeling and swiped for the phone. Slake cried out and I jerked in time to spot a pig galloping toward me. I fired. The bullet tore through the creature's flaring nostrils, propelling its head back as if punched. Three careening steps later, the pig collapsed, snorting a final crimson-coated breath across the dirt.

The other animals scurried backward as I whirled around in a circle, poking the gun out like a halo. When none dared to charge, I snatched the phone with ninja-fast reflexes. It weighed next to nothing, but as I shoved it into my jeans, it seemed to fill my pocket like a concrete slab.

A booming screech erupted as a line of pigs formed a few feet away. I seized the rope. My fingers pawed at the coarse fibers as I lunged up. The safety harness caught and tightened around my waist less than a foot from the ground. I jerked a second time, but remained tangled in place. Another growl zipped through the crowd, this time rumbling and low-pitched. I yanked once more, to no avail. The noise cut short, replaced by the thrum of trampling hooves. A deluge of pigs raced at me.

"The catch," Slake yelled, and I realized the safety lock was still engaged. I yanked the release, and as if springing open a reverse parachute, I bounded into the air. I glared up at the bottom rung of the ladder that appeared both incredibly close, yet miles away. My muscles seemed to pop from the bone as my legs caterpillared over the line. I whiffed an odor of decay mixed with a sweet scent similar to raspberries. A copper taste plunged down my throat as I climbed.

A shrieking howl exploded next to me and I flinched, turning just as a pig walloped into my ribcage. The blow knocked away my breath, but I managed to dodge in time to avoid its munching teeth. Another inch closer and it would've sucked away a mouthful of flesh, but its chomping mouth simply sprayed me with a runny streak of green mucus.

I heaved before another could soar in with these missile-like attacks, and after a few more bumpy tugs, my fingers wrapped around the bottommost rung. I scrambled onto the ladder with Slake's help, gasping fiery mouthfuls of air. The pigs swarmed, springing like bursting kernels of popcorn. I worried my trembling hands wouldn't steady enough to climb, but as Slake wrapped his arm around my shoulder, I maintained my grip.

My entire body pulsed while climbing onto the deck. I rolled across the platform, my legs unable to settle enough to stand. I patted my chest where the pig had walloped me, ensuring the skin hadn't broke, and swiped away the gooey neon-green snot. Biting at my lip, I steadied enough to remove the phone from my pocket. My shaking continued and I worried I might drop it, so I shoved it toward Slake. He took the phone from my unsteady hand and I flopped across the deck.

"No," Slake gasped, pounding the cell phone's buttons. I peered up as he smashed a reverberating kick into the railing.

"Easy," I replied. "If there's no reception, try going onto the outer-deck." A vile realization scuttled over me: *What if that downed transformer likewise killed the power for any nearby cell-towers?* I tried to recall whether the phone rang or not since we'd blown the transformer, but when Slake yelled again, I lost my concentration.

"Come on. No. Please. *NO!*" A thick vein throbbed across Slake's neck as he clutched the phone with a strangling grip. The dim light of the keyboard cranked off and I realized reception wasn't the issue. Slake held the power button and the phone purred a momentary chirp, buzzing back to life. It glowed for a five count before being cast back into darkness.

"Let me try," I said, but Slake ignored the request. He pressed the power button again. This time, the phone lasted for a single second, not even accomplishing the initial chirp before switching off. He continued this powering on and off dance at least a dozen times before collapsing beside me.

"Help," he cried out. "Help. *HELP!*"

His shouting must've sparked Victor to our failure, since he yelled down from the upper-deck. "I say we no leave, but you no listen."

Slake jerked his head up and curled his lips into a tight knot, but refrained from shouting a reply. Instead, he tugged me close, whispering into my ear. "If that fucker had mentioned the gun earlier, we could've gotten the phone before the batteries died."

Even though it was a whisper, he stressed every syllable with an iron tongue.

"We'll try again in a little bit," I whispered back. "Maybe it still has enough juice for one final call."

"Yes, we'll wait," Slake continued in the same staccato tone. He wrapped his arm around me, which, to be honest, felt kind of reassuring after everything. But when his hand reached over and removed the gun, the warm feeling mutated into a shiver.

"Hold on," I replied, as he waved the gun and steadied his aim toward the upper-deck.

"There's nothing else to do but hold on," he continued to whisper. "But come tomorrow morning, if we're still waiting, if help hasn't arrived, I'm going to kill that bastard."

Saturday 6:00 A.M.

 The alarm chimed like a hammer. I jerked, rolled onto my side, and pawed for the shabby nightstand where I normally placed my watch. Five more minutes, I hemmed, as my fingers brushed across the jagged metallic surface. *Metallic*? My wooden nightstand consisted of chipped paint and perhaps a couple splinters, but nothing like this. I sat up as the realization dawned like putting on a cold, damp sock.

I silenced the alarm, regretting I'd forgotten to switch it off when I lay down last night. The fact I'd set it specifically to ensure I wouldn't miss my bus made spotting the pigs, still rummaging below, more daunting. I leaned back, hoping to return to the blissful unawareness, but a harsh, throbbing pain made certain there would be no rest. Truthfully, I was a bit shocked I'd wangled a wink of sleep at all.

The entire night, I'd barely slept more than ten minutes at a time. If not roused by the raucous growls and thudding of pigs, it was the fiery agony shooting up my back. Worst of all, any time I came close to dozing I'd hear a noise, such as churning tires or a siren off in the distance, and bolt back to life. Except that whenever I looked, it must've been all in my head since there was nothing. Nothing ever, except those vile pigs.

I closed my eyes, but it was no use. Now that the sun had risen, the beaming rays pounded my skull like a volcano. I yawned, stretched my arms, and felt a pressure building in my bladder. My mouth felt like it'd been vacuumed and I began to wonder if my urge to pee was the final remnants of hydration. I was desperate for a drink, but not that desperate, so I crossed the deck, and urinated over the side. I was just a little bladder-shy, but pissing all over them oinking bastards was about the only enjoyable thing I'd experienced since climbing up.

Even this joy cut short as my good ole' bladder trickled dry. Nevertheless, the urge to urinate remained, seizing my innards, but as much as I pressed for more, only dust emerged. My belly moaned a hearty rumble, though I didn't feel hungry. The pangs had ebbed and flowed through the night, arriving in waves, churning my stomach into a mill.

I turned, hearing a whistle, and spotted Slake approaching. It took me a second to recognize the song he was whistling, but then I realized it was Harley's ringtone. Slake was grinning, though deep black pockets hung below his eyes like bruises, and I knew he'd slept about as well as I had. Even if I wanted to return the smile, my face had cemented into a puckered scowl, as if I'd eaten a bowl of rancid lemons. Shoot, if I could've been that lucky, I'd have traded my left nut for a moldy piece of fruit or a thimble-full of water.

"Top of the morning," he said with a smirk. "Ready for breakfast?"

I shook my head, not wanting to engage in any such games. One thing I'd learned inside was that it was best to avoid unattainable fantasies, particularly of simple pleasures, since they tended to break a man quicker than torture. The mind had a funny way or working like that. Although my stomach had other ideas and grumbled with the slightest mention of breakfast.

"One order of ham coming right up." Slake aimed the gun toward the pigs. I wasn't keen about the casual way he swung it around, especially after last night's comment about murdering Victor. I didn't spy Victor anywhere and assumed he must be on the upper-deck still since I would've certainly awoken to a gunshot or fighting of any kind. At least, I hoped I would've. From Slake's beaming expression, I was far from certain.

"We should save the bullets," I replied, hoping he'd holster the gun.

"Guess you're right." Slake dropped his arm, but kept a tight clutch on the grip. "Even if we shot one, the others would snap up the corpse before we could retrieve it. Perhaps we could tie a noose and sling it around one of those fuckers, hauling it up before the others got to it."

"I ain't that hungry." Not only did I lack the energy for any hunt, but that green snot gave me pause. Raw pork was hazardous in the best conditions and we sure as shit couldn't build a fire up here.

Disease aside, after yesterday's close encounters, I had no intention of getting anywhere near those vicious suckers.

"If the pigs are out of the question, I guess we can always chomp down on each other. You want to volunteer Victor for the honor?" From the way Slake smirked while peering toward the upper-deck, I prayed he hadn't done anything rash.

"I'm in no joking mood," I replied. "We need to keep our shit together until help arrives."

"I never would've believed it, but Victor was right." Slake spat a high-pitched cackle, more sinister than jolly. "The only one coming is death."

"Don't you start up with that nonsense," I said. "What about the phone? Any juice?"

"Ask them." Slake pointed at the pigs. "They sure have plenty of juice? Never run dry, do they?"

"Give me the phone." I reached out, but Slake swatted my hand away.

"It's like us, dead. So I buried it." He pantomimed throwing the phone over the edge.

"You didn't," I replied, but Slake patted at empty pockets. I wanted to fling him off the side, particularly considering I was still sore where the pig had walloped me while fetching the phone. Instead, I clenched my teeth while running my fingers over the bruise. My skin remained sticky from where the thing had slimed me and I hoped the infection couldn't be spread to humans, but if we didn't get off this billboard soon, a virus would be the least of our concerns.

"Choo-choo, the train has left the station. And nobody's aboard," Slake chimed in a sing-song voice.

"Stay positive," I replied. "Someone's bound to come for them wires. It's still early."

"If they didn't come yesterday, they won't ever." Slake broke into another cackle, this time more forcefully.

"You don't know that," I insisted. "Maybe the utility company didn't want to pony up for overtime, a union thing or such. Those downed transformers had to set off a bunch of alarms, so somebody's on the way."

"Do you prefer to be buried or cremated?" When I failed to reply to this morbid question, Slake continued. "Cremation for me. I never saw the appeal of pumping a body full of all those chemicals just to appear alive. It's like the world's worst Botox job." Slake pulled his cheeks back, mirroring a botched face-lift, before spitting another fiendish laugh.

"Speaking of pumping yourself full of chemicals, I'm sure you heard all sorts of promises in rehab that you thought weren't true at the time, but you made it through, right?" I grabbed his shoulder, attempting to relax his gun-clutching arm. "One day at a time. Up here, we need to take it minute by minute. But, I swear, we will get through this."

"A hundred and sixty-four," he replied. "I spent the last hour counting. You hear me? A hundred and sixty-four of those fuckers. *Oink, oink, oink.*"

I can't say I enjoyed the oinking, but it was a slight improvement to the laughter. "You survived rehab, so you'll survive this. Let's sit-"

"What the hell do you know about what I survived?" Slake interrupted, while giving the railing a firm smack.

"I know enough." I recalled my own troubles and almost felt envious that Slake had a cozy rehab, while my solace came inside the bitter bars of a six-by-eight cage.

"That's right. I almost forgot you're the guy with all the answers. But I have a secret, *Answer-Man*. Oh, do I have a whopper."

"I don't need to hear it." I glanced toward the upper-deck, really hoping that wasn't his secret. From Slake's rambling, I feared he'd done something irreversible. "Secrets are like children. Best keep them close otherwise there's bound to be trouble," I continued.

"Yes, yes, *YES!*" Slake repeated. "You wouldn't want me to *squeal*. Chew on that, *porky*. My mother did say bacon would be the death of me. *Oink-oink. Choo-choo. Oink-oink.*"

I eyed the gun, wondering if in his chaotic ramblings Slake might not see me coming. He noticed my glance and broke into a deep laugh, almost losing his breath altogether. Not knowing what else to do, I chuckled along with him.

"Don't worry, I'm not going to kill you. Those damn pigs are doing a good enough job. One hundred and sixty-four. Imagine that. I bet that's enough to supply footballs for the entire NFL. *Oink-oink. Choo-choo. Oink-Choo-Oink-Oink.*"

"Fine, what's this grand secret of yours?" I asked, but ignoring me, Slake howled while jumping on the creaky deck.

"I'm the big bad wolf. *Whooo-hooo.* I'll huff, and I'll puff, and I'll blow this whole billboard down."

I stepped back as Slake continued to howl. I'd seen my fair share of guys crack; mostly during my time in peels, and out of those, the controlling types always broke hardest. They'd swing from one extreme to the other, transforming from lizards into bucking bulls. Usually, a few minutes of ranting was all they needed to revert, but the key was to avoid any permanent damage. With Slake still brandishing that gun, I wondered if that was possible, so I shuffled back.

"Wait," he yelled, turning his attention back to me.

"What?" I froze.

"The truth is I never went to rehab."

"Okay, then. But you'll still get through this." I attempted to sound sympathetic, but as revelations went, this was far from the burning-bush kind and more of the no-shit variety. Indeed, drugs were my first instinct when he'd started to spout off all that crazy. Withdrawal rants were so kooky that even schizophrenics writhed with envy.

"You don't get it. I'm not an addict."

"I don't care if you are." If I had a nickel for every time I'd heard that, I'd have enough for a pretty good cocaine habit.

"No, I've never used drugs. It wasn't like I was supposed to go to rehab and ditched out. In fact, I've never done anything outside of a beer or two. Now, I'm going to die and the only thing I can think about is all the stuff I haven't done. Isn't that stupid? Most would regret never visiting Paris or making love to a model, but I just keep wondering what it feels like to smoke a cigarette."

"I'll buy you a pack when we get down, but let me warn you, it's a filthy habit."

"There's only one way down." Slake hoisted himself onto the railing. He stood there for a long moment, hovering over the edge. I yanked his arm, forcing him down. As his feet clanked onto the deck, he broke into another fit of unbridled laughter as though this had been the world's funniest joke.

"Not having a smoke ain't something to off yourself over." I shoved him onto his haunches, thankful he didn't resist.

"Do you remember Stu Sartain?" Slake asked as his heaving laughter puttered to a stop.

"I've heard of him, but he was before my time." I sat next to him, relaxing a bit, but keeping a keen eye on that gun.

"Yeah, I'm sure you heard about that bastard. Christ, even his initials spelled *SS*. He was the one who trained me. He sure loved sinking his claws into all the 'boys'. That's how he referred to me, always "Boy, do this!" or "Boy, get that!" Said it wasn't racist, since he called all the trainees that, but I knew better. I also knew enough to never call him out on it."

"Different times," I replied.

"It wasn't that long ago. The reason I brought it up is because on my first day, he trained me with another guy. Anton was his name. When we reached the top, Stu told us that from that point on he owned us. Anton, who was also black, didn't much care for this white asshole using the word 'own' and said as much. Stu didn't say anything and we went on swapping the banner as normal. You probably know the sign, it's that one just north of Chowchilla, across the highway from the shabby hotdog place that looks like it's haunted."

"Yeah, it's the one where the fourth rung from the top is missing."

"Precisely. So, we finished up and were about to climb down when Stu started to have this coughing fit. He motioned for Anton to come over and help, but when he did, Stu grabbed him, unclipped his harness, and flung him down the ladder. I'll never forget the way his head walloped against the rungs, splintering open like a watermelon. You can still make out the stain if you know where to look."

"Ain't that something? Did Stu go back inside for that?"

"No, I kept my mouth shut. I was fresh out of the pen and knew better than to challenge him. He was in with a group of old-timers who weren't much better and would use any excuse to bust heads. Those were brutal days."

"Sorry to hear."

"The reason I brought it up was because I made a promise right then and there. I'd never give those bastards an inch of rope to hang me with. I'd do whatever it took to be in charge and when I ran things, I'd be strict, but fair. Do you realize how difficult it's been? Trying to be perfect all the time? Living your entire life by the books? I've missed out on so much."

"The answer ain't slinking around in self-loathing."

"Do you think I don't know that?" Slake waved his arms and the one clutching the gun came dangerously close to aiming in my direction. Slake must've noted my panic, since he lowered his hands along with his tone. "It's just so fucking hard."

"Yes it is," I said, noticing Slake was shivering. The weather wasn't the cause, since the sun was glistening in the horizon like a toasty bath. It appeared to be another beautiful day. Damn, I'd never wished for rain more in my entire life.

"I obsess over Anton," Slake muttered after a protracted silence. "I can't stop thinking about it. I imagine how I might've been the one to backtalk Stu. How I could've easily been the one tossed over the side. How, if I had any courage, I might've dove to save Anton, instead of standing there like a dumb mute."

"It wasn't your fault."

"I've said that a million times, but nothing can bring me to believe it. I want to be angry at that murdering sonofabitch, but the emotions just keep turning in. What the hell is wrong with me?"

"Sounds like you were just scared. Ain't nothing peculiar about that."

"You know what *is* peculiar? The image I can't shake from that day? It isn't Anton's head bashing against the railing or any of the carnage. Nor is it how he flapped his arms, believing he might fly. Or how he didn't cry out. What I can't forget is his snap latch. How it whistled while scratching across the deck. How a single spark whirled out before toppling over the edge."

"That sounds horrible."

"No, it was beautiful. Do you know how much that single image has haunted me? I see that spark when I close my eyes. I hear that whistle in the shower. And the more I try to shake it, the more it possesses me. There's only one way to stop it. Do you know how many times I've stood up on a deck and scraped my carabineer hoping to see that spark again?"

My eyes turned from the gun and focused toward Slake's harness. The snap-latch was hanging loose, unclipped, and free. Everything clicked.

"Suicide," I muttered. "Why'd you tell everyone you went away for drugs?"

"You think I can show a single weakness? We may be on the outside, but some things never change. Guys respect addicts. Shoot, half of them were once and the other half still are. But nobody respects a suicide, especially a failed attempt."

"You tried? When?"

"It was during a job with Jake Fraden. I stepped over the edge and he caught my harness just in time. He knew it wasn't an accident and filed an incident report. I was taken in to a hospital for a fifty-one-fifty."

"Jake didn't mention anything. Nobody knows, so forget about it."

"I know. That's all that matters. I know I'm a failure. A failed boss. A failed husband. I even failed at being a criminal. A failure through and through. When I was a child, I actually believed I might grow up to do something special, but my only legacy is to die on this fucking billboard."

"What's this stupid talk about legacies? We've got to remain positive. It's only gonna be bit longer." I glared at Slake, daring him to challenge me, but he turned away, so I continued. "Until then, promise you ain't gonna do something stupid like climbing that railing again."

"Yeah, I'll respect life and all that shit. I know." He chewed his lip, mulling it over, and jerked up as if struck by a powerful realization. "We need to give Harley a funeral. That's positive."

"That's about the furthest you can get from positive. But if you want, we can have a moment of silence."

"What I want is a funeral. I'd expect the same for me." Slake stood, tucking the gun into his belt.

"Sure, whatever." I breathed a sigh with the gun's disappearance. "Guess sometimes you just need to get that heavy shit off your chest. That was sure some secret."

"Oh, that wasn't the secret." Slake pointed at the highway, but his eyes were glossy and dull, almost like he wasn't looking. "The secret is there."

I peered over, but didn't see anything. No parked cars. No cops with flashing lights. No utility crew. Not a single thing out of the ordinary. Slake motioned as if I was missing the most extraordinary sight. Really, there was nothing to see at all.

Nothing?

I bolted to the edge and scanned in either direction. Even on a Saturday, even at this early hour, there should've been at least a dozen cars snaking down the highway.

"They stopped coming a little bit after two in the morning," Slake said. "I couldn't sleep. Haven't seen a single car since then. Not even an airplane."

"That doesn't mean nothing." I peered out, waiting for a car to zip around the bend. The longer I stared, the more apparent the closed highway became.

"Yeah, it doesn't mean a thing." Slake chuckled and slumped against the railing. "Not a single fucking thing."

 Victor hollered from the upper-deck. The words were in Spanish, but from his tone, I took it for a curse of some sort. He followed this by a low-pitched groan, then a thud as he flopped down. I hadn't heard a peep from him all morning, so when he continued to whimper and thrash, I grew worried. I peered toward Slake, whose attention focused up in a similar manner except as he stared, a beaming smile unfolded over his face.

"You hear that?" I asked.

"I was wondering when he was going to wake," Slake replied, as if Victor's howling was as normal as a morning yawn.

"Maybe we should check in on him," I replied, as Victor's writhing grew louder.

"He's fine," Slake said, and as if hearing this, Victor's eruption came to a sudden halt.

"You sure?" I peered into the misleadingly tranquil air, waiting for Victor to start up again. Nothing but the sound of birds chirping. Even the pigs settled for a moment.

"I have to make preparations," Slake said, but before I could inquire what he meant by this, he stormed off onto the outer-deck. I peeked around the corner, noticing Slake's 'preparations' consisted of pacing briskly back and forth while muttering inaudibly to himself.

I kept my distance, having no intention to interfere; particularly after his admission of having been locked inside a padded cell. Better to walk off the crazy than revert to waving that gun around. I was about to return to my perch at the edge, but Victor groaned again and I detoured toward the ladder. Even if he'd gone bananas like Slake, I had to know for certain.

"You okay?" I asked, climbing onto the upper-deck. Victor sat huddled in a fetal position, rocking as he clutched his injured hand like a newborn. He gave no reply as I stepped closer. "Why don't I take a look?"

Victor nodded while rolling onto his back. He inched against the railing, resting his head onto the lowest bar. He gasped as I peeled away the bandage. My t-shirt was soaked with blood, some fresh, but most of the stain was dry and crusted. Victor's swollen hand glowed a dull purple. The veins running across the top bulged, appearing ready to snap free. He winced as I turned his palm face up. The red lines tracking up his forearm confirmed my fear.

"It ain't good, but with some antibiotics, you'll be just fine." I pressed on a bulging area right below his thumb, feeling a bubble of air trapped underneath. Unlike the other parts of his swollen hand, Victor didn't flinch as I rolled the skin between my fingers like a piece of bubble-wrap.

"I no worry," he replied, but the groan that followed appeared to contradict that. He broke from my grasp, tugging his hand to his chest. He cradled it for a moment before biting down on his lip and rewrapping the t-shirt around his hand.

I scanned the highway, looking for any movement. For a single moment, I marveled at the absolute serenity of the morning sky, but when the silence continued, a sense of uneasy dread washed over me. I scoured for any signs of life, telling myself if I could just see a single car, everything would be fine. None appeared.

"You stay?" Victor asked, curling his fingers around my arm. I nodded, plunking down beside him.

"You are in much pain," Victor continued, tightening his grasp on my arm.

"I think you have that backward," I replied. Thankfully, Victor released his grip and pointed at my face.

"I see in the frown. In your flushed cheeks. More, I see in the eyes. Much pain."

"Well, I'm not thrilled about missing my bus...or any of this shit for that matter." I released the clenched lock in my jaw and rolled my shoulders back. I decided to keep the detail of the empty highway to myself, figuring mulling over the situation wasn't bound to make anyone feel any better.

"No," Victor shook his head. "Even before, you never smile. You look into distance always, somewhere far away. You do not see in, to pain."

"I'm more worried about Slake." I motioned to stand, but Victor grabbed my arm again, holding me in place. "Listen, Slake isn't well and I think I should check in on him. He's down there ranting all sorts of crazy and I fear he might do something stupid with that gun."

"Slake is Slake." Victor tightened his grip. "You is you. We do not have much time. Must make peace."

"Make peace? That's all I do. I'm like a constant mediator between everyone's nonsense." I wrenched my arm free. Victor was wise enough to avoid swiping for another grasp.

"Yes, you find peace in others because you no find in here." Victor tapped his heart. "Trapped. Always trapped."

"If you need a single word to describe this entire cluster-fuck, yeah, I'd go with trapped." I lurched up, wondering why I'd even climbed up in the first place. Victor was right about one thing, I felt exhausted dealing with everyone's skirmishes and needed some peace. Not that there was a single inch of it up on this blasted billboard.

"I want talk, but go if you want." Victor motioned at the ladder. I paused, fingers hovering over the carabineer's release. From below, Slake shouted a profanity, followed by a thudding stomp. I couldn't hear the exact words, but understood he was raging hard, at the pigs, at life, at everything. I'd seen this before and had no intention of getting swept into his rampaging vortex.

"I don't feel much like talking, but if you want to sit here in peace, that I can do."

Victor nodded, and I released my hold on the clasp. As I took a seat, I made certain to remain outside Victor's reach. He folded his arms across his lap and leaned back. Not quite a comfortable position, but I mirrored it, staring into the cloudless sky.

I thought about what Victor had said, growing hot over the way he'd spun this mess into my issue. More than anything, I realized I was mad because he was correct. Of course, anyone who'd ever been locked up was pained in some way. Hell, even on the outside, I'd yet to meet any adult who truly felt at peace with this shamble of a world. No, what really bothered me, what really struck me as true, was the idea of being trapped. Indeed, I couldn't recall a single period where I didn't feel the bars of some prison closing in on me.

Guess I could blame my Pa if I was the blaming type, but I tended to believe we build our own walls. Though, I can't pretend he didn't pour a bit of cement onto mine. As a long-haul trucker, Pa spent the majority of time on the road, and even when he was around, he was more likely to greet me with a closed fist than a hug. Not that I didn't deserve a beating or three for all my misdeeds, but it was the arbitrary manner of his merciless justice that got to me. It never made a lick of sense.

For example, once, after a three-week haul, Pa had insisted on total silence during dinner and when I accidently spilled some milk, he erupted, breaking the glass over my head and splintering my arm with his fork. Then, on another occasion, when I'd almost burned the house down while igniting an old school textbook, he shook off the entire incident as kids-will-be-kids, pat on the back and a giant ice cream cone.

More often than not, his brutal attacks followed this same swift and unforeseen pattern. Any minor violation, real or imagined, could spark his vicious bite. Perhaps this was the reason Ma was so keen on following all his rules, no matter how crazy. And it wasn't as if she failed to dole out justice in a similarly ruthless manner. Once, she belted me for putting a pillow-case inside out while making the bed, another time for failing to separate the junk mail from the bills. At least with her, the reasons were clear, overly strict or not.

School was no better. Doc told me some kids found relief from their chaotic home life in their studies, but I was always six letters away from being an A-student. I didn't care much for any subjects outside of recess, but again, it wasn't like school cared much for me either. Most teachers passed me on account of my agreeable personality and that I didn't cause a ruckus in class. I learned I could skip as long as I frowned and acted real sorry anytime I got caught. By the time I was seventeen, I rarely went to class at all, and figured it best to abandon any hope of graduation.

For a fleeting moment, after quitting school, the feeling of being trapped faded. Chalk it up to youthful inexperience; but even with freedom from all responsibility, I failed to realize this would guarantee a life-sentence in a different style of prison. Years later, by the time I took that plea bargain and was locked inside a real cage, I'd already poured so much grout around my life that a six-by-eight was actually an increase in the size of my cell.

As for my old man, it wasn't all explosive rages and impulsive attacks. He did have a witty and seductive side, which at the right place and time, could charm the tail feathers off the most alluring peacock. At his best while cruising in his big-rig, the few times he took me along for the ride, I couldn't help grinning for the entire trip. He just had this way when it came to everyone he met on the road, joking with strangers like they'd grown up best buds, while commiserating in the drama of others as if sharing in their sorrow.

Never acted that way at home though, not with me or Ma at least. So when I quit school, I figured the road was the only path to happiness and followed in his footsteps. To be honest, it was real nice training for my CDL. Unlike all the boring books and abstract concepts in school, these classes taught real skills I could use on the job. No bullshit at all. So in next to no time, I was plopped down in a captain's seat of a semi-trailer and sent zooming down the asphalt.

At first, hauling was a pretty awesome gig. Far more than a misfit like me could've asked for, an abundance of alone time with no boss peeking over my shoulder, good tunes on the radio, and a fat wallet affording me my own place. I was even allowed to smoke on the job. It was like teenage heaven.

I won't pretend I didn't have my fair share of fun cruising from city to city. That heavy wallet was far from the only thing tugging down my pants, new girls were around every bend. But at some point, what appeared to be freedom, turned out to be the exact opposite. Where I once received a thrill wheeling down a new road, it lost its luster on the twentieth, thirtieth, one thousandth pass. All the towns began to look alike, the same truck-stops, the same diners, and worst of all, the same people. Everyone always chatting on about local sports, the weather, and whatever outrage the news was ginning up that week to get the most eyeballs. I despised them all.

Unlike Pa, who thrived on the routineness, I soured like roadkill in the blistering sun. Instead of chatting up strangers to share a brief moment, I disengaged entirely. The way I saw it, it was better to avoid conversation than endure the same litany of trivial complaints, stupid tributes, and implausible dreams. The faces could change, but the musings always remained the same.

Where once, while pulling into a truck-stop, I'd felt the pitter-patter of a beating heart, I suddenly experienced a throbbing rage. Unlike the towns with their superficial differences, the truck-stops had conformed into a uniform mediocrity. If it wasn't the same chain restaurants, the food was crappy enough to be indistinguishable. The shops hawked identical trinkets and knick-knacks, the only difference was the name of the state or sports team printed on the logo. Even the pay showers never varied, always dribbling out the same two temperatures, freeze or scald.

Then there was the greatest similarity of them all, the lot lizards. Sure, the prostitutes who lurked in the shady back row of every truck-stop may have differed in outward appearances, but they all shared that same stench. The smell of a few crisp bills that would unbind their bulging muffin-tops and drop their panties. The wafting odor of latex mixed with vinegary lube and semen. The choking fumes of idling diesel engines and the frigid taste of air-conditioning. I knew that stench, the one of pathetic desperation, mostly since it clung to me as well.

Patti was my sole release from this self-imposed prison. She was so stunning that night we'd accidentally met at Costard's Diner just east of Topeka. When she sat in the booth across from me, her glowing expression evoked a hope I hadn't seen since my first days on the road. I hate to admit it, but even so, I attempted to brush her off as I had with so many others. But she'd have nothing of it.

Turned out, she'd been stood up by her boyfriend that night and was determined to make something out of the wreckage with anyone who'd listen. Luck happened it would be me. So as she ranted over this fella named 'Mitch' who'd ditched out on her, I couldn't help from marveling at her curly blonde hair and silky black dress, wondering what fool could've believed he had better options. I told her as much and she beamed. I know it wasn't the proper thing, poaching this Mitch's gal but again, I don't have much respect for a fella who figured a choke-n-puke was the proper venue for a Friday night date.

Thank God I did. That was about the sole right choice I ever made in this stinking life. I'm sure glad Costard's was open all night long, since we talked into the wee hours, sharing giggles and, at times, deeper conversation. I even admitted my passion for building model airplanes, which bored every other girl I'd known, but Patti listened keenly and offered to help me paint one. I returned the favor, smiling as she went into the details of her knitting and agreed to wear one of her homemade winter hats. That was the best damn hat I'd ever owned, toasty and lasting far longer than any of this modern China-made crap they hawk today.

I took this wonderful accidental date as a sign, and less than a year later, a sharp gold ring was swinging from my left hand. Tyler came not long after that. Life should've been something sweet, all in all. Yet, inside, I couldn't shake the feeling Mitch had been correct in tossing in the towel on Patti and remaining free.

On the outside, Patti and I were real good together. Everyone commented on how we were soul-mates and how we'd struck aces finding each other. I couldn't disagree to that. At home, we weren't just peas in a pod, but like a puree whose ingredients were indistinguishable, but delicious together.

The troubles came when I was on the road, crisscrossing the country for a job I hated. Tensions arose when I couldn't help dragging this resentment across the doormat with my every return. For the first time, I understood how Pa felt that night I'd spilled that glass of milk. Not that I'd ever stab Tyler, I had made a promise to be better than my own father. That promise I'd kept. Even as I lied and broke every single other one in my life, I did keep that one.

Even so, according to the doc, sometimes a cold isolation from a son could be more painful than any blow. I wasn't sure I believed him at the time. The doc did say a few fine quotes between heaps of nonsense, as all of them do. But if Tyler's current attitude was any indication of my failed parenting, I guess there could be an inkling of truth. I've always hoped his resentment was the result of my later actions, but I've yet to muster the courage to ask him directly.

Back then, I lacked the insight even to question myself. I just knew I was angry and figured it best to withdraw rather than engage in the explosive alternative. So every time I'd arrive home, instead of cavorting with Patti, I'd retreat into silence, demanding my alone time. This sinking pit of silence was the only way to keep them evil hankerings in check. As long as I kept running from every emotion, I'd never be trapped. What I failed to realize was I'd likewise never be free.

I did have sense enough to know this crater of isolation couldn't endure forever, so I searched for any job I could take near Gelder. I snagged a few piecemeal gigs here and there, but never anything permanent. I'd even promised to commute as far as Oklahoma if the opportunity should arise, but lacking a high-school diploma, it was impossible to score anything that paid a living wage.

And that was when I found drinking. Or, as Doc said, my deficiencies allowed drinking to find me.

At first, I drank at home because it was forbidden while on the road. The *Department of Transportation*, DOT, conducted periodic testing, but as long as I dried up the day before my home-time ended, nobody cared. Plus, those so-called 'random' tests were usually given to the troublemakers and other undesirables at the terminal, so as long as I always arrived to work on time with a chipper smile, I avoided any suspicion. Perks of being a legacy, I guess.

My routine upon arriving home was simple, park the rig at the terminal, a quick stop at the liquor store, and polish one pint before pulling into my drive. Then I'd binge throughout my home time break as if Prohibition might return. I'd sober up on the final day before returning, but was usually too crippled by the 'liquid flu' to do anything useful. I was far from alone in this routine and it was so common that drivers even had a nickname for this, calling it "working the BT," meaning *Bottle to Throttle*. But for me, BT always spelled Big Trouble.

Of course, Patti wasn't keen on this arrangement, since I ended up blitzed whenever we were together. For the few hours I wasn't in a coma on BT day, she'd take the opportunity to nag about drinking, pestering about my responsibilities as a father and so on. The way I saw things, as long as I wasn't whaling on the boy and held down a decent gig, that was enough. Hell, she wasn't working and I was the one paying the mortgage on our ranch house, so nobody was gonna tell me how to live in it.

In a twisted sense, I saw myself as the victim, trapped driving the same mundane routes, chomping the same crappy food, and arguing the same fights about drinking, money, and chores, over and over. I justified my wretched attitude believing if I had to endure the prison of work, Patti best zip up and do her duty in this domestic jail. That only seemed fair.

When Patti started spouting off about the big-D, threatening to leave with Tyler, I doubled down on my opposition, rationalizing why I not only deserved to drink, but needed to do so. Everyone required a break, primarily after ten hours of the mundane grind. It was natural. Utterly human.

But somewhere in the pit of my dark soul, I knew she was right. I just grew weary of our constant arguing, the hangovers, all of it. What I didn't tire of was the drinking. And if Patti was giving too much gruff for doing it at home, that left solely one other place to blow off steam.

So I eased slightly during my home-time while jacking up my drinking while out on runs. As long as I avoided those random inspections, nobody was the wiser. In truth, if I had to pinpoint the source of my feeling trapped, it was the job rather than Patti. In a weird way, drinking inside my cab seemed justified. I can't say I never drank while driving, but it was mostly confined to those bitter nights alone in the cab.

God, I wish it'd stopped with the sauce. Sure, I still might've killed someone in a stupor, but I was far more likely to harm myself or get fired before things plunged dark. I could live with that. Oftentimes I dreamed about this. An alternative future with Patti and Tyler still tugging at my side. Dreams were nice like that, peering forward. But memories; well, after what was done, was done, the grim blade of truth alone can reflect in the rearview mirror.

"What you need?" Victor asked, breaking me away from this flood of hazy reflections.

"What's that?" I replied.

"What you need?" he repeated. "Tell me."

"What do you think," I snapped. "To get off this damn billboard and go see my son."

Victor chuckled, while shaking his head. "No, that is no what you need."

Saturday 12:04 P.M.

Slake clanked while clipping into the upper-deck, but neither Victor nor I glanced over. I stared down, hoping his appearance signaled the arrival of a rescue, and indeed, a flutter of movement emerged where the parking lot connected to the service road. I spied a white utility van circling into the lot. This flashed for a nanosecond, I blinked and the van disappeared. I scoured all over, waiting for the van to return, but after a moment, it dawned this had only been a hallucination.

I rubbed my eyes as if to dust off any delusional cobwebs, but this merely caused my vision to blur with a raw throbbing pain. Outside of my trucking days, where the interstate blacktop would transform into a liquid-like haze in the bright sunlight, I'd never experienced a mirage. Not even during the chaos of my drug-fueled days had I ever seen any vision this vivid, so I kept staring as if I could will the van back into existence.

I almost felt high scanning the landscape, which might've been pleasant if not for the headache. The heat was so dense that wavy lines sagged the air like a wash drying on a clothesline. And every color was brilliant, glowing brighter than anything I'd ever seen before. Moreover, the colors beamed out from the objects they reflected, creating a vibrant aura around them. Treetops glowed like flashing neon. The dusty fields pulsed a brewed-coffee-brown. While the asphalt of the highway plunged into a pitch-black abyss I'd only experienced in the deepest cavity of my dreams.

I wanted to believe the van had been real, but if anyone had arrived, the pigs would've whirled into one of their typical stampedes, which was the exact opposite of their current positioning. Most had downed for an afternoon nap, crusting the ground like a lumpy gravy that'd spilled weeks ago and soured. They smelled about the same. Even from this height, the stench was intolerable.

I stood to greet Slake as he approached, careful to keep my back pressed to the railing for support. Good thing too, since as soon as I straightened, a dizzy wave flooded across my vision. I held in place, panting, until the world dribbled back into focus. Standing required an arduous amount of energy along with my full concentration, so as Slake spoke, it took a moment to comprehend the words.

"Time," he declared, which sounded like a statement rather than a question, but then he paused, clearly waiting for a reply. I glanced at my watch and told him the hour.

"No, it's time," he corrected.

"Time for what?" According to my schedule, there was nothing planned other than sitting on our asses. Slake smirked, which was an unusual expression for him, so I wondered if he too might be in a heat-baked mirage. Or perhaps I'd broke for good and was having a conversation with nothing but wavy air.

"It's time for the funeral, of course." His reply was sharp and dismissive, as if we'd already discussed the matter. Maybe I had in one of my blackouts, but for the life of me, I couldn't recall any funeral talk.

Before I could ask Slake to elaborate, he started back toward the ladder. I did my best to chase after him, wavering across the deck as if drunk. Luckily, he noticed my staggering and slowed, but instead of offering any help, he just motioned for me to be quiet.

"What's all this about a funeral?" I whispered, while grabbing his arm, half to get him to stop, half for my own balance. "You ain't thinking about doing anything stupid, right?" I recalled his suicidal confession and how he'd climbed the railing.

"Not my funeral." He tilted his head as if I'd asked the stupidest question in the world. "For Harley. Remember? We discussed this. You okay?"

I nodded and released my grasp, remembering he had mentioned something about a funeral earlier, but I'd dismissed it as simply another part of his loony ramblings. From the way he leaned closer and raised his eyebrows...cockamamie idea or not, I sensed he was serious.

"We need to do it now while the pigs are asleep or they'll interrupt the ceremony. So come on." Slake hurried toward the ladder as if we waited a second longer Harley might stop being dead. I wanted to follow, but just standing in this heat took all my energy, so forget climbing down.

"What's wrong with doing it here?" I stood in place, clinging to the railing.

"We can't have interruptions." Slake shook his head while pointing at Victor. "Plus, I've made preparations. We're going to do this right and show Harley the respect he deserves."

"He was a racist and a drunk," Victor muttered, while cracking his eyes. As he sat up, I nudged Slake toward the ladder, but he spun back in Victor's direction.

"Harley had his issues as we all do. I think he'd want us to remember his most positive traits."

"I think what he want is to not be food for pigs." Victor chuckled.

"If you don't want to participate, that's more than fine with me, but I've had enough of your sarcastic remarks." Slake stepped toward Victor, but I moved between them and bumped my elbow into Slake, hoping he'd step back. He didn't and as Victor stood, proceeding closer, Slake jammed me away.

"Not sarcastic. Is the truth." Victor displayed none of the agony he'd been experiencing earlier when I first checked in on him and swung his injured arm as if wielding a hammer rather than a bloody bandage.

"Maybe a funeral ain't the best idea," I interjected.

"Nobody asked for your opinion, Russ. So back off." Slake shoved past and headed straight at Victor. I tripped, almost toppling as I pawed the railing for balance. How these two had the energy to tussle in this heat was beyond me.

"Look at you," Victor said, as Slake approached. He dipped his shoulders and widened his stance. "All you do is push, push, push."

"Is that another one of your mystical truths?" Slake inched closer, mirroring Victor's posture. "Because all I hear is talk, talk, talk."

"If you no make the peace now, you join Harley." Victor pointed toward the ground, but his eyes remained locked onto Slake.

"Go ahead, I dare you to try. Only one of us is going over that railing." Slake unclipped his carabineer, allowing it to dangle freely at his side.

"No, not fall to ground." Victor paused. "You join Harley in hell."

"Wanna bet?" Slake swiped for the gun, which was poking up from his safety harness. I lurched at him, knocking his arm back before he could grab it.

"You want a piece, too?" Slake asked. I swiped for the gun a second time, which was a mistake, since Slake easily dodged the blow and shoved me into the railing. I dropped onto my knees. Slake removed the gun and aimed at my head.

"Easy now." I held up my palms while crouching. "No need to add another funeral to your list."

"Yes, keep hiding behind the gun." Victor stepped closer. Slake swirled his aim toward him. Similar as I'd done, Victor raised his hand as if signaling to stop, but then pressed his open palm against the barrel. "Yes, be a coward. Shoot. I no give a fuck."

"Fine, we'll do this old school." Slake lowered his aim and signaled for me to take the gun. I did so quickly and scurried back.

"Training is over," Slake continued. "Now unclip. It's time for your final lesson." He swung his arms and twisted around, showing he was no longer bound to any of the safety lines. Victor followed his lead, not merely unclipping, but removing his harness entirely. He tossed it over the edge, while bouncing on the balls of his feet. A couple pigs awoke and dashed toward the harness, shredding it to pieces.

A flock of birds darted out of a tree nearby and into the air, swooping across the sky like a thick, black cloud. I figured Victor dropping his safety harness riled them, but then I heard the noise. I fixated on the horizon.

"Stop," I shouted, still clutching the gun. I guess I could've aimed toward them to emphasize the point, but the thought never crossed my mind. Plus, it was hardly necessary considering the noise.

Woo-wump. Woo-wump. Woo-wump. The noise clattered like a steel drum. A flutter of air swept over me, prickling my sore skin.

My heart exploded into a stampede. Both Victor and Slake dropped their arms and spun toward the whirling racket.

We all stared in unison, tracking it as it zigzagged across the sky before surging straight toward the billboard. The buzz grew deafening as a couple pigs squealed and raced into the fields. None of that mattered. Our entire focus stayed locked onto the helicopter.

5

Saturday 12:11 P.M.

Victor was the first to break the collective trance. He nodded once at the helicopter, sighed while clutching his injured hand, and then took a seat. Slake, in contrast, lurched up the railing, hollering, while flinging out a spastic wave. I joined Slake at the edge, but refrained from climbing even with my safety line clipped in. The helicopter zoomed straight toward us.

"Do you think it's the military?" Slake asked, but his voice was barely audible underneath the swelling buzz of the chopper.

I shook my head no. As he leaned further over the edge, I inched within grabbing distance. The last thing we needed at this critical juncture was for him to lean too far. From the helicopter's undeviating approach, it was obvious we'd been spotted, so I stopped signaling, wishing Slake would do the same.

"Maybe it's the police," Slake shouted over the whir of the chopper. When he decided to release his hold on the railing to wave with both arms, I grabbed his shoulder and tugged him back. This time, he had the common sense to follow my lead and jumped down from the railing.

"It's civilian," I yelled into his ear.

"How do you know?" Slake held out his hand to shade his eyes, but the blazing midday sun obscured the aircraft and its passengers into murky blobs.

"That's an Enstrom 480. Neither the police nor military deploy them. Solely for civilian use," I answered.

"You can't know that." Slake stared at the chopper with a locked expression as if the make and model was printed on the side and all he needed to do was look a bit longer to spot it, thereby proving me wrong.

"Don't tell me what I know," I snapped.

Slake whirled a suspicious gaze at me as if I'd sucker-punched him. The words had emerged more forcefully than I'd anticipated, but identifying the chopper reminded me of that foul period in my life where my obsessions had ruled over me like a gooey web. Where I masked my self-destruction through compulsive habits, one of which was reading those thousands of aircraft magazines. I'd wasted so many hours cataloguing the type of planes and variety of engines, as if studying for a final exam. When in reality, the only true test was how long I could be distracted and ignore the real problem.

"Notice how the pilot is seated on the left?" I continued, easing my tone. "That's a dead giveaway it's civilian. Plus, the semicircular skid guard under the tail rotor is another tipoff. I used to build models."

That was enough of an explanation for Slake, who nodded and turned back toward the chopper. I was relieved he didn't press for details, since I'd never built a model for an Enstrom, just military helicopters, but I'd flipped through enough aviation magazines to recognize the make even after all these years.

Back then, during the height of my obsession with planes, I'd pretended it'd all been for Tyler's benefit. Sure, he'd shown a passing interest, probably more for my sake than any real passion. Indeed, even I hadn't been all that entranced by them, I used those magazines as an excuse for isolating myself in the garage while I blasted my mind into oblivion.

The doc labeled these obsessions as my dark distractions, noting they were quite common among addicts. Some fellas started vast collections, some watched endless amounts of TV, some spent every night out dancing, some fell deep into religion, and some would just sit and stare at the wall, but reading about planes and making models was my compulsion. That and smoking crack.

"I couldn't care less who's in that whirly-bird," Slake said. "At least someone knows we're stuck on this rusty pole."

The chopper was a matte black, which blocked most of the sun's glare. As it approached, the pilot swung horizontal to the billboard, revealing a vivid red streak painted across its side in a lightning bolt pattern. The side door was missing or ajar, I couldn't tell for certain, but the men in the rear were unmistakable. Three sat together in a row, each wearing a yellow jumpsuit of some sort.

I didn't get much of a look, since the pilot swung the chopper's tail around in a sweeping motion. I locked onto the cockpit, realizing the pilot was also sporting a yellow jumpsuit. One with a hood obscuring his face. He waved with a gloved hand and I raised my arm to return the gesture when I spied the gasmask. I hadn't noticed it before, likely on account of its peculiar white coloring, almost ghostly in appearance. At first, I'd mistaken it for a pilot's visor or a pair of goggles. But no, definitely a gasmask.

"Down!" Slake yelled.

I thought he was signaling for the chopper to land, but then he yanked my arm, wanting me to drop onto the platform. That made no sense, so I broke away. As I reached for the railing to steady myself, Slake grabbed me again. This time, he patted across my back, neither shoving me down, nor bracing me. I froze, attempting to understand this odd manhandling. Before I could, his fingers swept into the small of my back and snatched the gun.

I slapped at his arm, attempting to dislodge the gun. Slake wrenched away, but I toppled straight into him. The gun tumbled from his grasp and skidded across the deck, sliding to a halt within arm's reach of Victor. He neither reached for it, nor looked over. His eyes stayed glued to the approaching aircraft. Slake scrambled past my side and lunged for the gun. I dove after him.

The whirling thump from the chopper shattered the air, drowning every other sound including that of our clambering bodies. Slake reached the gun first, snapping it up with a windmill motion. I shoved beside him, clawing at his whirling arm but grabbed nothing but air. He rammed my shoulder, spinning me onto my haunches, while pressing into the railing. As he steadied the gun, I wrenched away, but he wasn't aiming in my direction. Instead, he targeted the helicopter.

The thumping beat cranked louder as the chopper bucked, spinning around. The cockpit and the gasmask wearing pilot disappeared as the tail rotor whirled toward the billboard. Its rear blade drew so close the reverberations slashed the air like a whip. I tucked my head, fearing if it reversed any more, we'd be chewed into pulpy bits. Instead, the chopper jerked forward, hovering within spitting distance. A metallic grinding splintered out and it rocketed away with a bullet-like speed.

Before I could exhale, it'd soared across the highway and vanished within the shadows of the horizon. Only a thin gray mist remained as the thump of its engine dissipated behind the mountains. Even that faded a few seconds later.

"What the fuck?" I hollered into the newfound silence.

Slake panted while his aim remained locked into the empty sky. I stood, scanning for any sign of the chopper, but there was none. The entire landscape had settled into a dull void, not even the wind appeared ready to break this peace. I poked Slake's shoulder, hoping he'd lower the gun. He glanced from side to side before swiping a gooey handful of sweat from his brow, though his other arm remained frozen in its outstretched aim.

"Slake?" I continued, prodding him a second time.

"Relax," he replied, as if I was the one acting like a maniac. His shoulders dropped as he eased his aim, though he scoured the landscape one more time before turning around. He continued to hold the gun, tapping it against his waist in a frenetic pulse.

"Yeah, let's relax." I mirrored his sentiment while stepping back. From Slake's feverish movements, I feared he'd broken into a full-blown anxiety attack, and held up my hands in a calm gesture. He shivered and continued to peek over his shoulder, but at least his hands steadied at his side. I didn't dare swipe for the gun while he remained in this state, so instead, I leaned against the rear of the sign.

"They might come back," Slake muttered, as if this explained his shaky state.

"They no return," Victor countered. I winced, fearing this would spark their bickering anew, but Victor appeared worn and tucked his head deep into the railing.

"Let's sure hope not," Slake replied, shocking me with his agreement. Not only that, but he shook the gun with a bit of bravado while speaking, almost as if he wanted the chopper to return, not for any rescue, but to show them he was still the one in charge.

"Why not? How else are we going to escape?" I almost shouted, wondering if the pair of them had descended into a collective pit of madness. Perhaps that pig virus had spread and done a doozy on their minds. Slake tilted his head in what appeared to be earnest surprise.

"Didn't you see?" he asked.

"See what?" I replied. "What in the world could I've seen that would've justified scaring our rescue off like that?"

"The rifles." Slake chuckled. "That wasn't a rescue. It was a hit squad."

"I didn't see no rifles." I gritted my teeth, which was about the only thing preventing them from tearing into Slake's neck.

"All three in the rear of the chopper had them." He must've sensed my rage, since he stepped back.

"Is that true, Victor?" I spun toward him.

"What it matters? Rifles or no?" he replied.

"A whole fucking lot." I stomped to emphasize the point. "Were they armed or not?"

"I no get the good look," he answered, before closing his eyes like the discussion bored him.

"Why would I lie?" Slake asked. "They were armed. How could you've missed it? I couldn't tell the exact make, but the rifles were big. Why do you think I took this?" Slake shook the gun.

"Even if they had rifles, who cares?" I answered.

"I do when they aim right at us," Slake replied.

"I didn't see nothing like that." I turned toward Victor, hoping for a confirmation, but he just rested with his eyes closed.

"I swear it's true," Slake continued. "That wasn't a rescue, but goons hired to dispose of any survivors."

"Are you a hundred percent certain?" I stared into his eyes. He glared down.

"No, but-"

"But what?" I interrupted. "You can't be serious."

"I saw what I saw. I swear." Slake turned toward Victor. "Tell him. They had guns."

"I told you before, I no see nothing." Victor cracked his eyes and smirked. "But now that you chase away, they never return."

"No, we're not having a repeat of this." I stepped between the two. "Not worth the effort," I whispered into Slake's ear. He stood frozen for a moment, before stepping back. I nudged him a tad further and motioned toward the ladder.

"I saw what I saw." Slake stepped across the deck, though his eyes remained locked onto Victor, ready to leap if he should make any advances. Victor remained seated, but bent his legs, likewise preparing to bound-up if trouble should arise.

I pointed again toward the ladder and Slake proceeded across the platform. I followed behind, ensuring Victor wouldn't get any hot ideas as we reached the rungs. Before Slake started down, I tugged on his safety harness in a gentle reminder to clip in. He did so without protest.

"Listen, I know you believe what you saw," I began, as he fastened the clip. "Same thing happened to me right before the helicopter arrived. I saw a truck drive up to fix the wires, but it was only a mirage. Just the heat messing with my head."

"Don't tell me you're going crazy," Slake replied. "One madman is more than enough."

"All I'm saying is that during the excitement, you might've seen what you wanted to see."

"What I wanted to see was a cooler full of ice-cold water. What I did see was a helicopter full of men coming to assassinate us. Understand?"

I nodded, even though the more he protested, the more I felt he was hallucinating.

"Come on. It's time to memorialize Harley." Slake climbed down a couple rungs, but paused when I failed to follow.

"I think we all need a little bit of space to cool off and figure things out," I said.

"Don't tell me you're taking his side."

"There are no sides," I said, but really, I wanted to keep my distance. I wanted to be up here if that chopper should return, and if Slake was having visions of men come to murder him, best to stay far from that powder keg.

"Fine," he snapped. "But I'm keeping the gun. And don't expect me to come running up here to save your ass if they do return."

Slake disappeared down the rungs and I proceeded across the deck toward the portion closest to the highway. The road remained free of cars; a feat within itself, but what caught my eye the most was the mile after mile of barren fields. No sign of a single migrant worker, nor farmers of any kind. I kept scouring the countryside, waiting for the helicopter to buzz back around the bend, waiting for the triumphant return of its thunderous whir.

Instead, the only noise was that of the snorting pigs. For some wretched reason, that damn clatter never ceased.

Saturday 1:31 P.M.

 Over an hour had passed since the helicopter's departure, but I couldn't stop gazing at the sun-swamped horizon. I kept scanning and scanning, scouring every granular recess in the distant mountains, hoping to eye a single flash of movement. I stared so much that the throbbing in my eyes had grown into a slashing agony. With every blink, I feared missing the chopper's return, so I kept peering out long past the point where my vision had blurred. It was only when my sight grayed out of existence when I hung my head and relented.

Snapping my eyes shut hadn't provided the relief I'd hoped for and the slashing continued to splinter across my forehead. To be honest, the real let down was more psychological in nature. In an odd way, staring sparked a sense of reassurance, as if our deliverance rested on the intensity of my gaze. I'd convinced myself that as long as I kept watch, our rescue was dead ahead, moments from arriving. If I could just hold on a little longer, we'd all be saved. I knew this was a delusion but any hope, no matter how false, was sometimes all a man could ask for in this deplorable world.

I felt stupid standing there with my eyes shut, so I plopped beside Victor, who'd already resigned to an afternoon siesta. He shifted as I sat, but neither one of us spoke, about perfect for me. Even most of the pigs settled for a nap, producing a calm silence far from comforting, although not unpleasant considering the alternative.

So when Slake began to yell, his voice bellowing up from below, my initial impulse was to scream down for him to zip-it. But I held my tongue, not wanting to goad him into returning. One tussle this afternoon had already been enough.

Even without provocation, Slake's yelling escalated into a shrill pitch and he added a pounding beat to the mix. Perhaps he was only stomping, but from the clanking, I feared he'd broken into an arm-flinging wreck. He must've been on the outer-deck, since I failed to spot him right below, but I lacked the energy to peek over the top of the billboard and check up on him.

As Slake continued, it became apparent these disjointed words were a eulogy for Harley. I figured the reason for the ruckus was a passive-aggressive signal, or more likely, a demand, for us to climb down and join the ceremony, but that only worked to cement me in place. In my experience, forced accolades rang as hollow as the mouth spitting them.

"Stupid fool," Victor muttered.

"Don't egg him on," I replied.

"He wake the pigs," Victor continued. "He break the peace. He is the person egging the demons."

"Egging *on* the demons." I corrected Victor's broken English with a grin.

"The demons do not care about the words. He must stop."

"It's his way of giving Harley some respect." I watched as couple pigs staggered up and swung their mucus-crusted snouts in the direction of Slake's shouting.

"Harley no deserve the respect." Victor flicked his bandaged hand, either fanning himself or shaking off the pain. I couldn't tell which, but the aggression behind his gesture irked me. Sure, Harley and I hadn't been best buds, but I certainly didn't wish his fate upon anyone. Well, perhaps that dead-eyed man, but there was always one exception that proved the rule.

"Harley had his charming moments," I said. "Plus, it's best to avoid speaking ill of the dead."

"Why?" Victor asked, using a quizzical tone as if he really didn't understand. When I ignored his question, he stopped his fanning, tilted his head, and repeated the question.

"Why no speak ill of the dead?"

"Hell, I don't know." To be honest, I'd never given the idea much thought. It just seemed appropriate – the proper way of doing things. The way society functioned. Law, order, and all that other spunky stuff. Not that I'd been one to follow the rules, but I'd done my time, mended my ways, and saw no reason to stir the pot anymore. I guess if I had to answer, it was because I wanted the same for myself.

"If you don't know, why you say this?" Victor pestered, clearly wanting a quibble over some petty philosophical point. I faux-yawned, leaned back, and began picking at my fingernails.

"Harley was agreeable enough, decent folk, not the best, not the worst. Pissing on his grave don't do nobody any good."

"See the pigs? Down on the ground?" Victor gestured as if I could've missed them this entire time.

I nodded anyhow, figuring it best for him to ramble out his issues, similar to Slake's hollering. I found this worked best to defuse the crazy. Oddly, the kookier they got, the more they usually needed to spout off. And the louder. Maybe it was overcompensation for being ignored and the only way to get any attention was to put on a grand show. Funny how people required attention, no matter how off-putting or disagreeable. Hell, the fact I was even talking to Victor was proof of that.

"See the way the pigs sleep?" Victor asked.

I looked down, pretending like I hadn't previously noticed their peculiar groupings. Most of the pigs were paired into couples, pressed face to face, snuggling their snouts together as if that green snot was glue. Some slept in larger groups, but they all lay face-forward, even if there was a pool of slime between them. I couldn't peek for more than a moment before feeling revolted. Something about their intimacy crawled underneath my skin. Too friendly, too warm, too loving for such vicious beasts.

"Is how they pass the sick," Victor continued.

"Sure, I guess. What of it?" I couldn't care less how the disease spread or anything else about it, outside of a hope that it'd soon turn lethal and murder off all those bastards. I felt sick watching a pair off to the side. A thick bubble grew out from a puddle of green snot between them, rising and pulsating as they snored in sync. Nauseated, I turned away.

"Most animals want the clean, but pigs sleep in the filth." He spoke in a long, drawn-out manner as if this were a profound revelation.

"Can't argue with you on that. They are a grimy lot."

Until all this, I'd never fully realized why pigs were considered dirty. But dirty was a nice word for them. The first thing they did after stirring awake was roll around until they'd fully coated themselves with muck. Not only that, but in case they missed a spot, they'd kick up a cloud of dust, showering in the soot. They were literally filthy animals. Worst of all was the way the dirt combined with their snot, producing black globules that clung from their snouts like thick oil.

"They are full of the demons," Victor said. "Is why they come here. Why they attack Harley. Understand, no?"

"What does any of this have to do with Harley?"

"Harley was full of the demons also." Victor tapped his heart, but the gesture stung me like he was stabbing my own.

"Come on," I countered. "Harley wasn't like them pigs at all. Not a lick. Now if you don't got good things to say about him, fine, but best keep those other thoughts to yourself."

"Why?" Victor spat the question again, annoying me like a toddler who'd just discovered the word. Somehow I knew no answer would suffice, so I just turned and glared out toward the horizon again.

"Do not be angry," Victor said. "We all carry the demons. I have the demons. Slake have the demons. You have-"

"Don't you dare compare me to them loathsome creatures! I've never torn anyone apart limb-by-limb!" I shouted.

"You have killed, no?"

"What does that matter?" I snapped. "Whatever. This is absurd."

"Yes, this is absurd," Victor parroted my words. "This do not make sense. Pigs no eat people. But these pigs ate Harley. So why?"

Victor waited for me to answer, but I crossed my arms and closed my eyes. Victor was entitled to whatever kooky beliefs were rattling around in that warped mind of his, but I refused to think this was some divine retaliation for my misdeeds. My comeuppance was already served. With an ice-fucking-frigid-cold stripping away of my entire life like a crew of repo-men on speed. Not only had I lost the love of my life and soulmate, but that of my son. God had nothing to do with that. No, he'd been all too human, that dead-eyed bastard.

"God sent the pigs," Victor continued, confirming my suspicion this was only another of his nutty religious rants. "This is the end. We must use the final hours to repent."

"And that's best achieved by disrespecting Harley's death?" I smacked the railing, a bit harder than I'd anticipated, but enough to emphasize my point.

"Yes," Victor answered without hesitation. "Harley was full of the demons. He was racist and a drunk. Why celebrate his life? Not now. Not at the end with God watching. No, God want the truth. To be honest. To have faith." He crossed himself while peering into the sky.

"I don't think God wants judgments. Last I checked, He was keen on that whole love thing."

"Russ, you no full of love. Full of anger." Victor balled his fist and growled as if I needed a demonstration.

"I can't say I'm chuckled over this here pickle, but again, I'm not the one picking fights. You know what I think? You want me to be angry. That way, everything clicks into your warped vision. But I'm not gonna quibble with you, Victor. I don't have the energy."

"Yes, you angry because you can't fight. Always bringing the peace between others, but never in here." Victor tapped again at his chest. "I know you are angry, since you no say the truth. You never look into the eyes."

"If I fight, I'm angry. If I don't fight, I'm angry. If I stare, I'm angry. If I look away, I'm angry. You do see that revolving circle in your logic, right?"

"No logic, but is fate. Fate deliver us here."

"No, son, just luck." I sighed. "Just shit-ass luck."

Victor shook his head in disagreement, before lowering his chin into his chest. He chanted something in Spanish. I didn't ask for a translation, but he provided one anyway.

"Pray to the devil and he shall rise. But curse him and he will not fall. For when the devil climbs, never shall he return."

"Yeah, you already said that to Slake," I replied, recalling the peculiar chant. "I don't think it was meant to be taken literally."

"It was a prediction," Victor said, as if that explained everything. "My mother say this."

"I don't think your Ma would want you to give up all hope. She's probably praying right now for your safe return."

"No, she never pray again." Victor sighed a deep exhale. "She dead. And I am the killer."

"Shit," I muttered, as my mind exploded into high gear. I hoped to God this was a lie, since Victor didn't strike me as the reptilian mother-killing type. I had met a few guys who could fit that description in the joint, but they always radiated that fucked-in-the-head vibe, almost like they were proud of being callous monsters. Inside, they wore that reputation like a crown, ruling over anyone who dared to display a single ounce of compassion. Or worse, guilt.

"She not the first," he continued, as if I'd prompted a confession. But after that whopper, I figured it best to avoid interrupting. "No, the devil first climb with Felipe Dimas."

Victor paused and leaned back. He spat a harsh cackle, half laughter, half anguish. He arched his back, rocking in a compulsive shake.

"Pantalla," he muttered, while turning toward me as if this single word would explain everything. When I shrugged, he repeated the word, louder.

"*Pantalla. Pantalla. Pantalla.*"

"Does that mean pig?" I asked, mostly to break this spasmodic repetition.

"No, it mean a screen or covering. Like way the pigs use dirt. They wear like a coat, a pantalla, to hide from sun." Victor motioned like he was covering himself with a thick layer of mud.

"Maybe that's not such a bad idea," I replied, as the reason for the pig's filthy dirt-kicking behavior suddenly clicked. "In this heat, I'd use anything for sunscreen."

With the mention of the sun, Victor swiped the back of his hand across his forehead removing a gushing layer of sweat. He closed his eyes, slowing a bit in his rocking, but didn't stop entirely. When he stared back out, he shot me a look like he was surprised to see me seated there.

"Now, I say the truth. You listen?"

I nodded and his rocking steadied a bit. He exhaled and began by describing the true meaning of pantalla, which didn't have jack-shit to do with sunscreen. No, pantalla was just Mexican-speak for a front. He told how the drug cartels used them to hide their control over businesses, politicians, and practically every aspect of life when he'd grown up.

The pantallas hadn't always existed in Paso de Cresta, the fishing village situated on Mexico's Pacific coast where Victor had been raised. Before the arrival of the cartel, the village, whose name translated to *Beyond the Wave's Crest*, lived up to this reputation. Not only was the beachside locale beyond the sea, but also beyond pretty much all modern life. From the way Victor described it, the town consisted of steel shacks and a couple canoe-sized boats that barely passed for trawlers.

If any outsiders did happen upon the town, they were immediately bombarded by dozens of people, all hawking anything and everything they owned, along with some stuff they didn't. This, along with a dangerous, rocky, coast, where the surf was about as hospitable as a live volcano, ensured few ever returned. Of course, this isolation also provided the perfect location for the cartel to take root.

Victor was only a child when the narcotics traffickers first arrived, but he couldn't forget the way they wore fancy cowboy boots and glitzy oversized belt buckles. At first, the village welcomed the change, especially the newfound wealth that accompanied it. Not only did the narcos erect concrete homes and paved streets, but they planted row after row of palm trees, decorating the village like one of those fancy resort towns up north.

The vast majority of construction occurred atop a massive hillside overlooking the coast, which the locals referred to as La Sierra. It was here the cartel built its 'salsa factory', behind a row of sprawling, thorn-covered bougainvillea hedges. If that wasn't enough to detour any nosy strangers, they also constructed fences topped with concertina-wire and three parapet towers, each patrolled with armed lookouts.

Victor and pretty much everyone else in town, was entranced by the sprawling complex hidden behind these obstacles, far more than any real salsa factory required. And when a weird chemical stench drifted down from the hillside complex, some locals decided to snoop. Then the bodies of three local gossips were discovered in the village square, bound and gagged, with throats cut. The message was received. After that nobody dared to even glance in the complex's direction. Nobody but Victor.

He'd been out exploring the coast one morning and lost his bearings just south of La Sierra. As he attempted to find a path back home, one of the narcos appeared out of nowhere and snagged him by his shirt collar. Victor pleaded with the man, who threated to toss him over a steep edge into the pounding surf.

As the thug shoved him toward the sea, Victor complimented the man's giant belt buckle, which had the design of a vicious-looking spider on it. He told the narco the spider was fearsome and strong, just like him and he wanted to grow up one day to be exactly like him. When Victor nicknamed the narco "Tarantula Gigante," the man chuckled and loosened his clutch a little. Though, he did tell Victor he'd never be as strong as him, since that was impossible. That he was the most formidable man to ever walk the earth. Victor asked if this was on account of the belt buckle, as if it had magical powers.

The goon broke into a fit of hysterics over the idea that Victor believed his buckle was the source of some comic book-like power, so he released him. Not only that, but the narco removed the buckle and gifted it to Victor. This was a huge deal, since buckles were quite the status item among the narcotraficantes.

After that, Victor wore the buckle like a prize. He also kept loitering around La Sierra, hoping to be noticed by the other narcos and further rewarded. But when his padre discovered where he was hiding out, he used that same buckle to whip Victor, almost branding a spider-shaped scar into his back. Not that beltings were unusual since his father was real keen on beatings anytime he drank, almost nightly.

As Victor told his tale, I realized his padre's drinking was likely the reason he got so irked by Harley and kept calling him a drunk, but I kept this tidbit to myself.

Victor went on, describing an encounter with another boy he met near the complex who was also skipping school. The boy was a couple years older, but Victor had seen him around the village enough to recognize his face. He informed Victor that he'd run the occasional errand for the narcos and promised to make introductions as long as Victor agreed to keep his mouth shut. Victor promised, and they clinched the deal with a spit-sealed handshake. The boy's name was Felipe Dimas.

This was the point where Victor's madre uttered her prophetic warning, quoting a passage she'd supposedly received in a dream.

Pray to the devil and he shall rise. But curse him and he will not fall. For when the devil climbs, never shall he return.

After hearing about La Sierra's hilltop location along with the steady supply of violence dished out by the narcos, I realized the quote was a bit less metaphorical than I'd first believed. Her phrase had been in Spanish, but years later, with the assistance of a priest, Victor had it translated, which accounted for the odd verbiage and use of "shall." I guess every profession had it shop-talk, religious folk were no exception. I was just thankful there wasn't a "begat" somewhere in there.

Victor ignored his madre's warning and quickly fell in with the narcos, enjoying their brash and boastful culture. And there were also the perks, the expensive cars, the newest electronic gadgets, and best of all, the exotic women, some who were even pale skinned like northern gringos. A few of these scantily clad goddesses were indeed American, which to Victor was as exotic as spotting an elephant trampling down the street. He'd never seen such beauties in his entire life and adored the way they clung to the older narco thugs. Victor promised he'd do whatever it took to be in their crew.

He started by running "sobres", envelopes full of bribes to the local cops who were "sucio" or dirty. It was through the grumblings of these dirty cops where Victor heard the rumor that the salsa factory was only a pantalla to disguise the true product manufactured, "foco," or crystal meth.

This revelation was about as surprising as discovering the ocean was blue, but Victor asked Felipe to confirm. Instead of replying, the older boy grabbed Victor into a chokehold, cutting off his oxygen until the world dipped out of focus. As Victor dropped to the ground, gasping for air, Felipe told him that would be the last time he asked any questions about the business. Ever.

Silence was the prime rule and Victor learned to wear this muted mask as he drew deeper into the narcos' trust. He followed Felipe's lead, never questioning orders, nor back-talking to even the most outrageous demands. Soon, both of them were promoted to positions as "ventanas", or lookouts, which involved sitting around all night long atop one of the parapet towers.

During these prolonged shifts, boredom reigned since there was nothing to do other than sit around. Victor soon came to realize the monotony of the job was as vast as the star-blanketed sky. Alcohol and drugs of any kind were off limits, even though the older traffickers appeared to consume everything in record quantities. But again, after Felipe's warning, Victor didn't dare debate any of the restrictions.

He soon discovered that questions weren't the only thing off limits, but talk of any kind was seen as suspicious. Gossips were taken out just as quickly as any snoops, so Victor fell deeper into a taciturn pit of silence. He learned the special language of the narcos, consisting of evasive descriptions and vague replies, never broaching the heart of any subject. Caring little for the truth in words, as his truth…the narcotraficante truth, only came in the form of action.

And there was just one action that would cement his place in the cartel. One of blood.

Both Victor and Felipe always boasted they'd have no problem killing when the time came. Any other talk would ensure they'd be the ones killed, so Victor always said such with bravado and enthusiasm. However, they never saw action, killing or otherwise, while whittling away the nights as lookouts. They weren't even allowed guns, only lame whistles in the rare case trouble should arrive.

Since even banal conversation could get one labeled a chatterbox, about as good as dead, they spent most nights in complete silence. In order to fill the lingering hours until sunrise, they'd compete by lifting weights, and Victor transformed his scrawny frame, sprouting bulky biceps and a firm chest. He began to resemble the powerful narco he imagined himself to be, and pushed to be the most powerful man alive, spider-print buckle or otherwise.

Victor paused in retelling his story and turned toward me. He admitted the one man he really desired to be stronger than was his father, an obvious fact that'd eluded him at the time. He'd ignored his madre's pestering, and all but abandoned his home, refusing to return until his initiation was complete. He knew, when the time was right, when he did make his return, he'd be the one delivering the beatings.

His sole connection with his family was through his sister, who he gave a cut of his earnings. According to her, his father's drinking had only worsened in his absence, along with his temper, and a large chunk of Victor's cash went to fund his padre's binges and other debts.

Victor didn't mind, since this made him feel even more powerful, considering a single week's pay as a ventana fetched him five times the monthly salary his dad earned as a pay-toilet attendant. And if he paid for his father to self-destruct, all the better. What he failed to understand was how he was also seeding his own destruction in the process.

"The day arrive when they say it was time," Victor continued. "Nobody say what it was time to do, but Felipe and me knew. I remember I smile at Felipe and he smile back. We both so excited. We follow a group of narcos into back of La Sierra where we never been before. The room was gigantic, but empty also. I see dust and the floor have blood stains. We say nothing and they drag a man in front of us. He tied up and have a bandana on his eyes."

"Victor, I understand," I interrupted, allowing him an out for his tale. I'd been accused of being many things in life, but never a priest, nor was I in the mood for a confession. The picture painted itself clear enough, and considering all we'd endured, I didn't feel this was the right time or place to go trolling up ancient demons.

"No, you not understand." Victor shook his head. "I must say truth. Before time is gone. Before the end. As man placed in front of us, a narco hold a handful of hay. We, how you say, "draw straws." Mine more long than Felipe's straw, so I take gun. I remember it more heavy than it look, but I have no problems holding. I aim at the man with blindfold, but before I pull the trigger, I told to stop."

"Not bad advice," I muttered.

"The narcos demand I no shoot the man, I shoot Felipe." Victor cringed for a fleeting second, but then his eyes fell flat, almost vacant. He spoke in a monotone voice, hollow as if recounting a stranger's story rather than his own.

"Felipe no protest. He fall on knees, but he not beg. I sure if short straw was mine, I beg. Felipe say he want to speak, so I wait.

He say he hope hell was real, so he can find el diablo and use him for revenge. He look in my eyes and say he look for me. Always. Even as ghost, he will find me. He want to say more, but I shoot."

"Please listen," I said, as Victor bowed his head. "Whatever is happening here isn't some sort of cosmic revenge. Felipe has nothing to do with this. These are just sick pigs. That's it. Rabies or some other shit. The heat is messing with your mind. You're seeking order where there ain't none."

Victor broke into a fit of laughter, which lasted until he lost his breath entirely and started to wheeze. I pressed a reassuring touch around his shoulder, hoping his story had run its course.

"Order? Order?" he repeated. "Only silly Americans believe in the order. There is no order. No justice. No rules. Only fate. One day alive. The next dead. This is the belief in my world."

"Good. So we're agreed this isn't a punishment from God," I replied, folding my hands across my lap.

"All is God. Do you not understand? All life is a pantalla. Pantalla. Pan-taaa-lllllaaa." He spoke the word like it was burning his tongue. As he rocked in place, a wad of dark spit dribbled from the corner of his mouth.

"All pantalla," he continued. "Is why I no can speak good of Harley, since I must speak truth. I need take off the mask before time is gone. Look at the billboard." Victor gestured at the rickety planks that held up the rear of the sign. "The sign is beautiful, but a fake. Underneath, below all, is the rot. All is an illusion, a pantalla. Is why I will die here."

"Don't say that. You ain't dead yet."

"I die after I murder my own family. Now the only question is when to bury the coffin. Felipe was correct. He have his revenge."

Before I could even begin to debate this crazy, a racketing bang echoed out. A gunshot. I swung my head, scanning for the chopper's return. The sky was empty. Not even a cloud.

"There," Victor said, pointing down. A second gunshot exploded. I looked just in time to see a swarm of pigs racing away from the base of the unipole.

In the sliver of space vacated by the pigs, stood Slake. And he was on the ground.

Saturday 2:06 P.M.

The fool had jumped. Slake could've just as easily lowered himself with the safety line, but the rope remained coiled on the lower deck where we'd left it after snatching Harley's cell. No, he'd decided to take the plunge instead. That meant no retreat. No place to go other than straight ahead. Straight toward the cargo van, which was parked over fifty feet away. Straight into the mob of pigs.

I bolted up, almost clobbering my head against the railing. Not that this made a lick of difference since I felt just as woozy as if I had knocked myself. I grabbed the railing for support, which helped, but I still felt dazed and lightheaded. I stared toward Slake, but a haze of twinkling star-like points flooded over my vision, fading in and out like exploding fireworks. I retched and for the first time I felt thankful for a bone-dry stomach.

One sense remained keen. I could hear every bursting snap from the mayhem below. The pigs squealing. The shuffling clatter of their hooves. The crackle of dust detonating into the air. The strained breaths through mucus-crusted snouts. A pitter-patter of sprinting footsteps that had to be Slake's. And something that sounded like a needle grating a glass bottle.

It took a moment for my vision to clear. I zeroed in on a blobby shadow dashing away from the billboard. As Slake materialized through the blur, I noticed he was clutching the gun in outstretched arms. Unlike Harley, who'd waved his around while sprinting, Slake held the gun locked out in front as if it was a fishing pole reeling him toward the safe embrace of the van. He didn't even aim at the pigs, which didn't matter, since most had been spooked by the gunshots and were running off. I wondered how long this skittishness would last.

"Bolillo loco," Victor muttered. He remained seated, but craned his neck so far that the thick vein running across it appeared to be the only thing preventing his head from snapping right off.

I clung to the railing, half-transfixed by the events unfolding below, half-afraid I might collapse without its steady support. Watching Slake's galloping strides made my own legs feel wobbly and weak. This sensation doubled as the entire landscape zapped back into focus. Slake was sprinting straight toward the thickest concentration of pigs.

I gasped as he rushed right at a group of a dozen or so. A few peered up as he approached, but most flicked their snouts back, still shaking off the cobwebs from their midday nap. And of those who spotted him, only one failed to shuffle away as he stampeded closer. For a portly middle-aged man, Slake possessed more juice than I'd imagined possible, but the van remained looming in the distance like a remote oasis.

Slake must've spotted the one holdout in the group, since he lunged just in time to dodge the creature's snapping embrace. As he turned, he bumped into another who was fleeing, knocking this pig onto its belly. It skidded across the dirt like a beached whale, scattering the others to either side of Slake. I whooped and cheered at this minor success, but even as the sound left my lips, another group was forming at the margins. Hell, he was surrounded on every side, and in a sudden shift, the pigs pivoted, closing in like a deflating balloon.

Victor whirled toward me, a bandaged hand covering his gaping mouth. Through gritting teeth, I forced a reassuring smile, but hope was about the furthest emotion raking over me. To be honest, I was pissed. I didn't know what peeved me more, that Slake had decided on such a boneheaded escape or that he hadn't consulted me beforehand. What in the world had possessed him to attempt such a stunt? I despised this selfish act, while at the same time, hollered my honest support.

"To the right! Watch out to your right!" I pounded the railing, attempting to elevate my warning over the clatter. Though pigs were racing in from every direction, the closest cluster on the right of Slake was just feet away.

Either Slake heard me or spotted the pack himself, since he finally broke from his frozen outstretched grasp and whirled the gun to his side. He didn't appear to aim, but the first shot shattered into one of the pigs, spewing a cloud of pink mist. The creature squealed and attempted to reverse directions, but the others shoved it ahead until it buckled and collapsed. As soon as its legs caved, a dozen others pounced, sawing into its flesh. This bottleneck forced the remaining pursuers to detour, though many had spooked after the gunshot.

This reprieve lasted for a blink. As the lines bucked backward, oncoming pigs bashed into those who were retreating, and the scene transformed into a mashing pit of head-butting dominance. Snouts busted together in gnawing embraces. Stubby legs buckled as if dancing on hot coals. Green snot coated the air, adding to the dusty murk. For the first time, the vile creatures tore into one another, injured or not, heaping piles of corpses in their wake. And for every pig that stopped to devour its fallen companions, three others chose to pursue a tastier meal.

Slake raced ahead as a new group formed between him and the van. For a moment, it appeared as if he might be able to dash around the edge, but then the mass shifted. Out of the center of this pack, a dominant victor emerged.

The pig was double the size of the others. Its snout coated with the blood of its rivals. It used its hefty weight to ram ahead, shifting the entire pack. Only when emerging in front did the creature settle, locking onto Slake with ears pointing up defiantly as if they were spears.

The beast, for to call such an animal anything else would've been a disservice, howled as it darted straight at Slake. The cry was so shrill and resonating it was easily distinguishable from the others. No words could capture its force, since outside of a lion's roar, I'd never heard anything so full of raw and savage fury. A jet engine would've sounded more peaceful.

Both Victor and I yelled warnings, but no shouting would detour this monstrosity from its hunt. I somehow doubted a gunshot, hell, even a barrage of mortar blasts, would unnerve this beast. Having covered more than half the distance, Slake was just as focused onto his own prize. So entranced, he failed to turn as the pig galloped within striking distance.

But it didn't attack. Instead, the beast rushed right past his side. That caught Slake's attention. He peered back as the beast swung around in a circle. It spat its shrill cry once again while darting in from behind. Slake fired. The bullet zipped past the beast, connecting with dirt. The beast didn't detour a single inch. It drew up to Slake's kicking heels, close enough to skewer him. But still, no strike.

Instead, the grotesque thing galloped beside Slake as if racing him. At first, I figured the odd behavior was due to a preference for attacking from the rear, but when this too failed to materialize, I realized the beast was just toying with him.

Slake reached across his chest, aiming to his left, but the beast wheeled back. His right hand shook while raising the gun and the over-the-shoulder target must've proved too unwieldy, since he failed to take the shot. The creature used the opportunity to dart ahead, outpacing Slake's breakneck speed with an effortless stride. It skidded to a halt only feet from the van, pivoted, and glared up with desolate black eyes, almost daring him to veer off course.

To his credit, Slake didn't budge an inch, and galloped straight ahead. Had this been the heinous beast's intention the entire time? To lure Slake closer before assaulting him face-to-face, winner take all? Were these fuckers indeed that crafty? I clutched the railing tighter, squeezing my clammy fingers until they were numb. Slake raised the gun. His aim locked onto the beast.

Ka-bam. Ka-bam.

I flinched at the noise. Even from atop the billboard, the firecracker sound beat my eardrums like a whip. Both shots missed, but the noise was enough to startle the pigs back. A pocket of space emerged beside the van as the pigs scattered off. Every single one except for the beast. He remained. The fucker even looked like he was grinning.

Slake raced closer. The animal bowed its snout. Slake took aim again. The beast bent its hind legs, readying to launch. Slake fired. A spark flashed as the bullet lodged into the side of the van with a rusty pop. The pig lunged into the air. Another shot. The beast's mouth sprang open. A goopy line of drool tumbled from piercing teeth. Slake lurched, attempting to both aim and dodge. They collided. The creature wrapped around Slake's neck, causing him to stumble. They collapsed. Locked together.

No sprays of blood. Nor hunks of torn flesh. Odd. Slake raised to his knees with the pig still clinging to his neck. Slake jerked his head back. The beast's jaw hung limp. Slake tore the pig from his chest. It tumbled onto the ground, eyes fluttering, one leg twitching. Then stilled. Slake's shirt was ruffled, but no stitch was torn. A splash of green snot dribbled down his neck. He wiped it away. He stood.

What luck! Somehow that final shot had connected. I wanted to whoop in celebration, but didn't dare break this unsteady peace. Slake reached the van and pressed his back to it like a magnet. He whirled the gun out in front, daring any others to approach. They held steady. He shuffled toward the passenger-side door. Unlocked. He inched it open. The pigs charged.

Slake dove inside. A pig rammed the van. Slake fumbled for the handle, but the force of the pig's blow wrenched the door back open. Another pig nudged its head into the gap. Slake found a firm grasp and slammed the door against the intruder's head. It hissed an ear-splitting squeal, but remained wedged in place. Slake snapped the door wider before clobbering the thing a second time. Another pig crammed into the space. Then a third. Impossible to shut.

Slake hurled the door all the way open. The trio of pigs lurched closer. Slake fired. I don't believe he hit any of them, but the pigs scattered back. One even embedded itself into the sliver of space between the van and the ground. As its hind legs whirled, digging itself underneath, the van shook, scaring away any nearby lurkers. Slake slammed the door shut. Safe.

"Hot damn!" I whooped. "That's how it's done."

"No way," Victor grumbled, almost sounding disappointed in Slake's success. I glared over, shooting him a Bigfoot-sized hairy eyeball. He continued to grimace.

"No, no, *NO!*" He pointed toward the van. I spun back around. The door was open again.

"What?" I gasped. When Slake swung his legs out, I realized he was the one who'd opened it. Before I could even ponder his reason for doing this, another shot exploded. Any nearby stragglers darted off. Slake jumped out. I stepped back, folding my arms and watching as Slake raced across the lot.

The pickup sat parked about thirty feet away, his obvious destination. He'd only kicked a few steps when one pig squealed a deafening howl. The nearby animals skidded to a halt and joined the chorus. The noise was harsh and peculiar, sounding more like a pack of wolves than pigs. Slake sprinted ahead, not even glancing once toward the noise.

"No. Turn around-" I yelled, but trailed off. It was too late. Dozens of pigs galloped in from behind, swarmed past the van, and blocked any return.

Slake had crossed half the distance when a trio of pigs darted in front, swooping in from his right. They skidded to a halt, forming a line. Slake raised the gun, but the trio only huffed while pawing at the dirt. They raised their snouts in unison and shook their heads like a dog emerging from a swim. A soupy pool of green snot crusted the ground, almost painting a line of demarcation. Slake lunged closer. He motioned again with the gun, but this gesture was as futile as the first one.

"Shoot!" I hollered. "Shoot, dammit. Why don't he shoot?"

I glared at Victor, but he only shook his head. The answer was obvious. As if to confirm my fears, Slake hurled the empty gun at the trio in a last ditch effort to scatter them. The gun smacked the pig on the left in the face, but it barely budged with the blow. The others didn't so much as flinch. Slake peered over his shoulder, discovering what we'd already realized from our all-seeing perch. Only one path remained. Straight ahead.

Almost upon the trio, Slake dug in his heels. He shrieked a fierce cry. Not as formidable as that of the beast, but given the circumstances, I was amazed he was able to yell at all. I couldn't utter a single sound. Pigs flooded in from every direction, drawn by Slake's roaring charge. He crouched. And he leapt.

Too short.

Slake landed on the pig in the middle. The damn thing didn't even need to jump up to block. Slake crashed right onto the creature's back. The pig managed to keep its balance for a long moment before collapsing. Slake dropped along with it. I sure hope he crushed that damn bastard. Broke the fucker's back. Maybe he did. Maybe he didn't. I didn't see any more of that pig afterward, but then again, I didn't see my boss either.

I had to turn away as the first pig tore into his shoulder. By the time I mustered the courage to look again, the ground next to the pickup was overflowing with pudgy pink bodies. Even then, they moved in a blur similar to the beating of a hummingbird's wings. The sight wasn't all that disturbing, but the noise got to me. It sounded like a wet towel being shredded.

I was about to look away when I spied Slake's hand shoot out from the edge of the pit. For a split-second, I hoped he might climb free of the swarm. This wish evaporated as his arm drew further into sight. Instead of being attached to his body, it hung from a pig's mouth. As another knocked into this vile creature, the severed limb rolled free. My legs wobbled and I crumpled onto the deck.

"Why?" Victor whimpered. "Pinche pendejo. Why he leave the van?"

It was a valid question, but I lacked the strength to answer, even if Victor was searching for one, which I knew he wasn't. Plus, he'd come upon the answer soon enough. The van had no keys. Harley was the last to have them, so they were likely inside the belly of one of those bastards. Unless Slake knew how to hotwire the engine, which I'm sure was far more difficult than crossing two wires like in the movies, he was shit-out of luck. Hell, he'd been just as trapped in that van as he was up here. The pickup was his sole option.

No, my only question was why he'd decided to go at it all on his own? That irked me. Maybe we could've set up a distraction. Or perhaps tried in the middle of the night. Suspicion that success hadn't been part of his plan bothered me more than anything else. That made sense, especially after this morning's confession.

I'd been around long enough to know death rarely made sense. Doubly so when it came to suicide. I guess the same could be said about my own evil hankerings. I figure that was mankind's ultimate flaw. Why God made the instinct to kill stronger than to survive I'll never know. Perhaps those pigs had an answer since they sure appeared to live by this creed.

Somehow I doubted it.

Saturday 4:40 P.M.

 I hovered on the arches of my feet, steadying for the lunge. My target still remained at least a good two arm's length away, but sneaking this close had proved next to impossible. I paused, not wanting to ruin the progress I'd already made with some rash impulse to act. 'Rash', what a word for the urges smothering me. No, they were piercing, urgent, and more than anything, painful as hell. To think, I once considered those evil hankerings bad. Only one way to temper those, so I started the countdown hoping it'd work for this as well.

Twenty, nineteen, eighteen…

By the time I reached zero, my breathing had settled some, but it had done exactly jack-shit for the pain. My stomach churned, lurching like a jammed printer, while a stabbing sensation gored through my esophagus, charring anything in its path. I'd once heard true hunger resides in the throat, but I could feel the pinching knot through my entire body. As odd as it seems, the worst part was the constant ringing in my ears. This tinnitus made me want to jam a pencil into my head.

Tweet. Tweet. The bird's cry sparked me to jump. Not just because I feared it was onto my hunt, but because the chirp was so grating. You'd think the tinnitus would inspire me to relish any sound other than that fucking ringing, but it had the opposite effect, transforming every minor creak into the squealing of a semi blasting its air horn.

I missed. The flutter of wings zipped off before my heels even raised from the steel bars of the deck. I tumbled against the railing, grasping the air. The stabbing pain returned, doubling in intensity, almost mocking my futile attempt. Worse, the damn bird returned, landing a tad further down the railing, but forever out of reach. The shrill noise of its chirp screeched a vicious taunt.

Tweet. Tweet. Tweet.

I swiped, not in any real attempt to catch the bird, but rather to halt that jeering cry. It soared away, yet I found no relief in the newfound silence. I collapsed into a fetal position, hoping to ride through this agony. The pain came in waves, so I knew all I had to do was hold on until the inevitable release. The bird had other ideas and soared back onto the railing, whiffling down with its caustic trill.

Tweet-Tweet. Poor puddy tat. Faw down and go Ba-boom.

No. That quote was from *Tweety Bird*, from the old Warner Brother's cartoon. I rubbed my throbbing head, realizing the bird couldn't have said that. When I peered up, I saw no sign of the blasted creature. Christ, I was hallucinating again. The relentless heat, dehydration, and lack of food was playing tricks on my feeble mind.

Puddy tat. Tweet. Puddy tat-tat-tat.

At least this time I knew it was fake. But why this vision? These cursed words? I knew. Damn, all the pain in the world couldn't block that memory. Patti and her Tweety obsession. All those stuffed animal toys. And that fucking yellow parakeet she'd bought for Tyler. Some pet! The cursed thing had spent its entire existence shitting all over the house, tearing up the furniture, and filling the nights with endless chirping.

Pawr puddy tat! The wicked vision continued. *Tweet-tweet.*

Never a moment of peace, even up here where there was literally nothing. I focused on the memory of that heinous parakeet, hoping that might offer relief where everything else had failed. What had Patti named it? Golden Goose Gus. Yeah, that was it. Funny, I'd almost forgotten, which was odd considering all those nights I'd spent scheming up ways to murder the yapping critter.

Tyler, bless his toddler heart, had beaten me to the punch by 'petting' the bird too hard while I was out on one of my cross-country deliveries. When I'd returned, Patti was distraught, believing this to be a precursor to some psychopathic tendencies, but I was in heaven.

Chirp-chirp. Sad widdle puddy tat. Stuck on the tat-tat-tatwalk. Chirp-ca-chirp.

I recalled the parakeet's funeral and how Patti had crafted a ceramic statue. She'd given it to Tyler, hoping he'd be more careful with the ceramic bird figurine than he had with the real one. He'd been so proud, always chattering on and on about how he'd helped Ma paint it yellow as if he was the next Picasso rather than Dexter. Whatever the boy did, I couldn't help from loving him, so when he gifted the dopey statue to me, I agreed to place in front and center of my cab. To be honest, the statue's hollowed out middle proved to be useful hiding spot.

Tweet. I tawt I taw a whirly bawd. I did! I did taw a whirly bawd, bawt it flew uff, never to retawn!

"That's enough, you squawking bastard!" I walloped the railing. The chirping cut short, but the tinnitus return, hardly an improvement.

"Save energy. Make peace," Victor said.

I swung around and saw him seated only a few feet away. He was so silent, I'd forgotten he was there. I almost asked what he thought about the bird's remarks, but caught myself before revealing the hallucination.

"Victor, if you're so into peace, why'd you carry that gun?" The question had nettled me and now it'd disappeared along with Slake, I figured it couldn't hurt to ask.

"Ajuste de cuentas," he replied, as if I knew his Mexican lingo. He paused, waiting for me to ask about the meaning, but I just stared off toward the highway. Fuck it, I didn't need to know that bad. The road remained clear, just as it had all day. All damn day long.

"It mean settle a score," he continued. "To correct a wrong. And I make lots of wrongs, so I know muchos demons come to collect. I not stupid. I need the protection."

"And that clicks with the God you believe in? That don't sound very Christian to me."

"Demons no are Christian either," he replied. "God and guns. This is still America, no?"

"I guess you got me there. You think these guys out to get revenge can track you here?" To be honest, if men did arrive to kill Victor, I'd toss him over the edge in exchange for a bottle of water.

"The demons are everywhere. In here…" He tapped his chest. "And in you also."

"There's nothing in me. That's the damn problem. Aren't you worried about food? Outside of the pain, it's the only thing I can think about."

"Russ, you ask me a question, I can ask you one?" Though Victor didn't provide an answer outside of some religious mumbo-jumbo, I nodded for him to proceed.

"Who you kill?"

"That damn bird if I can get my hands on it." I chuckled.

"No, be serious. I know you kill, because when I ask before, you no answer. Man who not kill have no trouble saying that."

"If you're asking if I believe the devil sent the pigs to settle a score, the answer is no. I don't deserve this and you don't either."

"You no answer the question."

"Neither did you," I snapped.

Victor opened his mouth to reply, but then stopped. He scratched his chin before tugging on his earlobe.

"Si, I no speak truth. The gun is for protect the others. To scare el cartel if they come to where I stay now. To the church."

"Wait, you live in a church?" I jerked my neck up, and Victor nodded. "So somebody knows you're missing?" The realization flooded over me like a spilled oil drum. "Do you think they've raised the alarm? Is that why the chopper came?"

"Slake scare them before I can ask," he replied.

"Well Slake ain't gonna be a problem anymore. Why didn't you say this earlier?"

"Should we do a funeral for him?" Victor asked, like this was the most pressing matter at hand.

"I think we can hold off on funeraling for a while," I answered, recalling how well Slake's memorial for Harley had turned out.

"I think boss-man was okay."

"He ain't high on my list to be honest. What was he thinking rushing off without giving us a heads up? I mean, damn, he made it to the van. Why did he leave? What was he thinking?"

While spitting this barrage of questions, I kicked out and smacked the railing. Victor glared over and I folded my legs back. The outburst hadn't been my intention, but talking about Slake amped me up. His foolhardy escape attempt had not only taken his life, but our only weapon, so I felt like a hornet buzzing around without its stinger. Lacking the gun, our chance of steering through that horde was less than nil. If Slake hadn't wanted to live, fine, but that selfish bastard had doomed us along with him.

If we'd spent a single moment discussing an escape attempt, rather than jumping in half-cocked, I'm sure Slake would've realized the stupidity of heading to the van first. I recalled how he'd described himself as a failure. Damn, he couldn't have been more correct. A failed criminal. A failed boss. Fitting he ended his life as a failed savior. People never changed outside of fairy tales and why that delusional crank figured otherwise was beyond me.

"He want the redemption," Victor replied, as if I was truly searching for an answer, rather than venting off.

"Some hero he turned out to be," I said. "Really, it don't matter now. What's done is done and we got about as much chance of fixing it as a castrated bull bucking for his balls back."

"Yes, what is done is done," Victor repeated. "Is the tragedy of the life. Of *my* life, also. I must finish my story now. I never tell this to anyone before, not even the priest." Victor peered into the sky, but thankfully refrained from crossing himself for the millionth time.

"I'm all ears," I replied, though my true feelings about philosophizing was that it never solved a single problem outside of boredom. "But first, why don't you tell me about this priest. Does he know you work hanging billboards? Did you ever tell him about Soaring Banners? Will he notice your absence?"

"After I kill Felipe, I meet the devil," Victor continued, ignoring the volley of questions.

"Yeah, I also met the devil once," I interrupted, while knocking my fists together. "Mine was bald with a black bushy moustache and deep inset eyes like a skull. Dead-eyes, I called him. But let's focus on the here and now. Tell me more about this church. Is it just you and this priest? Or do others live there as well?"

"Only one thing matter about priest, *"in the here and now"* like you say." Victor smirked while repeating my phrase. "He one time tell me the only real diablo live in the mirror. Every man know this, but pretend to only see devil in other people. He was right. After I kill Felipe, I see el diablo everywhere. I always think all will be good when I was in el cartel, since they protect me from all the devils."

I crinkled my forehead and peered down as Victor continued with his preaching. At least I possessed enough self-restraint to avoid kicking the railing a second time, though my every impulse shrieked to do exactly that. I inhaled, counted down, and held my breath as long as I could. Made it all the way to zero, back up to twenty, and a couple ticks more before exhaling. I repeated this exercise until I relaxed enough to lean back. As for listening to Victor, I'd grown up with enough sermons to know how to zone out all but the most pertinent details, so I let my mind wander as he spoke.

From the bits I picked up, Victor wasn't altogether torn after murdering Felipe and it wasn't until another kid's initiation when the guilt really set in. Unlike Victor, this kid had refused to shoot his companion, which resulted in both of them being executed. That hit Victor hard. He no longer slept, ate little, and even stopped weightlifting. When one of the commanders inquired why he was acting so weird, he did the one thing he was told not to do and opened his mouth.

Of course, he wasn't foolish enough to suggest changing the initiation process, but he did propose building a church. He said it would be good for the town's spirit, sort of a public relations campaign, though he didn't use that phrase. Truly, the only soul he was really concerned with saving was his own.

To his surprise, instead of punishing him for his impertinence, the cartel latched onto the idea like gringos to cargo shorts (his metaphor). Instead of the bare-boned shacks that typically passed for chapels, they constructed a multimillion-dollar building. Every detail was lavish, right down to the pews, which weren't those ache-you-into-paying-attention ones, but rather cushioned with plush red padding like a movie theater. Even the Vatican showered praise on the chapel's completion and sent a representative to admire the work. Though that might've been on account of the cartel's hefty donation and all-expenses-paid trip.

Victor, being well aware of the source of these funds, figured it was better the money went to a church rather than indulgences such as gut-busting belt-buckles. He volunteered for the construction, but this was also to escape the mundane grind of guard tower duty. Unlike everyone else in town, he was never naïve about the cartel's intentions, knowing if a single priest ever spoke one ill word about the narcos, the whole complex might go up in flames.

Nor did he forget this same principle applied to him. He'd spoken up once, but doubted he'd ever get a second chance, so while the other workers were hammering up drywall, he built a small hinged panel in the corner of the atrium. It hid a tiny pocket of space, just enough to conceal a full-grown man. The trapdoor and hidden shelter would work in a pinch, not that Victor ever expected to make use of it. If the cartel wanted him dead, he'd probably be killed before having the chance to hide. All the same, it made him feel better knowing it was there.

For almost five years, Victor lived without trouble. The sole exception was a brief dustup with some soldiers who'd approached, firing guns in the middle of the night. Though, calling the incident a battle would've been a stretch, since the soldiers had fled at the first sign of return fire. Nobody was hurt, outside of a few oversized egos, and all the soldiers wanted was a cut of the action. They'd mistakenly believed they could blast off a few rounds and force the cartel to capitulate without anyone getting hurt. Amateurs.

Outside of one who had a background in special-ops training by the Americans, Victor never heard anything more about these soldiers. That guy was sent far across the country to do God-knows-what for the cartel. Unlike these dolts, Victor avoided stirring the pot in any way after the church incident. All in all, life as a narco was turning out to be pretty damn swell.

The trouble began when someone emailed the federales. Whoever it was claimed to live in Paso de Cresta and accused the narcos of all sorts of misdeeds, half of which were true. The federales were working with the gringos to clean up the drug trade, which really consisted of spending their money on military toys and taking down any token players who weren't smart enough to mix their funds with the oil industry. Anyone with true power did that, since the gringos never fucked with oil money. Not once.

Of course, the cartel had a few policia on the take, so they were informed about the email weeks before the scheduled raid. By the time the federal agents showed, the entire La Sierra complex had been rolled up, transformed into a make-shift food processing plant. They even bought a chemical spray that somehow smelled exactly like fresh salsa.

On the final day of closing the complex, after loading crate after crate filled with guns, drugs, and all variety of world currencies, Victor was ordered to meet at the dock after sunset. But when he witnessed dozens of boats zooming away down the coast, he knew better than to show. His fellow low-level narcos, most were locals, failed to spot this obvious warning. That was the last anyone ever heard from them.

Closing shop with the cartel meant tying up all the loose ends. And if Victor wasn't on one of those boats, he was a loose end. The entire town would pay for whoever snitched, not because it was fair or just, but because that was how life worked. Everyone knew that.

Victor certainly had. He packed a small satchel with some canned goods along with a couple guns and climbed into his hiding place inside the church. He didn't expect to last long, the cartel always won out in the end, but he hoped to take out a few of his pursuers before buying that ticket for the carnival upstairs. In fact, escape was never his intention, rather he saw a quick death in a shootout to be preferable to whatever would happen if he was taken alive. That was just his fate. The agreement he'd signed that night after killing Felipe.

So when they did arrive, search dogs in tow, he lunged out guns blazing. Bullets peppered everywhere, painting gore across the church like a mural. The multimillion-dollar chapel was shredded, yet not a single bullet hit Victor. So he continued to fight, not even taking the effort to dodge, picking off narco after narco…until none remained. Somehow, by a miracle, he was able to kill all his pursuers. Every single one. He was so flummoxed, he immediately dropped to his knees, and pledged the remainder of his life to God.

Not that this was much of a commitment, since he knew reinforcements would soon arrive. He doubted he'd live until nightfall. So he waited. And waited. When the sun dropped and then rose again without a peep, he slipped outside. Perhaps he could give his mother one final kiss in this brief remnant of his life. He'd tell her that her prophetic warnings not to join the cartel had been correct. Drop down to his knees and plead for her forgiveness. For her love, for redemption, one final time. He was convinced that was God's true plan for him.

What a dope. God had a far more devious scheme in store.

He was smiling when he knocked on the door of his mother's shack. Almost hopeful. He'd never imagined he'd make it across town, even by the back routes he'd taken. At the worst, she'd curse him, screaming and throwing a tantrum, before the inevitable embrace. His mother was fiery and brash, but always forgiving. She acted the same with his father any time he returned from one of his benders. She was lovely like that.

Redemption would not be found behind that door. Neither would his mother. Instead, Victor discovered carnage that made his massacre at the church appear paltry. The body of his youngest sister was the first he spotted. She was hanging from a beam on the ceiling, her fingerless hands bound above her, legs severed clean, her intestines splayed underneath. All that remained of her face were ribbons of flesh barely concealing her gray skull. The sole reason he recognized her was her tattered yellow floral-print dress, which hung by threads. And she was the most intact of the bunch.

The bodies of his other five siblings were likewise pulverized, as if tossed through a shredder. The carnage splashed everywhere, on the floor, on the walls, in the beds, across the frying pans, hell, there was even gore oozing out of the dresser. Only a single picture frame remained unmolested. It was a photograph of him.

He dropped to his knees and vomited, even though he hadn't eaten for two days. Identifying the others proved to be impossible, even if he had wanted to do so, which he hadn't. He counted the skulls, noting their small stature and realized one was missing. His mother.

He ran out the door in a daze. He headed toward the village market in the center of town knowing somebody would be there. Though he doubted anyone would speak to him, he had to try. If there was any hope of finding his mother, the answer rested there. And boy, had he been right.

In the center of the market, between the dilapidated stands hawking trinkets and fresh fish, someone had constructed a make-shift wooden cross. His mother, or what remained of her mangled corpse, hung from its bar.

Her hands were cleaved away along with her feet. Bones stuck out from the end, smothered with pulpy bits of dark brown flesh. Her mouth hung open, almost gasping, and just two teeth remained, poking from the center of her desiccated gums like tombstones. The gooey remains of her tongue rested at her feet, splinted in half. Patches of scorched flesh peppered her exposed torso, both nipples missing. The worst were her eyes, colored a cloudy white. The result of being charred by a propane torch.

An elderly man sat a nearby bench and pointed out her eyes as if Victor hadn't noticed. He didn't recognize the man, which was odd for this tiny village, but was about the least of his concerns. The man told him that his mother had been alive when they torched her eyes and throughout much of the grisly proceedings. She'd put up a fight, he'd continued, adding that most of them do. Elderly or not, Victor wanted to pulverize this man for watching as his mother was tortured to death.

The man must've sensed Victor's outrage, since he revealed that Ramon Gutierrez was responsible. Victor had never heard this name before, but thanked the man for providing a newfound target for his wrath. The man chuckled, telling Victor where this Ramon character could be found in a town up the coast. He also added how Victor shouldn't procrastinate, since if he failed to go soon, Ramon would implement this same fate on his uncle's entire family. He also said something about Victor's father, but considering Victor hadn't seen that vicious drunk in years, he couldn't care less what happened to him.

Four days later, Victor arrived at the front steps of Ramon's colonnaded mansion, his feet aching from the lengthy hike. He didn't need to knock. Ramon, a chubby, baby-faced man, greeted Victor with a wall-to-wall grin before he reached the front gate. Victor smiled right back at the narco, though the expression was pained and forced.

A pair of armed guards rushed to either side of Victor, but he hadn't come for a fight, so he raised his arms in submission, offering himself up to the brutal torture he'd have to endure in exchange for the lives of his family. As they patted him down for weapons, he pleaded to save his uncle, dropping onto his knees in capitulation. Ramon simply chuckled, motioning for him to stand again.

Ramon led Victor inside and informed him that the pozolero, or stew-maker, had already made a pit stop at Cuervo, the town where his uncle and his family lived. Victor gasped, flinging his arms over his head. The only stew the pozolero made consisted of acid used to dissolve dead bodies. He had come too late.

Ramon flicked his hand, signaling the guards to throw Victor to the ground. He didn't put up any resistance, even as Ramon dug his heel into Victor's neck. Ramon offered two options; either he die now, slowly suffering a fate worse than his mother's, or live as a pantalla. Victor knew there were no other options, so he told his captor he'd do whatever this sadist wanted.

To his shock, Ramon raised him from the ground with a tremendous hug, thanking him profusely. He told Victor he was impressed by the slaughter at the church and wished he had more men like him. That by showing such initiative, he'd made himself an invaluable part of the organization. He beamed while describing Victor's new role.

In the United States, the DEA was investigating a member of the cartel named Tito Lanuza. He was an American-born narco who'd been caught on the wrong end of a wiretap and was the lead focus of their investigation. Any further digging might jeopardize their operations and considering the DEA had no idea of Tito's appearance, only his voice, Victor would serve as the perfect replacement. As crazy as it sounded, he agreed to his new identity.

"I thought I will avoid the torture," Victor continued with his tale. "But no. After the beatings, I smuggled into the USA and have a new ID. They say I to meet someone at cheap motel, where I sure I will die. But, the police arrest me for drugs. I think Ramon scared the real Tito snitch, give info for sentence more short. I know nothing, so I say nada."

He slumped his shoulders, paused, and dropped his arms to his side. "I go to prison as Tito for eight years. Ocho long years I do to protect this criminal, for killing my mother. It no feel long enough."

"If it's any consolation, you don't look much like a Tito to me," I replied. "Now that's done, can you tell me more about this church where you live?"

"Russ, this no matter. I suppose to see parole officer today, so they know I gone. But nobody care. Understand?"

"That's great news. We're going home soon."

Victor shook his head as he slouched, before raising it with a groan. The red streak of the infection trailed well above his elbow, growing quite a distance from this morning. Without antibiotics, it'd soon reach all the way to his shoulder. He strained while stretching out and grabbed my arm.

"Now you say who you kill. Confess and we find the peace."

"I think we've had enough storytelling for one afternoon."

I wrenched free from his grasp. The ringing still throbbed in my head and as much as I thought Victor's words might help, they did the opposite. I stood and proceeded down the deck. Victor attempted to rise, but buckled and collapsed. I rushed back to assist him.

"No push!" he screamed. "You no push me!"

"Victor, I'm not going to push you." I drew back, perplexed at this crazy notion. Victor waved his arms as if I was attacking.

"Yo comprendo," he continued to yell. "I understand. I die and this is hell. You are the diablo."

"I'm not the devil. I'm your, your," I stammered, wondering if the word 'friend' even applied. "I'm your coworker."

"You are liar. I see the horns. Why you have the horns if you no are the devil." Victor persisted with his flailing, even though I was a good ten feet away, almost half the distance to the ladder.

"I don't have any damn horns." I parted my thinning hair, displaying nothing but a bald scalp underneath. "See."

Victor's eyes widened and he inched further back. He was panting and his arms punched the air as if fighting an invisible boxer. He muttered something in Spanish while clawing at the deck. I inched my way toward the ladder.

"It's merely a hallucination." I clipped into the ladder's safety line.

"Liar," he screamed. "You speak and smoke come out." He pawed toward the edge, inching so close I feared he might topple over.

"Okay. I am the devil," I cried out. "And you're dead, but if you don't sit still, I'll torture you and eat your soul."

168

That grabbed his attention and he froze. I growled while sporting my best savage expression. This must have done the trick, since a look of terror splashed over his face.

"Your punishment is to remain up here," I continued in my growl. "Don't move or I'll come back for you."

Victor nodded and I descended the rungs. As I reached the lower platform, I chuckled, recalling his madre's quote. Maybe I blew his mind by having him watch the devil climb down. But again, I doubt there was much left to blow. I feared there wasn't much of mine left either.

Saturday 9:33 P.M.

The sun had set, but my eyes stung worse than they had in the blazing rays. Every blink felt like sandpaper was grating over them. Not that there was a single part of my body that didn't hurt, but my eyes were the worst. To top it off, a glowing dot appeared in the corner of my vision and disappeared if I tried to look at it. A miniscule hallucination compared to the others, but awful in its persistence, especially since staring was the only thing to do up here.

The other option was to sleep, but that damn glowing dot remained even with my eyes shut, always shrouded just out of sight. As I lay sprawled across the deck, I pressed against my closed eyelids like I'd done as a kid, wishing this might erase that blasted dot. My muddy vision transformed into a blast of colors and geometric patterns, which was real nice, so I kept pressing and pressing until the pain became too overwhelming. That cursed dot remained though, bruised eyes or not.

I took a deep breath, counted down, and daydreamed, believing this might help distract from the physical symptoms. I fixated on drinking a tall glass of water and how the icy liquid felt rumbling between my cheeks. The daydream didn't end there. I imagined every kind of water. Ponds. Rain. Gushing rivers. The neighbor's sprinkler that I'd skip through on those muggy summer afternoons in my childhood. Snow. Sleet. Ice cascading from a glacier. Hell, I even licked my lips thinking about that peculiar tasting well-water from my grandpa's farm and I'd hated that stuff.

Shit, I was so parched, I'd probably ask Victor to piss in my mouth if I had the energy to climb to the upper-deck. I'd beg for it, though he had to be as shriveled and dried up as me. The last few times I'd attempted to piss had resulted in dust. It sickened me, but even thinking about urine made me lick my lips.

Every last ounce of moisture had evaporated from my mouth, leaving flaky skin across my lips. I bit off a tough piece, chewed, savoring the fragment of flesh like a gooey piece of chocolate. I couldn't bring myself to swallow, so I spat, but lacking any saliva, it remained lodged underneath my tongue. I hacked a couple of times to no avail.

Unable to settle, I decided to pace. I couldn't move faster than a stumbling lurch, but every step helped as a distraction. I felt like I was sloshing across wet cement, but even a second of relief was worth the effort. The tally was twenty-four paces from side to side, forty-eight if I counted each foot, which I did since this kept me more occupied. Keeping a steady pace proved to be a challenge, though I felt special the few times when I managed to end with my toe pressed right to the edge.

The more I paced, the better I became. When I hit the edge five times in a row, I shortened my stride, attempting to bring the tally to an exact fifty steps. This turned out to be far more difficult than I would've imagined, since I always arrived at a fifty-five or fifty-six count and a few inches off. I compensated with a longer pace, but then I barely maneuvered forty steps and almost lost my balance in the process. I kept at it and after a couple dozen tries, I did arrive right at fifty, though about two inches short. That was good enough, so I celebrated with a loud cheer.

As soon as the noise left my lips, I regretted it, since Victor lurched to life from above. He pounded at the railing, shrieking gibberish, a few words in English, some in Spanish, but mostly an animalistic howl. A pitter-patter grunt of nonsensical sounds, all sharp and pained.

He'd broken into this madness a few times since his murderous confession, the most considerable flow arriving just after sunset. I knew this wasn't all too unusual having witnessed my dad's own descent into dementia. The docs had called it "sun-downing," since Pa's paranoia and madness had grown worse at night. Though, he wasn't much better during the daylight hours either.

Ma described an assortment of vivid episodes during those days in the hospital with him, while I'd taken a brief stay from work to watch over him at night. Not that he required 24/7 supervision, but I'd used him as a convenient excuse to escape my deteriorating home life. I'd spent those nights sneaking out for 'breaks' that entailed crack-smoking sessions along with a hit of speed. At the time, I told myself I needed it to endure the psychological pain of losing my father, but really, I was an addict and just needed to get fucked up.

Not that there wasn't plenty of psychological trauma to be endured. I still can't forget that one night when Pa ripped out all his tubes and flung his dirty diaper at me, hollering how the shit was proof the nurses were raping him when I'd gone out for my breaks.

Of course, that night the nursing staff had been all female, so when I pointed out this inconvenient fact, he'd changed his story, insisting the rapists were supernatural goblins hiding in the walls. He'd validated this insanity by claiming the reason I couldn't see them was on account of my age. Once I grew older, I'd noticed them for sure. Many years have passed since then and I have yet to spot a single sodomizing goblin, but perhaps I still might. I'd already seen stranger things up on this cursed billboard.

The only real takeaway from these episodes was how they grew worse with time, which didn't bode well for Victor. With that infection creeping up his arm, I figured I have to prepare for his madness to become more unpredictable. If my dad's descent was any hint of things to come, accusations of being the devil would be the least of my worries.

I paused in my pacing, hoping the silence would settle Victor back down, but he kept screaming "Diablo Oro," over and over. This was followed by a booming thud, sounding as if he'd attempted to stand and collapsed. I didn't dare climb up to check on him, not while he was in this manic state.

Sparked by Victor's outburst, a group of pigs shook awake, and galloped around in a circle. The more I watched, the more I became entranced with the motion of these trampling animals. Their flow increased and my vision transformed into that of a flowing ocean. I stared, memorized by the hallucination, and imagined diving over the edge into its deep blue waves. I envisioned rocketing through the air, the pigs parting, and instead of splattering across the ground, I'd drop into the water, splashing up a geyser. My entire body would soak the moisture like a sponge.

My hand inched toward the carabineer and I broke from the spell. *It ain't real, not fucking real*, I thought, dropping the clasp. Plunging into that slimy pit would spell instant death, but I found no comfort in this. Maybe death was better than these gnawing aches and delusions. Maybe.

Tyler. The boy's name thundered in my head. No, I'd stick it out for him. I zeroed in on this thought, remembering that magical evening when Patti had given birth. His infant body soaked in goop as his peach-fuzz hair sprouted into existence with a yapping wail. How we'd spent those extraordinary days afterwards, cuddling with our breathing merged in syncopation. Together. Forever. At least, I'd thought so. I spun back into the bleak gloom. I'd never get that back. Merely glimpses. And even those mired in the hazy murk of memories.

My racing mind failed to stop. The deluge of memories, mistakes, and lies, choked over me like a leaky hose I couldn't switch off. I began to pace once more, if only to be doing something other than drowning in them. I stared down again, willing the hallucination of the ocean to return. Sometimes smashing the walls of reality was the only way to restore one's sanity.

When the vision failed to return, I kept staring and lost balance. My legs buckled and I grasped the railing. I peered at my wobbly feet and the thought struck like a boxer's fist. Why had I been so dense? Here I was starving and I was prancing around on a damn buffet. Sure, the leather of my boots was weathered and grimy, but I didn't care one lick. I dropped to my knees and pawed at the laces. My hands shook so much I could barely grasp the knots, let alone untie them, but I kept yanking and yanking until the boot shivered and slipped free.

I chomped at the boot's tongue, grinding the rough leather between my teeth. My gums burst open as I chewed, filling my mouth with the coppery taste of blood, but I couldn't break off a single piece. I was chomping so hard I almost missed spotting the headlights.

They poked up from a bend in the highway, illuminating the barren road. I dropped the boot and rubbed my eyes. I shook my head, wondering if this was another delusion, but the headlights zoomed closer, hovering over the road like a magic carpet. When they slowed approaching the exit for the billboard, I lurched up and raced toward the outer-deck.

"Victor! Victor!" I hollered, while staggering out front. After all the other hallucinations, I needed confirmation I wasn't heading into sodomizing-goblin territory. Victor heard me, since his gibberish pitched louder, but he remained just as unintelligible. I couldn't tell if this was in response to the headlights or just more of the same. I didn't care, really.

The headlights turned down the service road, drawing closer as I stood underneath the giant half-hung banner. I waved and yelled as they reached the turnoff for the parking lot. The dull red of the brake lights flashed at the intersection, pausing as if wondering to proceed. I hollered "HELP" as loudly as my aching chest would allow. To my delight, the headlights turned into the lot.

The pigs scrambled to their feet, squealing a drumming din. Either my hallucination had grown to epic proportions or they too spotted the lights. A dozen scurried straight toward the vehicle, while another group dashed into the safety of the tall grass. Most trampled in a circle, not approaching nor retreating.

As the lights wheeled perpendicular to the billboard, I spotted a cutaway van similar to an ambulance. The front chassis was that of a van, while the rear was a truck. But unlike an ambulance or a cube-truck, this cutaway van had a curved roof. People sat in both the driver's and passenger's seats, but were indistinguishable within the shadows. The rear lacked windows or markings, so I couldn't tell if anything was inside. The ghost-white van screeched to a halt a few yards from the base of the unipole. It flicked off its lights.

"Hello!" I repeated a number of times, receiving no reply, I craned up toward Victor. "Are you seeing this?"

"I kill them all," he shouted back. These were the most coherent words he'd yelled in quite some time, but around the last thing I'd expected to hear. I hoped he'd return to his gibberish, or better yet, zip-it altogether.

"Victor, do you see the van?" I yelled a second time.

"I kill all. My family all dead. I kill, I kill, I keeee-llll…" He dragged out the word with a throaty roar.

"We know you're up there," a husky voice said, amplified by a megaphone or speaker of some sort.

"Yes, we're here." I banged at the railing. "Up here!"

A narrow beam of light glided across the sign, swooping over the dangling banner and onto the outer-deck. It was too small to be a spotlight, so it was likely a flashlight or reflector of some sort. I bolted toward the beam, but overshot it as it swiped in the opposite direction. I swung around to chase, but lost my balance and stumbled. A sharp, stabbing pain crashed down my back and I rolled onto my side. I reached for the beam, but it slid further down the deck.

"Show yourself," the amplified voice commanded.

"Here! Here!" I waved as the beam swirled back in my direction.

"Kill! Kill!" Victor shouted, almost parroting my cry. Before the beam reached me, it swung up toward him. I couldn't see if he was peeking over the top, but it didn't sound like it. The beam swept across the top as he continued to rant, this time in Spanish. The flashlight flickered off.

"No, down here!" I yelled. "Here! I'm down-"

Gunshots peppered the air. The whizzing bullets exploded to my right and somewhere over my head. I scrambled across the deck as another volley blasted, this time a little further back. I rounded the corner onto the inner deck and huddled into a ball just behind the billboard. A third barrage cracked, but sounded distant as if they were shooting across the lot.

"Stop shooting!" I scrambled further down the deck, my head tucked low in case my pleading went unheeded. When the gunshots failed to emerge a fourth time, I shouted again for them to stop.

"Toss down your weapons," the amplified voice commanded.

"We don't have any," I yelled.

"We know you do. Toss down your weapons or we will be forced to take further action."

I whirled around, searching for anything to throw that might be mistaken for a gun. We'd already flung all the tools while trying to down the power lines, so the deck was empty. Off on the corner, I spied one of the ratchet straps we'd used to hang the banner.

"I kill them. Listen you devils. I kill!" Victor moaned, not helping matters any.

"Zip-it, Victor." I yanked the ratchet strap free and clasped the frigid metal between my shaking palms. I ducked around the edge, anticipating another barrage of gunfire. When none came, I tossed the strap over the side.

"I threw the gun," I yelled, while crouching behind the sign.

I don't know if the strap would've fooled them, since a whooshing flutter drowned out the noise of its landing. In my rush, I'd yanked one of the few remaining straps holding the banner in place. Without it, the vinyl tumbled free. As it fell, it lashed in the wind, spitting a loud crack before slithering to the ground. A small portion landed on the curved top of the cutaway van, but only remained there for a moment before momentum shook it free.

"Okay, then. You made your choice," the loudspeaker buzzed.

The cutaway van switched on its headlights and wheeled in reverse. A group of pigs that'd gathered at its side scrambled back, screeching at the sudden movement.

"No, I threw the gun!" I yelled. "Don't go."

"We'll be back tomorrow," the loudspeaker squelched over the noise of the braying pigs. "And you won't be able to hide in the light."

"I kill! Kill! Kill!" Victor pounded at the deck as the van lurched down the drive.

"Stay!" I screamed, but it was too late. The van disappeared onto the service road before zooming back down the highway. A minute later, its headlights curved around a bend and disappeared.

"Fuck you, Victor!" I shouted, while likewise adding my own pounding to the racket. This simply drove him into a greater frenzy as he spat more gibberish in Spanish. I matched his hollering, yell for yell, but eventually my lungs caved and I wheezed, struggling to breathe. I dropped and shook as if bathing in ice water. My stare was spastic and blurred, but I kept looking, waiting for any sign of the van's return.

"Keeelll. Keeelll," Victor continued to holler.

"Oh, I'll keeelll, motherfucker," I promised. "Just you wait until morning."

Sunday 2:18 A.M.

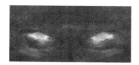

I couldn't sleep. Not one wink after that. My eyes just wouldn't close for more than five minutes before peeking to see if the cutaway van returned. When it failed to materialize, I'd check the time on my withered wristwatch in what had become a compulsive habit, wishing to put a cork in this dreadful night forever.

The way I figured, there were two possibilities for tomorrow. Either they'd return to rescue us or blast us into oblivion. That is if they do return at all and considering everything that has happened, it is far from guaranteed. Hell, I wasn't together enough to know if the entire damn incident had just been a vision.

I peeked again at my watch, only a single minute passed, but at least that truth remained. Time always clicked ahead, perhaps at a plodding pace, but forever forward. As everything else deteriorated around me, I could always count on that. Although, stuck in my thoughts, in my memories, I sometimes wished otherwise.

If there was a single moment I'd like to spin in reverse, it would be that morning outside the truck-stop in Fort Collins. That morning I made the choice. When the evil hankerings really took root. When my addiction began.

Compulsions were twisted like that, always bending toward control. In this calamitous existence, when life was outside anyone's command, one option always remained. Until the moment it arrived, the choice still existed. Fuck freedom, this was the true universal human right. The bet that always paid out no matter the odds. The single part of this blasted life always under my control. The choice to die.

And I chose wrong.

Sure, my self-destruction had a little more finesse, more lies and more fun, than most, but it was suicidal nevertheless. I guess that was why I was so furious at Slake. Not that I agreed, but worse,

I understood. I knew how it felt to crave. The inherent power in those evil hankerings. The relief. The escape. The control.

Similar to my compulsive pacing, step counting, and time checking, I was no fool when it came to desiring control. Any addict can talk on and on about the magic of being high, the soaring feelings, the pits of self-loathing, the numbness of that vast void. But only honest ones will ever mention its true roots. And addicts, by nature, aren't honest. I sure wasn't. Because at its heart, the evil hankerings weren't about doing or feeling anything at all. They were about relief.

Addiction wasn't about cravings, but avoidance of them. For those brief moments under the drug's spell, all my hunger, my greed, my lust, my pain, my every need went missing. Not fulfilled by any means, but just plain gone. It was death by any other name. Once I had a taste of that devil, heaven could never compare. Only fools wanted eternal bliss. I desired the emptiness.

Pray to the devil and he shall rise. But curse him and he will not fall. For when the devil climbs, never shall he return.

Victor's peculiar phrase popped into my head and I think I understood. If there had been a time when I'd prayed to the Dark Lord and received his grace, it was that morning outside of Fort Collins. And unlike the dead-eyed man who came to collect later, this particular fellow appeared bright and positive, almost innocent. Hell, the bastard even wore cargo shorts.

I find it amusing how people seem to recall only the positive moments in life during retrospect. Nobody ever said they were having the best day of their life while in the moment. At the same time, the opposite was hardly ever true. Tragedies such as the death of a loved one, being arrested, or being jacked of a prized possession, tended to get noticed the instant they occurred. Nobody ever had to be reminded they were having a shitty day. People were born complainers, I guess. They just had a keen sense when it came to disasters. I sure did that morning.

To call me a disaster when the devil found me would've been an understatement. Not to make excuses, but I was particularly vulnerable that morning. For weeks, I'd barely spoken a single word to Patti that hadn't come with a combative wrapping. Our issues were the same as all young couples, no money. So when Tyler came down with a nasty case of croup, forcing us into an insurance-less visit to the ER, we reached a tipping point into our financial abyss. No money. No sex. No fun. That was the lowest I'd ever been and I didn't need Patti's yapping to remind me of it.

Not to mention, by that point, I'd been drinking at least a dozen beers every night, likely more while in a permanent stupor. This didn't help our budget, nor my temper, and before the Fort Collins run, we had a skirmish that would've made a general dive ten feet deep into a foxhole. Words flung like grenades and I wish they were the only damage. Glasses, picture frames, and even the TV got blasted into shrapnel.

By the time I jumped into the rig, squirreling off for Fort Collins, I was raging like a bar-fight drunk with chewing tobacco in his eyes. Lacking funds for sauce merely poured kerosene onto the flames. I couldn't sleep a wink that first night and just lay in my cab, quivering and drenched in sweat. While driving the following day, my hands shook so hard, I almost considered using a bungee cord to tie them to the steering wheel.

So in my infinite wisdom, I detoured into a less than respectable neighborhood. I found a miserable deli with boarded up windows which stunk of cat-piss. The only positive trait was that the teenage clerk didn't appear to be armed, so I pinched a bottle of bottom-shelf vodka.

I'd never stolen a single thing my life before that, not even as a kid, and discovered the enthralling rush of a successful score. That would turn out to be the first of many criminally induced highs, an addiction itself. I'd been so jacked afterwards, I chugged an entire bottle that night.

Of course, the results were anything other than pretty. I ended up weeping like a baby over how much I loved Patti, how I had to change and be the perfect dad for Tyler, and how I'd never make such a stupid mistake of falling for the sauce ever again. Straight and narrow from now on, I promised, but as with all gargle guarantees, this oath was about as strong as a wet piece of toilet paper.

So that dreadful morning outside Fort Collins began exactly as one might expect. I didn't even manage to exit the sleeper before the first round of vomiting painted my cab a chunky yellow. I crossed the truck-stop's parking lot, shirt drenched, pants hanging to my knees, stumbling like a hobo on a ten-day binge. Every head swung in my direction, all pretending not to look, but watching my every staggering step. In my haze, I waved like a rock-star, and lurched into the bathroom.

There was no way I could arrive at my delivery in such a state, so I cleaned up the best I could. After the nausea died down enough for me to stand, I tottered out to gather some cleaning supplies for my cab. The single positive that morning was how the cashier provided a slop bucket and dishwashing soap free of charge.

The cleanup proved to be far more difficult than I'd anticipated. Not only was the stench beyond rotten, any time I could hold my breath long enough to clean one spot, another gut-churning wave would overtake me, adding to the mess. It was a losing battle, so I exited for some fresh air, and plum fell asleep leaning against the truck.

That was when the man in the cargo shorts arrived. He spotted me snoozing while standing up and it didn't take a detective to know something was wrong. He was bone-skinny, but wore an oversized t-shirt with a logo of two wrenches crossed in an X. That, along with a pencil-thin brown moustache, distinguished him from the typical obese drivers and other cretins who usually loitered around truck-stops.

I awoke as Mr. Cargo Shorts tapped my shoulder and asked if I was okay. Instead of answering, I spat a mouthful of vomit, which I guess was an answer in of itself. He remained at my side and said he had something that would "right me." I assumed he meant the hair of the dog that bit me, so I shook my head, refusing the offer. Forget the previous night's promise to quit, at that point just the thought of any more alcohol sickened me. On another day, I would've told this fella off, maybe even with my fists, but I lacked the will to stand up straight.

Somehow I was able to tell him all I needed was five minutes to recoup and I'd soon be on my way to Wichita for the afternoon delivery. He laughed something fierce at this, wheezing almost as much as I was. He replied that I wasn't gonna make it to the onramp, let alone four-hundred miles down the road, adding a high-pitched chortle.

I turned to climb back into my cab when his laughter cut short. He straightened and peered over each shoulder, all suspicious-like. I assumed he was going to jack me, though the joke would be on him considering my empty wallet. Maybe this was why I didn't even flinch as he reached into his pocket.

To my surprise, he didn't pull a gun, but rather, a small glass tube containing a couple white crystals. I'd never done drugs before, but I knew what it was when I saw it. Crack. He was holding a vial of crack cocaine.

He declared himself a 'Good Samaritan' assisting a fellow traveler in need, insisting this was the medicine to clean me up good. Before I could protest, he removed a piece of foil, and placed one of the rocks onto it. He held a lighter underneath the foil, heating the crack until it bubbled and turned all gooey. In his other hand, he clutched a small glass tube, similar to a straw, calling it a tooter. He hovered the tooter over the steaming goop, and though it didn't appear to have much smoke, when he inhaled, a massive grin spiked across his face.

He took three hits before handing the tooter to me. I wish I could say there was some pivotal emotion or reason for taking up the offer, such as feeling reassured that Mr. Cargo Shorts appeared respectable and nothing like those druggies on TV, but really I was just curious. More than anything, what drove me to bend over and inhale was because I knew he was right. Unless I cleaned up, I was never going to make my delivery, and hell, with that ripping nausea, I couldn't feel any worse.

The buzz hit me on the first breath. All of a sudden, I jolted awake as if hopping out of a wet cotton-ball. Everything focused into brilliant colors, sharp and precise, yet pleasant on the eyes. While the typical truck-stop clatter, all the grinding, squealing, and hissing that typically annoyed me, transformed into a harmonious chorus. My thoughts spun into overdrive as though time had frozen for everyone but me. Best of all, that churning in my stomach up and left. It was a Goddamn miracle.

Mr. Cargo Shorts slapped his thigh and spat another high-pitched chortle. This time, I couldn't help from joining in the laughter. After the forth hit, I knew I had to get my hands on more of this mystical crack, but my wallet remained empty. I asked for a freebie, but he simply laughed harder at this request. He asked if I had a company gas card that might work for a trade since he was an independent and had to buy his own diesel. I whipped my card out and left with a handful of rocks, the tooter, and some foil.

He didn't stick around after gassing up, but that suited me just fine. I had to finish cleaning the cab. I scrubbed as if my arm might fall off if I paused. The vomit no longer bothered me, not even the rancid smell, and lickety-split, the cab was sparkling as if brand new. The entire time, I kept wondering why I drank when I could feel like this while high on crack.

Making the delivery in Wichita that afternoon turned into a joyous race. I couldn't wait to unload the pallets and zoom back home. The guys at the terminal didn't seem to notice I was high and everyone was upbeat, even though I did arrive late. Perhaps my newfound positivity was contagious. When Patti greeted me the next day, she sure seemed to believe so, returning my smile for the first time in what felt like years.

Overall, my brief high turned out to be a spectacular success. Even coming down wasn't as awful as everyone pretended. I was just tired to be honest. The one bad part was the paranoia my adventure sparked the following week. Sure, I'd cleaned up enough for the delivery, but I couldn't shake the fear at any moment I was going to be pulled aside and be drug tested by the DOT. My fears grew obsessive, overpowering me to the point of reoccurring nightmares where I'd have to pee for a test, but could never go.

By the time a month passed, I was so nervy that I'd be drenched with sweat whenever I pulled into a weight station. It was as though a glowing neon sign reading *crackhead* marked my forehead. Worse, I'd shake and stutter during the most innocuous conversations and picked at my nails until my fingers became red and swollen. I even yelled at Patti for things that normally didn't bother me, such as leaving her knitting needles on the couch. We were arguing worse than even before my Fort Collins run.

I couldn't live like that for much longer, so I concocted a tall tale in order to get info on drug testing from other drivers at the yard. I said I went to a party where this scruffy hippie-looking fella pulled out a joint and puffed away all out in the open. I pretended to be worried over inhaling second-hand smoke and asked how long drugs remained in your system. I said it wouldn't be fair to test positive for something I didn't do.

Sure, the story was a bit transparent in retrospect and I wasn't much for fibbing up to that point, but I figured it'd do the job well enough. I couldn't have been more wrong. When the fellas began to mock me, I wished I'd kept my fat mouth shut.

One after another, they poked holes in the story, grilling over the minute details, such as the color of the hippie's hair and the music playing at the party. They even busted my chops for failing to call the police, pretending like I'd witnessed some major crime and was obstructing the investigation. I received a lot of ribbing, but what I didn't get were any answers.

After that verbal lashing, I dummied up over the whole matter, but the story must've circulated, since one of the old-timers named Ray said he needed to have a word with me. Ray and me hadn't ever spoken before in private, so I knew something was fishy, but on account of he was a real stand up fella and not one to give much lip, I decided a meeting behind the terminal wouldn't do any harm.

Unlike the other chuckleheads, Ray was about as virtuous as they came. Not only did he have a perfect record, which qualified him for some of the pricier hazmat runs, but he was in terrific shape, didn't smoke, and always attended the Sunday services without fail. Hell, I'd never even heard him spit a single curse.

So that was why I almost toppled over at our powwow in the back alleyway when Ray sparked a joint. I mumbled something innocuous, my voice cracking as I shivered like I was the one breaking the law. Ray snickered, offered me a hit, but considering the paranoia that'd come after smoking that crack, I politely declined. More than anything, I worried it was a set-up and kept peeking around in search for hidden cameras.

Ray sensed my jitters and told me not to fret. He said a number of guys here shared my predicament and that he'd been smoking grass for over thirty-years with none being the wiser. I started to repeat my secondhand smoke fib, but he cut me off, saying he wasn't a pasture, so save the bullshit. That was the first harsh word I'd ever heard him speak, so when he handed me a slip of paper with a phone number scribbled across it, flustered, I dropped it. He snatched it up and said to call a fella named Kirk who'd hook me up with the solution.

As soon as I left the terminal, I raced to a phone. Kirk answered on the third ring. He was friendly enough, and unlike the other drivers, he answered all my questions without jokes or insults in a straight to the fact manner. I can't believe I was so worked up, since he told me crack flushed out within three days, and by that point, weeks had passed. He went on, informing me that if I needed to be certain, he could sell me some dried urine that would fool any drug test. I agreed to this offer, willing to pay anything for peace of mind at that point, however, I did decline his offer for more crack.

I drove over to Kirk's house and he even took the time to demonstrate how the dried urine worked in his kitchen sink. All I had to do was rip open the packet, dissolve the mixture in hot water, and presto, I had some faux-urine. Unlike the strict drug tests they did while on probation where the parole officers stared at my cock while I pissed, the ones in the yard weren't so rigid. My supervisor would hand me a cup, show me the bathroom door, and once inside, I was always alone, so sprinkling the packet into some tap water was easy-peasy.

Even though the crack had flushed from my system, I still had the dried urine in my pocket when I arrived at the terminal the following day, awaiting my schedule of upcoming runs. Ray hadn't been the only one who must've heard my tall tale, since I got pulled aside and singled out for a 'random' drug test. That made me real cranky, especially knowing how much lip I'd already endured from the other drivers joking behind my back. I decided to get my revenge by turning the whole rotten system on its head and used the dried urine.

It was a risk, since I was far from certain I hadn't purchased some snake-oil, especially considering how much fun the other guys already had at my expense. Somehow I trusted Kirk and poured the concoction into the little plastic cup. After all that ribbing, I enjoyed my sneaky protest, reveling in my new secret. When the test came back negative, my elation grew.

I assumed that would be the end of it, but a week later, I got yanked aside for a second so-called random test. And again, three days after that. Not once did the supervisors outright ask me about using drugs, so this struck me as rude and I lost any respect I had for the cowardly terminal management. After all my years of loyal service, this was how I was treated. Unbelievable! So as they kept handing me those plastics cups, even though I was in the clear, I kept filling them with dried urine along with an upraised middle finger.

After three months of this nonsense and always testing clean, I grew so peeved, that I took Kirk up on his previous offer and purchased some crack, if entirely out of spite. At least, that was what I told myself to justify it. The true reason was far simpler. I wanted to get high.

The first time felt so grand, I needed to know if that was only a fluke. I'd heard all those stories how the first hit was the best and after that it couldn't get any better; that the addict was merely trying to recapture that initial rush, which would inevitably fail. What a crock of shit! I'd be damned if the second time wasn't just as marvelous, perhaps better since I didn't have a hangover to dampen it.

I became bold after that. Alcohol was too visible, too easy to smell, and left too many empty bottles as evidence. All the clerks at the trucks stops knew the drivers, so buying alcohol meant either stockpiling beforehand or taking unscheduled detours while on route. No matter how careful, the cab always ended up reeking like a urine-soaked bar.

Crack eliminated all that. Not only was it easy to conceal, I hid mine inside that hollowed out Tweety Bird statue Tyler had given me, but the chemical stench only remained for a few minutes before evaporating forever. Unless a DOT agent caught me as I was lighting up, there was no way to prove anything.

Most of all, for the first time in over a decade, I loved my job. I felt free, just as I had when I was green and driving the routes with a sense of unbound exploration. Even Patti noticed this uptick in my attitude and we sparked a passion that'd been missing since we were young lovers. She adored how I'd ditched the sauce and in our newfound bliss, I lacked the heart to tell her it was for a different fix.

The more crack I smoked, the more I realized the media was full of lies about it. No, I didn't transform into a haggard bum with no teeth, willing to blow strangers for another hit. Sure I was an addict, but some days I didn't smoke at all, solely to prove I could. As for work, with that extra sizzle blasting through me, I kept providing for my family, which I figured was more than enough.

What I failed to realize was that devil resting on my back, the one who whispered sweet temptations into my open ear, was just biding his time. See, the true heart of addiction wasn't craving the high. No, the transformation occurred when I started hungering for the relief the high brought more than the high itself. And if them evil hankerings brought relief, even temporary, even at the expense of everything I loved, even though I found that I no longer enjoyed the high, I allowed that devil to run amuck. That was when shit jumped off bad.

I sat up realizing no good could come from reliving the past, not up here. But I couldn't help myself. Though the wave of pain lulled a bit, never quite disappearing, I couldn't stop thinking about crack. The relief it offered from all the pain, depression, and isolation. It'd be perfect now. One hit was all I'd need to ride me through this dreadful night. One Goddamn hit. One final dance with the devil.

That hurt the most. After all the misery and destruction that horrific drug brought into my life, how it'd transformed my evil hankerings into a warped reality, stripping all the good, and perhaps, cursing my soul forever, I would've lit up if I had any within reach. Tyler be damned. An addict forever.

I stared out, scanning again for the cutaway van, but the highway remained empty. Until it arrived, I knew I'd find no rest. The sharp pain wheezed again in my stomach and I doubled back over. I tried praying to God, but in the agony, words failed to form in my mind. Hell, I would've prayed to the devil if I thought it'd do any good.

Sunday 7:16 A.M.

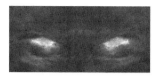If someone had told me I'd be spending what were likely the final moments of my life scraping away bird shit on account of what some guard told me in the pen, I'd think they were insane; yet this was exactly what I was doing. Crazier still, I was enjoying the dirty job.

I hadn't managed a single minute of sleep throughout the night, so when the sun dribbled over the mountaintops, spraying the horizon with a dazzling array of blood orange streaks, I'd immediately perked up. That was, until I spotted the bullet holes. This was all the confirmation I needed to know the cutaway van had been real.

The fact they'd showered bullets and demands without offering a single helpful word didn't bode well for their intent. I kept mulling over Slake's theory they were a hit squad come to cover-up the outbreak, and the more I thought about it, the less crazy his escape attempt appeared. Better to die trying rather than sitting around, waiting for our execution. Nevertheless, after witnessing both Harley and Slake being mauled by those savage pigs, I wasn't certain being shot wasn't the better option.

The biggest problem was the boredom while waiting for them to return. Even the swine appeared listless as they staggered awake and peered up to see if we were still stuck. I'd stared back, shooting the best vitriolic expression I could muster, but it felt flat and was exhausting to hold. Not that the pigs seemed to care one way or another. Their gaze was just as blank as their foggy black eyes.

My mind kept merry-go-rounding in an endless circle of no escape. I knew the one option was to wait, but that idea made me want to plunge over the edge. The more I thought about it, the more fond I became of this suicide solution, and even the idea of seeing Tyler again couldn't pull me from this rift. I'd gone as far as dangling my legs over the side and allowing my half-chewed boot to topple down into the horde.

The pigs had torn into the boot, almost shredding it before it hit the ground. The worst part was how I hadn't felt anxious or afraid, but rather jealous over the ease of their chomping. I'd spent a good portion of the night trying to break off a bite-sized morsel and had managed to swallow a chunk of the lip, but I'd almost choked and my stomach seethed afterword. Though, the pain wasn't half as bad as that time I'd swallowed two crack rocks after being pulled over by the cops while driving Patti's minivan. Now that had been agony.

Luckily, I had a moment of clarity and recalled the advice a guard had given while I was inside. Unlike the other COs, Terrell had been quite popular with the prisoners on account of his jovial storytelling. He'd begun his career at a super-max facility, thrown into the sharks right on day one, so he had all sorts of vivid tales. Everything from gang wars, insane suicide attempts, abusive torture by the other guards, and the mentals who'd act in mind-blowing ways, such as a schizoid who'd severed off his thumbs to use as earplugs.

All that aside, according to Terrell, the most agonizing part was the boredom. Nothing broke an inmate faster. Not violence or torture, not even being sodomized. And the most brutal boredom came in solitary. I was housed in a minimum security prison, so we didn't have an isolation unit and I'd mistakenly called it "the hole," since that was what I'd seen in the movies. Terrell corrected me, saying it was sometimes called ISO, short for isolation, but mostly it was the SHU, an abbreviation for *security housing units*, and because it provided a firm kick in the ass like a shoe.

He told how the toughest thugs broke into crying babies after spending a single week in the SHU. How one fella had captured a fly, befriended it, talking to the bug for hours on end, and even cried when it'd somehow escaped. Or how common it was for the inmates to scribble incoherent messages across the walls using either shit or their own blood.

"Delusions are similar to lizards, always growing to the size of their cage," he'd told me, while describing the case of an especially creepy inmate who'd spent so much time compulsively masturbating that he'd ejaculated blood. "The more a guy lets his thoughts flow free, the more likely he was to end up with a big-ol-Godzilla on his hands."

The secret to surviving the SHU was keeping busy, according to Terrell. "Do anything. Exercise. Pace. Count the cracks. One guy told me he'd take a random number, say 4,208, and then subtract 7, just to keep focused. And he fucking hated math. But that's better than daydreaming, 'cause that's where the demons live.

I'd always been on good behavior, so I never gave Terrell's warnings much thought, not until this morning. After dangling my legs over the side, I knew I had to do something. I decided to pace, but when unable to hit the fifty-step mark, I just lost it. I started screaming and pounding at the railing. When my hand crushed atop a pile of bird shit, the thought struck. "Clean house, clean mind", as Patti had always said, so I'd decided to spend my final hours scrubbing the deck clean.

And it worked. I felt fantastic. Even the pain in my belly subsided as I used the heel of my remaining boot to chip away the dried bird poop. I worked across the deck, slowly and methodically peeling off the grime. When the boot proved to be too unwieldy of a tool for the job, I tore the button from my jeans and dug even deeper. I was about a third of the way across when Victor began to shriek.

I ignored it, still peeved over last night's outburst. Maybe those men wouldn't have shot if he'd kept his fat trap shut. Maybe I'd be soaking in a bath right now, sipping on a tall glass of water, eating a fucking ham sandwich, instead of remaining trapped on this jinxed billboard. If the van returned and his hollering continued, something would have to be done. I didn't know what, but something.

I closed my eyes and counted down. Victor's hollering grew louder, sounding more despondent than the yowling of a cat in heat. I reached zero and grabbed the button to clean some more. Victor kept yelling. I grated at the deck, rubbing so vigorously, the metallic button grew hot. Victor persisted. I slammed the button against the beams and a spark erupted. *Must keep going*, I told myself, *must keep-*

"Russ, Russ," Victor repeated, penetrating my hypnotic trance.

"Shut up," I yelled. "If you know what's good for you, you'll shut the fuck up."

"Russ." Victor pounded at the deck. "*Russ!*"

"What?" I spun toward the highway. Unless that cutaway van was pulling down the drive, I saw no reason for the interruption. No fucking reason at all.

"You hear me?" he hollered.

The highway was empty. Nothing in sight.

"Whaaa…TTT!" I snapped like a whip.

"I wish say something to you."

"What's stopping you?"

"Come here, I request."

"Shove that request up your ass. I'm busy." I bent over to clean. My hands were curled into knotty fists, so when I began to scrape, I lost my grip on the button. It twirled across the beams and I swiped for it, missing as it dropped between one of the cracks. It plunged noiselessly into the throngs.

"Russ, please," Victor pleaded.

"Look what you made me do," I cursed.

"I climb to you if I can, but I stuck."

"You're stuck?" I yelled. "Do you think I'm not? Where the fuck do you think we can go? So zip-it, unless you have something useful to say."

"Who is dead-eyes man?" Victor asked.

"What did you say?" I pounced onto my feet. "What in the world did you just say?"

"The dead-eyes man, who he is?"

"I'll be right up," I replied, through the corner of my mouth. So that was that. This problem had to be resolved once and for all. I climbed onto the ladder, not taking the time to clip into the safety line. Whatever, falling was a better alternative than slowly withering into a prune. But I held on. I needed to hear what that bastard had to say. And if he kept playing games, he wouldn't be speaking for long.

"Thank you for come up, thank you," Victor repeated, as I stomped toward him. He knocked his head to the side, almost flinching from my approach, but only his neck shifted, while the rest of his body remained frozen.

"What do you have to say?" I asked, stringing out the words.

"I no can move." He sighed and bowed his head. "No arms. No legs. Toes just a little." He wiggled his toes to prove this fact, as if I give one shit about his condition.

"What's your game?" I snapped. "Who are you?"

"Is me, Victor." He swung up his cheek and curled the side of his mouth into an O.

"Or are you Tito? Or maybe you prefer federal agent? Did he send you? Did *he*?"

"What?"

"Answer the fucking question." I towered over Victor's outstretched body and inched my foot above his hand.

"I no understand. Why you so mad?" Victor peered down at his hand, but didn't yank it back from my hovering foot.

"I don't need to explain myself to you." I stepped down.

"No, Russ. No!" Victor screamed. "*Stop!*"

"Who are you?" I eased back, but kept my foot pressed onto his hand. "Did he send you to spy? Is that why you're so keen on getting a confession? You wearing a wire?"

"Russ, this not you. Please," Victor whimpered. "I am not spy."

"Confidential informant, snitch, whatever bullshit label you feds call it now." I patted at his chest, raising his shirt, while searching for any bugs. I knew they made them small these days, sometimes the size of a button, so I couldn't be certain when nothing stood out. I did notice his infection had tracked up to his shoulder, pulsating a bright red glow. If he was working for the feds, they'd have to evacuate him soon or he wouldn't make it. Perhaps that was the reason for the van.

"Russ, you think wrong. Brain is all muddy."

"Yeah, I'm the mud-brained one." I chuckled. "Wasn't taking my family enough for you bastards?" I pressed my nails into his inflamed arm, dragging him to his feet.

"Si, I kill my family." Victor wheezed, misinterpreting my accusation. "I admit, yes, I admit. Now please release me."

"Not until you tell me what that dead-eyed bastard wants." I shoved Victor against the railing. His legs slipped, offering no support, so I heaved him higher.

"You yell about the dead-eyes bastard," Victor replied with a moan. "Last night, you say 'dead-eyes bastard' again and again. Maybe in the sleep."

"I didn't sleep, so cut the bullshit." I inched him closer to the edge.

"Who is dead-eyed bastard? Tell me, I am a friend."

"Friend?" I hollered. "*Friend*? You aren't my fucking friend. You're not a confidant. Shit, you aren't even much of a coworker. I barely know you. You're a Goddamn stranger."

"I am here. That is enough."

"No, it fucking ain't," I yelled. "And you're a liar to boot. I never said nothing about the dead-eyed bastard."

"Why I lie? Tell me, Russ. Why I lie? I tell you all. Demons and everything."

"Stop. I didn't tell you about him. Not one lick." Did I? Surely, I would've remembered that. Another one of those blackouts would've been a relief last night, but I'd waded through the dark agony counting every minute. I glared at Victor. He was gasping, barely breathing as his eyes blinked out of control. His mouth was hanging open and his lips were shaking as if chewing on an ice cube.

"Do it," he muttered. "Throw me to pigs. I want to see my family again. I am ready. Si, I am ready."

"I was awake all night," I repeated, as if to reassure myself of this truth. "I wouldn't have said that."

"I ready to see my mother now. She can forgive me."

I released my grasp. Victor toppled onto the railing. He neither recoiled, nor shouted out in pain. Instead, he just closed his eyes.

"Victor, my God, I don't know wha...what came..." I stammered.

"Is okay, Russ. I understand." He looked up at me. "Demons are inside. I not know this dead-eyed bastard, but he haunts you."

"Yeah," I muttered. "He sure do."

"Please help me sit." Victor nodded at his contorted body. I shifted him onto his back and into a more comfortable position. Or at least as comfortable as it could get up here, which wasn't much.

"Victor, if that van returns, I think they're going to kill us." I stared out toward the highway, but it remained empty.

"Yes, I believe that also." He closed his eyes, leaning his head into the railing. A moment later, he stilled, either asleep or dead. I didn't know which I preferred.

No mistaking it, the cutaway van was the same: same curved roof, same unmarked trailer, same ghostly white paint, and the biggest giveaway, the same squealing brakes as it spun into the parking lot. There was one major difference though, now four pickup trucks followed. The exact number of people crouched inside the truck beds was unclear from this distance, but what was impossible to miss were the dozens of semi-automatic rifles poking up beside them.

The van slowed while approaching. Two pickups followed it. The one to the van's left sped up and raced directly at the pigs. They brayed and scattered off. A few darted into the fields, but most dodged and circled back. They stomped their hooves, almost daring the men to emerge. A couple even banged into the side of the truck as it wheeled to a halt.

As this truck parked, the one to the van's right broke away from the others in the convoy. It spun in a wide circle, kicking up a gritty cloud as it stopped with its rear facing the pigs. The taillights sparked as the truck switched into reverse, backing into the throng. It didn't roll far before the animals swarmed in, forcing it to stop.

I peered over the top, thankful the thick grouping of pigs was preventing the convoy from circling around to the rear of the billboard. I could still duck behind the wooden panels if picking us off was their intent, and from that arsenal amassed in the trucks, I was fairly certain this was the intention.

God, if it'd only been that simple.

As the pigs swarmed the trucks, a man stood in the bed of the truck with its tailgate facing the horde. He wore a cream-colored gasmask along with a full-bodied biohazard suit, not too dissimilar from the men in the helicopter, except decorated with a desert camouflage print. I almost chuckled, considering a virus wouldn't be thrown by some blended colors, then realized the disguise wasn't intended for the pigs. It was for us.

The man in the gasmask grabbed what appeared to be a hose with a gleaming silver nozzle at its end. He steadied himself in a wide stance while grasping the handle with both hands. Even if they'd come to murder us, I had to smile at this, thrilled to watch him drench those slimy bastards first. To my surprise, instead of water, an orange jet of fire blazed out.

The pigs squealed and galloped back as the man sprayed them with the fire. The slower ones weren't as lucky and the flames engulfed them. They scampered a frenetic dance, jerking spastic circles, their howls pitching over the din of the others as their skin bubbled and browned. A few even launched into the air like crackling fireworks before collapsing into limp heaps of charred flesh.

When the area around the pickup cleared, Mr. Camouflage extinguished the flames. The swine gathered into a tight row facing the truck, but remained outside the flamethrower's range. The incident spooked the animals gathered around the other truck since they too backed off.

The van revved the engine, scaring off the stragglers remaining nearby. As a path cleared, it lurched forward, driving between the two trucks, but instead of stopping at the billboard's base, it swung around to the side, heading into the rear. The van stopped though, before swinging around back.

The four trucks lined between the van and the pigs, occasionally sparking a flamethrower if any should rush too close. Each had a metallic cylinder in its bed, the obvious source of the flamethrower's gas. From the number of rifles, I'd assumed they were full of men, but upon closer inspection, I realized the trucks were mostly empty. One didn't even have a single man in the rear. I counted five men total, excluding the drivers.

"Good morning. It's swine-time!" The voice on the loudspeaker was the same from last night, though I couldn't tell if it emerged from the van or one of the trucks.

"Up here," I yelled, shooting a short-lived wave over the top. It wasn't as though they wouldn't eventually find us, so I saw no reason to hide.

"I no do that," Victor grumbled, still sprawled across the deck to my side.

"On the top," I yelled, ignoring Victor's protest, but I did refrain from waving a second time. That did the trick, since all five of the men glared up, swinging their rifles in my direction. I grinned and nodded, as if this might placate any murderous desires.

It didn't. A barrage of bullets tore into the billboard. I held still, perhaps out of shock or a death-wish. I certainly felt both, as the volley detonated to either side. It wasn't until they stopped that I mustered the energy to move. Even then, I didn't duck, instead opting to shoot them an outstretched middle finger.

When the second barrage arrived moments later, I squatted, but lost my balance and tumbled onto the deck. I spat a pained yelp, though the fall hadn't hurt anything other than my naïve hope we might emerge from this pickle alive. I knew I should scramble away from the whizzing bullets, which splintered through the billboard's wooden paneling with ease, but I just sat motionless.

To be honest, I saw no reason to hide. If these men decided to circle around back, we'd be as transparent as a politician hoping to explain away a sex tape. So as a third barrage shattered overhead where I'd just been standing, I took a deep breath and closed my eyes.

Twenty, nineteen, eighteen…

"That was a warning," the loudspeaker hollered, though it felt quite the opposite. "Throw down your weapons and walk out front with your hands raised. This is your final chance."

Baloney. I didn't move. I'd spent my entire life ignoring orders of one sort or another and saw no reason to break a perfect streak, particularly when it came to making my death more convenient for the killers. I wasn't holding out for any real reason other than a pestering notion that my final moments should be best spent enjoying myself.

"If you don't come out, we'll be forced to take action," the loudspeaker continued, as if those gunshots hadn't counted as action. If they'd wanted to talk or rescue us, they sure as shit wouldn't have opened with a flurry of bullets. I wished they'd just shut up already since it was killing the mood.

"Remember, we warned you." A loud static click followed, indicating the loudspeaker had been shut-off. I could hear the vehicles rumbling below as they drove closer, but my eyes locked onto the horizon.

I stared at the mountains with their majestic snow-topped peeks. A vision of heaven. I could almost feel the crisp air whisking across my sun-scarred flesh. I thought about the tumultuous earthquakes that must've occurred to propel them into existence. Odd how the world worked in such a manner, springing disaster after disaster, and yet we called it beauty. And, in a way, it was beautiful.

The van honked twice and, without thinking, I glanced down and saw it parked with a direct eye-line to us, just beyond the base. The rear door opened. I blinked, waiting for the gunmen to emerge; their instruments of death tuned and ready for that first note of this final symphony of carnage.

Heaven knew I deserved such a fate, and from what Victor told me, so did he. I reached toward his limp, outstretched body, and squeezed his hand. When his shaky fingers tightened, returning the gesture, I smiled. I'd never felt such a divine touch in my entire life.

A figure emerged at the rear of the van, but this was no armed soldier, rather a hooded man with his hands bound behind him. He looked like a captive. Another man appeared beside him, wearing the same gasmask-biohazard suit combo as those in the rear of the trucks. The captive bucked forward as the gasmask-guy shoved him from the rear.

The hooded man grunted while rolling across the cracked earth. He bucked and writhed, attempting to free himself from the restraints. The van's rear door snapped shut and the driver honked three times. The pickup trucks, all four still out front, echoed in a wailing chorus of horns. The sizzle of flamethrowers followed, wafting up a stench of burnt pig. A group rushed in from the other side, clearly driven by the fire.

The captive staggered upright and twisted around in what must've been an attempt to gauge the location of the pigs. Their grunts seemed to penetrate from every direction as they charged. The fact these men hadn't removed his hood before tossing him out to die told me all I needed to know. There would be no rescue.

Hooded or not, the captive determined the direction and sprung toward the neighboring field. As the first pig descended onto him, it hissed a high-pitch squeal, but rather than attack, it sprinted beside him. Hearing the noise, the captive careened to his left, but the pig didn't give chase, instead opting to rush into the fields, more interested in its own escape over hunting any prey.

As it disappeared into the tall grass, one truck zoomed across the lot, blocking the path of any others who might share a similar inclination. A showering from its flamethrower likewise reinforced the point. Not that the pigs needed much prompting, since a dozen or more descended onto the captive, knocking into his racing legs. He toppled with a brisk cry and kicked one final time in a fleeting attempt to ward off the beasts. A couple crunch-filled seconds later, only pulpy bits remained.

"That's what happens to those who refuse to participate," the loudspeaker declared. "Your only hope for survival is to compete in the SHARK."

"Shark?" I asked, and Victor shrugged. Whatever their meaning, I had no intention of participating in any of their warped games.

"And for you up there," the loudspeaker continued. "If you climb down right now, you'll be eligible to play in today's contest. It's your only chance to live."

The van honked again and the trucks wheeled into motion. They drove in a circle, pinning the pigs into a densely packed group with the van at the center. Each truck parked, forming a rough square, again with their tailgates facing the pigs. They were evenly spaced from the van, around twenty yards or so, though with all the animals huddled between them, it was difficult to be certain of the distance.

Beep-beep. One truck honked. *Beep-beep.* Another echoed. The third and fourth copied this double honk. The succession of beeping was way too precise to be random, so I took it for a signal. The pigs must've figured the same, since they all settled, perhaps fearing another fiery blast. They kept their distance from the vehicles, including the van, even though it was smack dab in the center of the corral.

The van's rear door opened again and the masked man stood at the edge. The pigs, spooked by the door's motion, bucked as far back as they could before packing too tightly to move. The man disappeared into the rear and I feared he was readying another captive to be tossed out for prey.

What emerged was far worse.

"Time's up," the loudspeaker blared. "You've missed your opportunity to participate in today's shark. Don't fret, it should be one terrific show. Contestants on your mark."

A group of bare-chested people lined up at the rear of the van. Each had a number spray-painted across their torso in black. They were mostly men, but two women I could see, hugged their arms over exposed breasts. A couple of these "contestants" peered up at us, but I had to look away. I just couldn't return that glance.

"A vicious germ has swept across our land, infecting all who come in contact with its barbarous touch. The cure is in limited supply, so only the most physically fit, the toughest in spirit and mind, the most able are deserving of it. This, dear contestants, is your chance to prove your worthiness."

"I hope you sick fucks rot in hell," one of the female contestants screamed over the blaring loudspeaker.

"Nobody is forcing you to be here. If you wish to withdraw, we'll honor your request."

"Just like you did with Keith?" Another male contestant yelled, while motioning at the bloody stain left by the first captive. He sneezed and wiped a trail of neon-green snot from his nose before continuing. "You call that a choice? He had a daughter named Nora, just so you evil shits-"

The man's rant cut short as he was flung from the van. The pigs eyed him as he rolled across the dirt. He took one peek toward the line of drooling swine and spun back toward the van. As he clutched the rear bumper to climb back inside, a gunshot exploded. The man toppled over, dead before hitting the ground. A second shot kept the pigs at bay, preventing them from rushing in to devour his body, though a few pressed closer.

"A disqualification. Does anyone else have questions before we proceed?" The loudspeaker paused, but when no more contestants spoke up, it continued.

"We couldn't ask for a finer day to race. The rules are simple. Anyone who makes it to a truck lives. The others, well, take comfort in your sacrifice. You will not be forgotten, maybe digested, but not forgotten."

A chorus of laughter wheezed from the men in gasmasks at the rear of the trucks. One even fired a round into the air.

"Enough delay, it's time for the Stock Human Alternative Racing Kontest, or as we all so adoringly call it, the SHARK."

"SHARK! SHARK! *SHARK!*" the men in the pickup trucks chanted. I gritted my teeth, not giving a shit what they called this monstrosity. The only label that fit was pure evil.

"Contestants prepare yourselves. This could be your chance to join our other winners, such as Landon over in truck three." One of the gas-masked men waved, but I had doubts anyone had ever won this twisted race.

"Ready. Set. *Go...oooo!*"

A shot rang from inside the van, but I couldn't see if anyone had been killed. Though, this was enough to force the contestants to climb from the rear. As they emerged, the pigs lowered their snouts, readying to charge. There were around twenty contestants total, though the numbers painted across their chests went as high as eighty-six. This unsteady peace lasted until the van's door slammed shut.

One of the armed men shot a burst of flames into the air and the horde shifted. A pig at the front kicked up its head, and hammered toward the contestants. The nearest contestant dove from its galloping path, but it didn't even glance over. The pig's focus locked onto the corpse of the contestant who'd been shot. It shoved its snout into the man's stomach, flinging out pieces of severed flesh and drooping entrails.

Pandemonium erupted. The pigs charged, propelling a wave of snapping jaws. Most of the contestants broke to the side, but two stood frozen. One shrieked when knocked to the ground, while the other dropped without a sound. The beasts in front tore into them, but the pigs racing in from the rear plowed them away. A rampaging ripple of chomping teeth splintered any flesh within sight, both human and pig alike.

The contestants fanned out into the stampede, galloping at a breakneck pace. Their bare torsos bobbed above the writhing horde like buoys in a rapid current. Most dropped into the tsunami of pigs, being instantly shredded. Severed body parts - hands, feet, and even one head - bounced atop the throngs, coasting through a spray of green slime that hovered above the mess like a cloud.

A single pig felled several contestants in an open space while other contestants barreled through the thickest pigs without a single scratch. It defied all logic who the pigs chose to pursue. To my amazement, a fat man (number twenty-six) emerged from a crowded area and climbed into a truck. He stood unscathed; his massive gut drooped over a pair of baggy jeans. I couldn't help wondering if the pigs had some odd bias against fat. However, when dozens of pigs ravaged a woman equally as large, I expelled this notion.

Of the twenty contestants who darted from the van, three were all that survived. The fat man, a scrawny teenager, and a woman with gray hair in terrific shape for her age. My mind raced, trying to discover any connection, a reason the pigs ignored them, but I came up with nothing outside of pure luck.

"We have our winners," the loudspeaker announced. I wondered if this was for our benefit or if more poor victims sat huddled inside that wicked van.

"Let's give all our SHARK champions a round of applause."

The elderly woman and the teenager, who'd raced to the same truck, stood together as a clapping-cheer echoed over the loudspeaker. A man in a gasmask grabbed them in order to raise their hands in a victorious salute. The woman resisted, breaking from his grasp, but the teenager beamed as if having scored with a girl for the first time. The fat man, in a different truck, not only didn't raise his arms, but was no longer standing, having collapsed into a gasping fit.

"A well-deserved victory," the loudspeaker continued. "Now it's time to whisk our winners away to the safety of our medical tents. Once treated, they will continue on with their lives, full of hope, and more importantly, the knowledge they are indeed true champions."

"Medical tent, *pftt*." Victor snorted. "I no believe that."

I tended to agree with his cynical assessment. Anyone holding such a deplorable contest sure wouldn't allow survivors to live long enough to tell about it. They wouldn't be whisked to any hospital, not unless there was a morgue inside it. The armed men forced the winners to sit as the trucks drove across the parking lot and disappeared down the service road.

The van remained.

"Fear not potential shark contestants. We haven't forgotten about you," the loudspeaker announced.

"Climb here, you devils, and I show you the fear!" Victor yelled.

"Quiet," I hushed. "If we don't rile them up, they might just drive off."

"We are your only hope," the loudspeaker continued. "This is restricted space and we are the sole crew authorized to enter. Nobody else will be coming for you. *Nobody!*"

"After you, nobody sound real good," Victor added.

"Way I figure, you fellows must've been stuck up there since Friday. Imagine that! Two whole days in the direct sun without any water. Do you realize the longest anybody can survive from dehydration is around three days? Four if you're lucky. But if I had to guess, I'd say your luck has run dry. *Dry*. Get it?" The voice in the loudspeaker laughed.

"Eat the shit and die," Victor yelled.

"Oh, I have something far better than shit to eat. A nice frosty beverage." A snap hummed over the loudspeaker, clearly a can pried open. This, followed by a gurgling swig. The sound grated my ears, stinging worse than even seeing that vile carnage.

"Get out of here before I piss my own beverage all over you," I hollered, while standing up and grabbing at my crouch.

"That's just the type of enthusiasm we need for SHARK. We'll be back tomorrow, same time. And in case you fellows need to hydrate before the big race, I have just what you need."

The van's window rolled open and an arm reached out, clasping a bottle of water. The man inside pitched it toward the unipole, though it landed quite a distance from the base.

"Fetch, little birdies, go fetch." The man tossed around a dozen more bottles. One bounced to a stop almost directly underneath the ladder.

"See you tomorrow," the loudspeaker continued. "That is if you live that long."

Before either one of us could holler back some snarky response, the van jerked forward and raced across the lot. As it exited back onto the highway, my eyes locked onto those bottles of water. I kept looking, even long after the pigs swamped back underneath and obscured the bottles from sight.

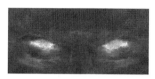 I'd tried everything, but fetching those bottled waters was impossible. No, that was a lie. I hadn't attempted anything more than climbing a few steps down the ladder. As soon as my feet hit the topmost rung, the pigs surged, overrunning the area around the base. Their whirling shadows instantly submerged the bottles. I'd made it about a third of the way down before realizing it was futile. Plus, I figured those bastards wouldn't have left the water unless they knew there was no possibility of retrieval.

Not that this helped to relieve my mind from obsessing over the water, but no matter how much I pondered, no answers came. With Victor paralyzed, any assistance from him was out. Nobody would be there to steady my line. Not to mention, the brief climb had taxed me to the point where I'd been afraid I might lack the energy to return. Forget any prolonged maneuvers, perhaps a day or two ago, but not now.

That, too, was a lie. My gas tank hadn't run plum dry yet, at least nowhere outside of my mind. I guess I could've tried to tie some lasso-type knot with the safety line, but really, I didn't see the point. The only thing water would do was delay the inevitable. Sure, I might get an extra hour or two of life, maybe even an entire day, but it'd still be pure agony. I refused to play that game. *Their game.* This was my life, my death, my grim choice, so I figured why not kick back and avoid any unnecessary stress. Not heroic, but again, I never claimed to be a hero.

"I'm not a monster." I said the words aloud without realizing it. They'd emerged sharp and penetrating, almost too convincing. I guess I'd really wanted them to be true. Now, more than ever. Though, some lines, once crossed, could never be undone, but there was something human about believing that lie.

"Are you a dream?" Victor asked, kicking back into consciousness. He'd been knocking on and off ever since this morning's excitement, and as crazy of a question as it was, this was the most coherent thing he'd said in hours.

"Sure," I answered. "Whatever skedaddles your storks." The expression was one of my Pa's favorites, meaning something similar to *whatever floats your boat*. I guess it was Pa's little flair for the language, but I'm not sure why it popped into my mind, since even in my childhood, it didn't make a lick of sense. Must not have to Victor either, since he shot me an upturned glance.

"Naw, you ain't dreaming," I clarified. "How you doing? You have any feeling in your legs?"

Victor shook his head, and I didn't doubt the answer. He hadn't moved his legs, nor shifted from his slumped over posture all day long. Not an inch.

"Let me have a look," I continued, and before he could protest, I rolled up the end of his khakis. I had to stop before reaching his knee, though. Not only had his skin transformed into a pale blue, it was frigid to the touch. I pressed on a thick vein running up his calf, but it felt mushy like a piece of gum. I didn't notice a pulse and when I released my touch, instead of springing back, his skin remained indented.

"Am I shot?" he asked, probably noticing my appalled look.

I patted up his thigh, wondering if he had taken a bullet from this morning's barrage, and if so, why he'd waited to tell me such a thing, but I found no wound. Nor a single thread out of place.

"No," I answered, but left out the part about his cold rubbery skin. We couldn't do anything about that, so I saw no reason to drudge up those demons. Best to remain positive.

"I am in the church?" he asked, continuing with the peculiar line of questioning.

"Do you see a church?" I wondered if calling it *the church*, rather than just *church*, was out of a misused pronoun, or a hallucination from back when he was hiding from the cartel.

"What I see is…" He paused and chewed his lip as if struggling to form the words. He kicked his head back and grimaced before turning back to me. "Is this hell?"

"No, we're still stuck on the billboard. Do you see that?" I knocked on the deck to emphasize what was real.

208

"I do now," he replied, without an indication of what he might've seen before. I didn't ask.

"Best you relax." I leaned back, hoping he'd follow my cue.

"I not know if what I see is real. Strange, yes?"

"Yeah, strange." The understatement of the decade. I doubted hell could be more bizarre than this cursed billboard.

"I already confess. Why I am still alive? I no understand," he continued.

"I don't think it works like that. Don't stress about it and just close your eyes."

"Russ, I understand. You must confess. Who you kill?" He glared at me as if his eternal soul rested on my answer.

"Fine," I snapped. "I went inside for reckless endangerment of a minor."

"Your son?"

"No, it wasn't my son. He's still alive, remember?"

"Who, then? Russ, who?"

Jesus, did this guy want my entire jacket? He was worse than Patti's cousin, Carly. During one of her weekend visits, that buttinsky had sensed I'd fallen into the crater of my crack addiction and done her best to drive a wedge between me and Patti. Her pestering had gotten so bad I'd given Patti an ultimatum. I'd won that battle, but the war did turn in Carly's favor. That was, until her own meth addiction came to light. The nosiest ones always had the biggest secrets. Somehow it always worked like that.

"I killed a kid while driving. That's the long and short of it." Of course, this was far on the shorter side, though technically true. And that was all that mattered, being technically true.

"An accident?" When I didn't answer, Victor provided one himself, declaring it as if it was a fact. "No, you kill the child, how you say, "on purpose, no?"

"Yes, on purpose," I lied. If he wanted a confession, I'd give him one. Anything to shut him up. I flapped my hands and cleared my throat. "The brat was bullying my son. He stole Tyler's lunch money, but what threw me over the edge was when he took his bike. I'd worked overtime, taking extra runs to afford a really expensive bike for Tyler, so when I saw that bully riding around on my son's bike, I lost it. I only meant to scare him, but I got a bit too close."

I paused, not out of any dramatic effect, but rather to leave the details mostly unfilled. Lies worked best like that; kind-a like justice, religion, and love. Best observed in the abstract. Victor nodded, chewed his lip a tad more, before cocking his head to the side. "How many years your son have?"

"Fourteen," I replied without hesitation. Patti asked me that once, and I'd given the wrong answer while high, so I made a point of never screwing it up these days.

"And you no see your son for ten years?" Victor craned his neck forward, blinking so rapidly it appeared like he was signaling in Morse code.

"Who cares? Ten years? Five years? A hundred? What matters is I wasn't there. If I could escape this hideous billboard, I'd make it right. I sure would."

"Four is young for bike and school, yes?" Victor asked.

"In civilized countries, we have pre-schools and training wheels." I balled my fist, but then felt dizzy and had to rub at my temples. A throbbing headache shattered down my cheeks, pinching my sinuses.

"To be there not equal to being a father," Victor said.

"What do you know about it? You have a son?" I crossed my arms, pulling my legs into my chest.

"No." Victor sighed. "I have no family anymore."

"Then I'd zip-it on the parenting advice."

"Yes, you say all when ready. Time not over yet."

"I'll set my fucking alarm," I quipped.

Victor added something else, but I'd stuffed my ears with cotton by that point. Patti always said I was a master of that, being able to hit mute on the world. I guess I was keen at it, since even the doctor had some fancy words for my failings, calling it *proximal separation*. Similar to Victor's accusation, the doc had said this was being physically present, but emotionally distant. Said most addicts were like that, isolated and removed.

Hell, maybe if life stopped handing me shit sandwiches and calling it steak, I might've found a smidge less comfort in being isolated. Everyone ranted about how drugs made one lose friends, jobs, relationships, and whatnot, but nobody ever said how none of that mattered compared to the joy of being left the fuck alone. I had yet to experience a better sensation within this rotten existence.

No, isolation was always my goal and crack was just the delivery boy. If addicts cared about losing everything, they wouldn't lose it. None of that means piddly-shit while stoned. Friends, family, community; those were sober problems. Later on, they came tied with a bow along with a huge helping of regret.

On the other hand, nobody ever said the biggest regret wasn't losing my family, or going to prison, or being distant from my son. It was no longer being able to get stoned. To feel that complete isolation, to be solely inside my head, a complete outsider to the world and all its problems. No, they don't advertise that shit, since most folks wouldn't understand it.

I was isolated long before I turned to drugs. Crack just made it easier to tune that dial to zero. My fondest memories with Patti, if I had to be honest, weren't our activities together. No, it was those hours I'd spent in my man-cave garage, building those model airplanes. There was a reason I was so meticulous when it came to categorizing all those plastic parts, how they glued together, the exact color of paint to use, memorizing their real-life prototypes and all that crap. Patti had called it an obsession, never realizing the cause.

The scariest part was if I had total control, if Patti had submitted to my every whim, I would've had her just sit quietly beside me as I smoked crack and assembled those airplanes. That would've been my ideal relationship. No protests over missing chores, no hassles over money, and no damn complaints over the stinky electrical smell. I never did tell her the stench came from crack smoke rather than the refrigerator as I'd always claimed. No more lies. No more fighting. No more communication.

Alone with my best friend. The addiction.

That didn't mean I lacked the craving for friendship back then, I just had to be picky about it. The only person I could trust with my secret addiction, who I could be totally honest, was with another addict. They understood. But they also shared that same desire for isolation, so discovering them was always a grueling quest. Unlike those images plastered on TV, most crack heads don't stagger around toothless, muttering to themselves as if wearing oversized sandwich boards advertising their addiction.

Sure, I'd heard rumors of other drivers who might be freebasers and chasers, but no matter how many drug tests I passed using fake urine, I was wary of the word getting out. Hauling was a tight-knit community, and similar to every small group, there were no shortages of gossips and snitches. The last thing I need was some nitwit base-head getting all chatty.

The exceptions were the tommys. I'd known a lot of them. For the uninformed, a tommy was the nickname for the men, and they were always men, who'd act as go-fors at truck-stops. Basically procuring sensitive items from the local market that a visitor might not know how to get, mostly prostitutes, drugs, and guns. Though they'd probably deliver a pizza for the right surcharge. And that was the one and only rule with the tommys: everything had a price. Everything.

I guess, if pressed, another rule was they weren't really called tommys. The only drivers who used that term were the ones who did so in a derogatory manner, such as a warning. For example, an old-timer might tell a newbie, "Don't go wasting all your hard earned cash on them tommys," or "If you take your eyes off the road for a second, a tommy will have his hand in your pocket." Indeed, the only time I used the phrase was while trying to score. I'd approach the most scraggly fellow in the lot and ask if his name was Tommy. After that, if we did business, we used our proper Christian names.

Don't misunderstand, tommys were far from trustworthy when it came to matters outside getting high, not really confidants in any real sense of the word. Even so, they served a purpose. I never met one who wasn't down for a hit, meaning both drugs or to light-up a mouthy gal. And there were a lot of girls. Prostitution was by far the majority of their business, preying on drivers who were away from their old ladies. Unlike drugs, that never showed up on any test, except maybe one for STDs.

So, seeing that being secretive was in their nature, these guys became my only true friends. They made perfect smoking buddies. I'd whittle away hours with them during my truck-stop breaks, lighting up and chatting all night long. Tommys always had the best stories, and for the same reason I could open up to them, they likewise told me everything.

Most had epic mommy issues, running away from broken homes where their caretakers were either addicts or prostitutes, which helped to explain their chosen line of work. Nearly all admitted to being abused, victims of violence and all types of sexual mischief. They idealized a nomadic lifestyle, and I never met a single one who'd grown up in the same city where he currently worked.

The stories they told were so revolting, I sometimes had difficulties believing them. The most peculiar thing was the darker the story, the more likely a tommy was to spill it. You'd think it'd be the other way around, but it wasn't. Maybe the doc would agree that telling stories was their way of saying that their past didn't bother them anymore, that if they owned it, it couldn't own them.

Whatever the cause, I heard all kinds of lurid tales, such as one where a tommy hid underneath his bed while his mom and her boyfriend tussled, only to witness the boyfriend pulverize his mother's head into hamburger with a fire-extinguisher. Afterwards, that monster sprayed the extinguisher all over, maybe in a drug-fueled attempt to clean the crime scene. The boy was splashed with the blood-stained suds and explained how even to that day, he'd taste a vile soapy-flavor anytime he got upset.

That was one of the numerous stories I heard throughout the years, and similar to crack, once I had a hit of a tommy's sordid past, I kept wanting more. I hung around the lots so often, taking extra routes to escape my dreadful home life, I do think some considered me a friend. They certainly rewarded me by offering up free trixies – a code word for prostitutes – time and time again. Sure, this could simply have been an insurance policy for keeping my trap shut after revealing a dark secret, but I tended to believe it was their peculiar way of showing friendship.

I was no saint, but previous to crack, I was a faithful husband. The road could be tempting, but most lot-lizards were wider than my rig and spewed even more venomous exhaust, so they weren't that tempting. Previous to my marriage, I'd partook enough times to bleach away any allure, even while drunk. However, while high, my every hesitation disappeared. Any girl, no matter how big, hair-lipped, or skanky, was fair game.

And what a game. Crack for girls, a simple equation. After basing with a tommy, a trixie would knock on my door and introduce herself. Some lied, pretending they'd just been dumped or only wanted to talk, but we both knew the deal. One time, a trixie even admitted she needed more "seasoning" before handling any real johns. Used that very word, *seasoning*. Imagine that.

I rarely declined their services, since after the drugs eroded all my internal boundaries, external laws and morality didn't mean anything either. For example, I never cared one lick about age unless a girl told me outright she was under eighteen. So if some stringy gal with tiny knobs for breasts approached me wanting to party, I wasn't pressing for any details. The sex was always consensual, not that it made a difference. For the few moments I was sober, I despised myself, so my only solution was to be high more often.

As I said, everything with the tommys had a price. One rock of crack might be cheap, but doing it all the time started to add up. Same went for the trixies. Even in my crack-fueled haze, I wasn't a cold-hearted lizard, and knew it was proper to tip, even with a freebie. Worse, I grew so accustomed to the girls that if none came to me, I sought them out. In that world, for a few extra bucks, there was always a new conquest, another hit, one more addiction to experience. Always more.

So when funds started to run low, I decided to supplement my income and created my own underground hauling business. The plan was set in motion with the assistance of a tommy I'd met on the outskirts of Junction City. He introduced me to a crew of shady Nigerians who had connections to suppliers in the Middle East. They smuggled the drugs, mostly pills and smack, into the States, and it was my job to trek them cross-country.

I typically met up with a local biker gang in Vermont or upstate New York and loaded their packages among my other cargo. I heard rumors they used Indian tribal areas to sneak across the border, same as Russian spies had used during the Cold War, which made sense considering the location, but being on a need-to-know basis, I never had confirmation of that.

After the pickup, I'd crisscross through the Midwest, dropping off packages along the way. I never knew my exact route until contacted through a burner phone. In fact, after that initial introduction, I never saw much of the Nigerians at all, so I wasn't sure who was really in charge. I did suspect someone in our dispatch office was being bribed, since suddenly I was assigned a ton of routes out East.

Unlike in the movies where one racial gang battles another for control, my experience was quite different. I made drops with all sorts of gangs, every color of the rainbow, depending on the region. In urban areas, I'd deliver to black street gangs, while in the country, Hispanics dominated, and in the south, white power groups controlled the market. All very multicultural when it came down to the green. Hell, one gang in Canada even called themselves the UN since anyone could join.

As long as I made my deliveries, nobody cared if I did a bit of business for myself on the side. Hell, it was expected. A perk of the job. So I bought a black duffel-bag and stuffed it to the brim with goodies: pot, pills, and powders. You name it, I dealt it. My nickname became Roadside Russ. I even had my own motto, *Trust Roadside Russ, he don't give no fuss.*

After that, I was the one doling out favors. It was as if every day was Christmas and I had my pick of presents. No longer did I have to search out girls, they approached my rig at every stop. Like clockwork. Most weren't even trixies, but addicts searching for a fix. Me and the tommys called them "Strawberries" and would say, "Time to ripen the fruit," whenever we desired a juicy bite. The strawberries got to know me so well that most knew my routes better than I did.

Of course, considering how it all fell apart, I should've kept a keener eye. I guess I placed too much faith with the Nigerians, or whoever was really pulling the strings. The process was so organized, so controlled, so monitored, I suspected someone more powerful might be running the show.

I remember being terrified the first time I noticed a tail while on route. I called the Nigerians in a panic, ready to dump the cargo, but received confirmation they'd hired extra muscle for security. After that, any time I spied a suspicious vehicle, a single text would confirm or deny any trouble. They never warned me beforehand, but I grew so accustomed to the presence of these minders I learned not to worry.

I grew to know these hired men and even though every single one radiated that vicious-as-fuck vibe, they were quite helpful. They called themselves "guardians," and guard me they did. They kept me in the loop on the local cops who needed to be greased along with the areas to avoid. If a pickle-park - what we called truck-stops known for prostitution and drugs - was under surveillance, a local guardian would always give me a heads up before I arrived. When all else failed, they'd race ahead of my truck in a heat vehicle, busting the speed limit like the sound barrier, thereby drawing out any law-and-order cops seeking a bust.

The operation was so organized that most times I drove on autopilot, oblivious to any real danger. The crack also helped in this. However, the knowledge of this covert underground world drew me into another addiction, one far more robust than even crack. That was power. Nothing in the world could spin my head into a blast of intoxicating bliss faster than a hit of pure power. Since power meant freedom and freedom was the strongest of all addictions. And, at the same time, the biggest lie.

To be honest, I was wary of law enforcement, but drugs were like any other business, so the real concern was never the law. Cops, judges, all that shit could be bought. What didn't have a price was the competition. The worst the police could do was lock me up, but the competition could kill both me and my family. Or worse, torture us beforehand.

Power protected that. The Nigerians and their guardians alleviated my every concern. A single mention of a suspicious car, a twitchy strawberry, a disrespectful tommy, or even an off-putting glance from a stranger, would whirl their machine into action. I never knew exactly how they solved the problems, but if I spoke up, whatever trouble I'd mentioned disappeared forever.

Troubles, though, were rare. On the few occasions I did spot a stranger scouting the area, or was tipped off to the competition, a single text message would solve the problem. I could count on one hand how many times that had occurred, but the deeper I grew into this side business, the more I demanded protection. In fact, by the time it all fell apart, trucking was my side business. Smuggling and dealing was my bread and butter.

As with every small business owner, I had dreams of expansion. The money, the women, the drugs, the whole damn country was mine for the taking. Yet at the same time, I was obsessed with the notion others were lurking nearby, waiting for one misstep. Then they'd be the ones doing the taking. I started to demand guardians on typically safe routes and after receiving my first denied request, my paranoia grew. Of course, the drugs didn't help matters none.

So I began to carry my .45 everywhere, tucking it into a black leather vest with a built-in holster. Hot or cold, I wore that vest everywhere. At restaurants, I insisted on being seated with my back to the wall, so nobody could sneak up on me. I even paid strawberries to act as lookouts while I slept. Actually, it was one of them who first spotted the dead-eyed man and provided the nickname.

"He circled twice in a gray Buick," she told me. "He was bald and wore a t-shirt with a sports logo. Must've been from out of state since I didn't recognize the team. But those eyes, Jesus, they were the worst. Almost blank, as if death was staring right at me. Dead-eyes, I tell ya, dead, dead, dead."

I thanked her with a generous tip and contacted the Nigerians. By that point, I'd cried wolf a few too many times, so they brushed my warning aside. At least, that was what I concluded in hindsight.

I didn't hear another word about this stranger for months. Trixies, even paid lookouts, weren't known for their sleuthing skills, so I'd chalked up the incident to either being resolved or plain paranoia. Then I spotted the gray Buick in that lot near Omaha and at the wheel was a bald man whose listless, deep inset eyes could only be described as dead.

He circled three times through the lot. By his forth pass, I was back on the highway. I didn't have guardians for that part of the run, so I drove through the entire night without stopping, arriving at Grand Forks an hour before the terminal was open for deliveries. I made the typical calls, providing a partial license plate and car make.

Again, the situation settled, this time for three more weeks. Then I spotted a gray Buick on the highway just north of Lubbock, but it flew by so fast, I couldn't get eyes on the driver. Perhaps it was a different car, since the plates didn't match, but somehow I knew it wasn't. If the man had trailed me from Nebraska to Texas, then there was no way he was a local boy in blue. Either he was a fed, or worse, the competition.

Two weeks after that, I was certain I spied the dead-eyed man at a rest stop off I-70 in eastern Pennsylvania. I scoured the lot, searching for the gray Buick, but there wasn't one. My paranoia grew to the point where I started a journal, scribbling down the make and model of every vehicle I encountered. Even ones who trailed my rig for a little too long were jotted down. Every night, I scanned the list in a vain attempt to spot a pattern, but none ever emerged.

It didn't stop there. I started writing descriptions of anyone I encountered who appeared even slightly off-kilter, dead-eyes or not. In the drug business, that included pretty much everyone. Hyper alert and frenzied, all this journaling became a full time job. I was so consumed with conspiracies that when another threat emerged, I was oblivious. She wasn't a cartel member, or fed, nor were her eyes dead. In fact, they shone like marbles, a marvelous sky blue.

The girl was beautiful. She radiated an extraordinary aura with every floating step, confident and bold, yet gentle and affable at the same time. Unlike the other strawberries who'd puckered up into shriveled messes, the drugs hadn't time to steal her allure yet. Not everything was perfect, she dyed her hair a trashy blonde and her gaunt frame screamed "eating disorder." But the way she held her style, perfect in her imperfections, reminded me of the first time I saw Patti in that rundown diner.

I should've known something was wrong when I asked if she was mature enough to party, and she removed a driver's license stating she was twenty-two. None of the other strawberries had ever done that. I bet most lacked any ID. From the girl's youthful appearance, I figured it was a fake, probably an older cousin had let her borrow it to buy beer on the weekends. But again, with that stunning beauty, I wasn't asking questions.

She shook a bit while climbing into my sleeper, but that wasn't odd, especially for the younger ones. By that point, I'd graduated from smoking crack off of foil and used a glass tube that truck-stops sold plastic roses in. I stuffed it with a wad of copper wool like a Chore Boy, which worked as a filter, and heated the pipe until the rock bubbled into a brown goo. Unlike cigarettes or pot, the key to smoking crack wasn't inhaling, but allowing the vapors to flow into my mouth. From the way that girl sucked on the end, I knew she was green and would only end up with a pair of burnt lips.

My attention focused on her inexperience, along with those sparkling baby-blue eyes, so I failed to notice as she reached into her purse. Having taken a couple hits, I was already in a trance, so when she yanked the gun out, at first, I thought it was a joke or even a toy. That changed as soon as she aimed the cold steel at my head and yelled for me to hand over the duffel bag. In my haze, I just laughed.

She hollered again, demanding I hand over my bag a second time, but the louder she yelled, the harder I laughed. How absurd that this fair maiden, this spry youth, this inexperienced beauty would try to rob me. I knew I should be taking it seriously, especially with a gun pointed at my head, but I couldn't help myself. I told her to come back in a few years when she was all grown up.

That was when the gun fired.

I don't know if she meant to miss, maybe she figured the gunshot would scare me into taking her seriously, but from the grimace splashed across her face like a wet towel, I had my doubts. Plus, in my laughing fit, I'd bucked at the exact moment she'd pulled the trigger. With the discharge still ringing in the cab, she smacked her hands over her ears as if she was the one who'd been hurt. That single moment of lost concentration was more than I needed.

Before she could fire a second time, I grabbed her arm, slamming her hand into the dash. Her gun dropped onto the floor and I kicked it underneath the seat. She glared at me with those big baby-blues, then turned toward her empty palm. She appeared befuddled as if she couldn't understand why I'd done that instead of handing over my product and cash all easy-peasy. She looked back at me, all sweet and innocent as if this was just a misunderstanding.

It wasn't. I slammed my palm against her cute button-nosed face and grabbed a handful of that trashy dyed-blonde hair. Then I shoved and I bashed her head into the door. Over and over.

Thump. Thump. Squishy thump.

I did this until blood squirted out from a gash on her forehead like a geyser. She opened her mouth, allowing it to hang there as if waiting for a scream. She gulped and gulped, struggling to spit any protest. No sound emerged. That caught me off-guard, so I paused. But I knew I wasn't done yet. Not after this cunt tried to shoot me.

I shoved her face into my crotch, rubbing it all around. A coating of blood stained my jeans. I hate to admit it, but the warm dampness aroused me. I had some real rotten thoughts. I hollered I would lube myself up with her blood and fuck her whore snatch like she was a virgin again. That got her attention and she glared up at me.

And she grinned.

Thwack.

I hadn't heard the cab door open, but I sure as shit felt the bat as it clobbered my shoulder. I spun around and spotted a boy holding a bat. He looked no older than twelve, but he sure swung like a major leaguer. He pivoted for a second whirl. I ducked just in time as the bat walloped into the cushioning behind me. With my back turned, I didn't see the girl kick until her feet bludgeoned my torso. The air exploded from my lungs. I crumpled onto the seat. The boy didn't miss with the next swing.

The bat landed across my jaw, peeling a couple teeth from my gum. A splash of vertigo whirled over me. My vision faded. I jerked, but every twitch felt like a shower of razorblades. The boy yelled something, but damned if I could understand him. He socked me again, this time in the kneecap. I held on by a few strained blinks, paralyzed.

The boy yanked at my legs. I slid across the seat and out the door. I toppled onto the frigid asphalt. Lucky, while I was falling, my head folded into my chest, otherwise my brains probably would've spilled out. I didn't try to stand. The only movement I could muster was a shaking similar to a seizure.

Both the boy and the girl shuffled through my sleeper, but I couldn't see what they were doing. A moment later, the boy leapt out. He dropped the duffel-bag beside me, almost daring me to make one final swipe for it. Last I counted, inside there was a little over forty-grand in cash, double that in product.

The girl jumped out right after the boy. Unlike him, her goal wasn't the pavement, but my outstretched shin. As she landed, the muscle tore from the bone. I screamed in agony. The boy knocked me again with the bat, and I shut up. He raised the duffle-bag, swinging it over my head like a guillotine.

"This is better than you deserve, pedophile," he said.

The words trembled against my blood-soaked ears, thrumming worse than the blows. I detested that word. *Pedophile*. Sure, I had my fun here and there, but I wasn't that. Was I? I'd seen myself more of a rock-star, cruising across the country in a nonstop party, bouncing with any fans interested in dancing to my hits. Those guys, those twisted men, hid in dark shadows, waiting for their unwitting prey to stagger by before they snared them with their evil claws.

Yet, the kid was correct.

I could barely hold the pain at bay, let alone had the energy for deep self-reflection, so I lay there as the two of them scurried off. I rolled over just in time to see them leap into a rusty red Honda with a gaudy tailfin. They cranked the engine and wheeled across the lot.

They had everything. I cursed. Sure, I'd already made my drops for the Nigerians, but without my personal stash I would crash like the Titanic. Shit, freezing to death in the north Atlantic would've been preferable to coming down from that high.

I spat the loose teeth floating around in my mouth and staggered to my feet. A man on the other side of the lot rushed up, hollering like he was the one all banged up. I ignored him and waddled back into my cab. He grabbed the door, but I smacked his hand away, and slammed the door shut. Before jamming into gear, I popped open the middle compartment on the dash and removed the .45.

Tractor-trailers weren't the swiftest vehicles, especially when it came to accelerating, but once they got going, they had a huge advantage, momentum. Nothing in this world could stop a thirty-ton semi barreling down the freeway at eighty m.p.h. Every sane driver will swerve out of the way lickety-split. For those who didn't, a couple blast of the air-horn always did the trick.

So as I raced down the highway in pursuit of that red Honda, cars parted to either side like I was Moses at the Red Sea. From the way those kids jumped in their seats when I rolled up behind, I knew they hadn't expected a chase. I flashed my high-beams and kept blaring my air-horn over and over, like I was shooting a volley of audible cannonballs.

The Honda swerved from side to side, barely remaining on the interstate. I did my best to follow this erratic driving, but no rig could manage those tight swings, so I backed off a bit. They keened in on this fact and took sharper turns, almost spinning over the side before hurtling back onto the road. When the freeway curved into a long bend, I felt the trailer swaying behind me, but I couldn't ease off the accelerator. Not if I wanted to see that duffel-bag ever again.

And I did. Fuck yea, I did.

They miscalculated the bend and smashed right into the concrete divider. I didn't have time to react. I thought they'd crumple into a thousand pieces of jagged metal, but somehow they managed to spin back onto the road. However, they were facing the wrong direction. And careening straight at me.

I hit the air brakes and swerved to the right, but it was a futile gesture. The Honda's headlights sliced across the cab. I flung my arms over my face without realizing I'd even done so. My ears exploded with a clamorous roar of metal shredding, brakes whistling, and the grinding of rubber searing to the road. Sparks burst like zillions of miniature fireflies.

We skidded to a halt with the Honda glued to my semi. Only a second after we stopped, a gigantic thud walloped from behind. I flung across the steering wheel as the trailer jackknifed, smashing into the cab.

Silence ensued. I peered again. The Honda had dislodged and was parked no more than ten feet in front of me. The boy was at the steering wheel. He peeked up. Our eyes locked. He grinned and shot a wave. The Honda revved into reverse and spun around. I could only watch as those little fuckers rocketed down the road.

I didn't stare for long. Another jolt launched me into the air. The cab shook like I'd rolled over a landmine. My nostrils filled with the stench of diesel. Glass detonated into a stabbing mist. The truck shimmied one final time before settling into its final grave.

I wasn't so lucky. The entire cab crushed like an empty can of beer. The windshield was missing. Shards of glass dusted the floor in a thick, icy coat. The Tweety Bird statue on my dash, the one Tyler and Patti made for me, cracked in half, exposing jagged yellow bits as its head dangled from a piece of string. I attempted to move, if simply to assess the damage, but my arm was pinned behind me. Shadows blurred my vision, and I blinked and blinked, but the world remained out-of-focus. In the distance, I heard a woman screaming.

What I hadn't realized at that point, but would become abundantly clear as soon as I awoke handcuffed to that hospital bed, was another car had crashed into my truck from behind. And inside it, a child, a three-year-old toddler not much younger than Tyler, had been in the rear seat. He'd been thrown from the car, right through the windshield, and splattered across my trailer like one of a thousand bugs.

"Russ," Victor said, tearing me from the memory.

"Yeah," I replied, scratching my chin.

"You lie about killing that kid. The bully," Victor clarified as if I'd forgotten.

"What the fuck do you want me to do with that information?"

"I need you to know I know." Victor hacked a deep cough, struggling for a breath. "I also know I no live to tomorrow. I no want to die."

"Neither do I," I replied.

That was about the most honest thing either one of us had said since climbing up on this cursed billboard.

 When I spotted the headlights trailing down the service road, I yanked on Victor's shoulder. His neck bucked, rolling his head into a wobbly pose, similar to a seal balancing a rubber ball on the end of its nose. He steadied a bit as his eyes fluttered to life, but his body remained glued to the deck, same as it'd been since this morning.

"Oh, stop," he murmured, before snapping his eyes back shut.

"Are you kidding?" I poked his shoulder again; this time on an inflamed portion. Victor yelped and craned his chin into the air. I signaled toward the service road where three sets of headlights came crunching southward across the dirt. Victor's sight locked in the opposite direction though, somewhere across the deck. He gasped.

"You see?" he asked. "Is real?"

"That's why I woke you," I answered, as the three sets of headlights slowed to a crawl. They were approaching the intersection where the empty police cruiser sat.

"So is real, yes?" Victor remained focused on the opposite side of the deck.

"You tell me," I answered, while nudging his chin toward the lights. "Do you see them as well?"

"See what?"

"The headlights!" I cried out. "Do you see them?"

"Lights no matter," he replied. "Be quiet or it will hear."

"It matters," I snapped. "They could mean either rescue or death, so of course they fucking matter."

"Please, stop." Victor lowered his voice to a whisper. "Or it will hear you."

"Help," I yelled, waving my arms. "Help, help!"

The three vehicles circled the police cruiser before stopping, all aiming their lights at it. From the illumination, I spied two pickup trucks, while the third vehicle appeared to be a sedan. I couldn't tell the exact make, I believe it was a Ford, but for certain, it wasn't the cutaway van.

"Stop. Fuck a whore. Silencio!" Victor yelled.

I froze, shocked over Victor's outburst. For the entire day, outside of his banal platitudes, he'd spat nothing other than groans. This was the first sign of anger I'd seen since bickering with Slake and that felt like months ago.

"Are you okay?" I whispered.

"No, I am not wanting the death," he muttered.

"It looks like they're more interested in that police car than us," I reassured, though this was far from reassuring to me. I knew the police wouldn't send pickup trucks to check on an empty cruiser, so I feared these were the same sadistic men from this morning. My suspicions grew when I spied a man creeping toward the cruiser with outstretched arms, clearly holding a gun.

"You have energy to fight the pig?" Victor asked, still speaking in a barely audible whisper.

"Fighting those bastards isn't an option. Pigs or otherwise. If you haven't noticed, we're a bit outgunned and outmanned."

"You can stop one pig, yes?" Victor remained turned away as he whispered the question, not focused down on the pigs, nor toward the parked vehicles on the service road.

"One, sure. But I think our problem is larger. Do you see those cars?"

"If I stop the look at the pig, it do charge."

"The pigs can't get you up here." I sighed, as if explaining how a scary movie wasn't real to a toddler.

"That pig can." Victor flicked his chin, signaling toward the opposite side of the deck. I glanced over, but even in the pitch black, it was obviously empty.

"You see a pig there?" I asked, but before Victor could answer, I continued. "Because there isn't one."

"Oh, no." Victor choked, fighting for a breath, as he shook his head in a spastic burst. "You work with pig. You attack together and eat me. No, *NO!*"

"Victor, you ain't thinking right." I wrapped my arm around his shoulder in what was supposed to be a comforting touch, but he craned his neck as if to bite me. I wrenched back.

"There's no pig there. They can't climb. What you're seeing ain't real," I continued. Thankfully, he jerked away, but he continued those twitchy nods.

"Why it no attack?" He leered across the deck as if one of those vile things had grown fingers and climbed up to feast upon us. "Come on, do it!"

"There's nothing there," I yelled. "The Goddamn deck is empty. Settle down. It's not real!"

"Real, *real*?" Victor shrieked the word. "Russ, you are fake one."

"Fine, believe whatever nonsense you want."

I stood and was about to step away when a gunshot rang out. It came from the direction of the service road, so I spun toward it in time to witness a man lunge into the police cruiser. He slammed the door before I could get much of a glance, but I failed to spot any reason for the panic. The area around the cruiser appeared free of pigs, but in the dark and from this distance, it was difficult to be certain.

"Where do the pig go?" Victor hollered. "Where is it?"

I shushed him and stared at the cruiser. The light-bar on the top illuminated for a moment before switching off. The cruiser's headlights then popped on as the engine revved to life.

"Must not be cops if they mistook the lights," I said, mostly to myself.

"Police or no, how they shoot this pig from there?"

"Shoot what…" I paused, realizing Victor believed that gunshot had killed his imaginary pig. I lacked the energy to convince him of the truth.

"They must be expert marksmen. So we should keep a close eye out for them," I continued.

Victor nodded in agreement, before settling into a watchful stare. The vehicles aligned into a row, all beaming their headlights south in the direction of the billboard.

"You no move," Victor insisted, as if that was my intention. "If they can kill pig, can see us also."

There was a twisted logic to this brand of crazy, but that gunshot was a far better reason to keep a low profile. After this morning's race, I had no intention of signaling anyone I wasn't certain was here to rescue us.

My mistrust grew as one of the vehicles honked, and in unison, they all snapped off their headlights. As the vehicles faded into the murky shadows, I could make out the faint hum of their engines, but determining their direction was impossible, especially as the wind spiraled into a snapping flutter.

"The smell," Victor said, breaking my lock on the service road.

"What smell?" I asked.

"Take it off, the bandage." Victor nodded toward his injured hand. Even from a couple steps away, I could sense the stench from his rotting wound. I guess I'd just grown used to it and only noticed it after he pointed it out.

"It'll only smell worse if you take it off." I had no intention of touching the crusted t-shirt I'd given him as a bandage. His infection had grown so rancid that just looking at it made me feel queasy.

"Is the smell of death," Victor continued.

"Can't argue with that." I scanned again for the vehicles, but spotted no movement within the dark.

"Is how the pigs find us. They smell the death. Is the truth," he declared.

"Must have top-notch noses to smell through all that snot." I nodded anyhow, even though I didn't care one iota how they knew we were up here.

"We must take off the clothes or more pigs come. Help, Russ, I no can do alone." He rubbed his chin against his collar as if wanting to release the buttons.

"There ain't no pigs up here," I said, having no intention of engaging in any more of his insanity. "What you saw was a hallucination."

"Hallucination?" Victor tilted his head and shot me a look like I was the crazy one. He blinked rapidly while grinding his jaw as if puzzling out a complicated math equation.

"Think about it. If someone had shot that pig, there'd be a carcass. Then we'd at least have something to eat."

"No eat the pig!" Victor shouted, as if that'd been my intention.

"Maybe I'll do that," I yelled back.

Victor shook his head as if certain I would chomp down on his imaginary foe. An idea clicked and I figured a way to put a stop to this madness.

"Yeah, I'm going to eat that entire pig," I continued. "And there's nothing you can do about it. Just try to stop-"

I held my foot in the air, ready to step over Victor when a siren interrupted me. I yelped, swinging my attention toward the ear-shattering noise. The police cruiser's light-bar erupted to life, slashing a dizzying dance of blue and red streaks across the shadows. The other vehicles joined the ruckus, adding a chorus of honking horns along with a spat of gunfire.

I didn't have time to duck before it all ended. Even though the clatter sounded directly underneath, I spied the vehicles on the service road just beyond the parking lot. Within those whirling lights, it was impossible to make out any details, such as the exact number of men or the amount of guns. The one thing I did know for certain was that, unlike Victor's pig, they were indeed quite real.

I knew this because the pigs also startled at the noise. They stomped to attention, braying and kicking. A stampede formed around the perimeter as they raced in a circle. A dozen broke from this pack and galloped straight toward the vehicles.

"Don't stay up too late," a loud-speaker blared. "You need plenty of rest before tomorrow's big race."

I cursed, slinking low across the deck. The voice was different from this morning, perhaps distorted from the police cruiser's PA system, or a different person entirely, but the identity of the convoy hadn't changed. It was those same depraved bastards.

"So my little chicklets, it's time to end the slumber party and go to bed. We'll be back bright and early, so sleep tight and don't let those nasty pigs-"

The man on the loudspeaker paused as a pig barreled against the cruiser. The siren chirped again, scaring the pig back. Before the others could likewise attack, the vehicles switched on their lights and raced down the road.

"That's right, shoo," I yelled. "And take some of those slimy demons with you."

Indeed quite a few chased after the fading taillights, but it only took a few minutes before the pigs gave up and returned to their sludgy nest at the base of the billboard.

"Is true you eat the pig?" Victor asked after a long moment.

"There's no pig. Never was one." I sighed. "God, I wish there was, since I would eat it at this point. Hell, I'd eat about anything, even broccoli."

"Anything?" Victor tilted his head.

"Sure, give me a single morsel and I'd be grinning like a possum chomping a sweet tater."

"You eat me?" Victor stared right into my eyes.

"No, of course not. Don't be stupid."

"Not stupid. You need food before race."

"Victor, that race is just like the pig you saw. A mirage. No amount of food, or training, or mental focus, is going to make a lick of difference. We're not gonna make it if-" I paused and exhaled. "-when they return. Best I end my time here on the planet with some dignity."

"I wish to die with the dignity also. After all the lives I kill, I want to save one. You can to eat me after the soul is gone." Victor pantomimed chewing on his shoulder as if I somehow could misinterpret this grisly request.

"Your soul ain't going nowhere soon, so forget about it."

"I know you lie to be nice to me, but why you use the word ain't?" he asked. "You smart, but always pretend to speak the stupid."

"Do you really care how I speak?" I replied. "Anyhow, those fools had their fun winding us up, but I don't see them returning tonight, so best we cut this conversation short and get some rest."

"No, please continue talk more. We must keep talking."

"I can't hear any more of this shit about confessing. Not tonight," I snapped.

"No, the reason, um, the reason…" Victor chewed at his lip. "If I sleep, I not wake again."

"Considering our troubles, that might be for the best."

I closed my eyes hoping I might be as lucky as to find that final eternal rest. Otherwise, I'd have to face the dawn. I'd already made my decision. I wouldn't live through that sadistic race a second time. When they returned, before they had their chance, I would end it all.

"Please not sleep," Victor pleaded, and I glanced back over at him. "You think I can be forgiven? By Him?" He nodded toward the sky.

"I can't speak for the great man upstairs, but from what I've heard, forgiveness is His specialty." I rolled toward Victor, not because I felt like engaging, but rather out of an attempt to find a position that didn't shoot splinters up my back. Though, that side wasn't a lick better.

"Any tips?" Victor asked, obviously noticing me fidgeting. "What to say to be forgiven?"

"Maybe say you're sorry. But I'm about the last person with an answer to that."

"No, you perfect. When you plan to see your son, you want to be forgiven, yes? So what you think to say to him?"

"Can we deal with one issue at a time? For now, let's worry about getting some shut eye."

To be honest, I hadn't thought about what I'd say to Tyler. Just getting the chance to see him in the first place was enough of an ordeal, so my plan was the same as always, wing it and hope for the best. Not that this had done me any good in the past, but if Tyler wanted me to ask for his forgiveness, I'd do it. Hell, I'd do anything for that boy.

"Russ," Victor began again after a brief moment of silence, but I interrupted.

"Go to bed. Ain't nothing more to say."

"So you no talk?"

"Yes, I no talk."

To emphasize the point, I swung onto my back, which was about as comfortable of a position as I could muster. I yawned and stretched, but the woozy trance of sleep remained elusive. My mind wouldn't settle. I kept mulling over the idea of forgiveness, its meaning, and how Tyler would react to seeing me. That bothered me even more than those sadistic men. They were easy. I could just jump down and die. I didn't have the faintest clue where to begin with Tyler.

How could I explain my past? What reasons could I give for taking that toddler's life? For abusing all those girls? Some monsters couldn't be forgiven. We just survived.

I guess that was enough. It had to be, at least for tonight. I rolled over and glanced at Victor. I guess talking wasn't such a bad alternative considering my careening thoughts. At the least, I could match his morbid offer, and inform him he could eat me if I was the first to go. It wasn't much of a conversation starter, but it was something.

Victor remained upright with his back pressed to the railing, but his eyes were closed as he puttered in shallow snores. I lacked the heart to rouse him, especially with *that*, so I sat up and waited for him to stir. And I waited, and waited some more.

Monday 12:18 A.M.

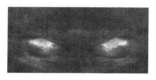

Midnight passed and Victor hadn't blinked once, forget waking long enough to hold a conversation. He continued in that choppy panting, almost breaking into a deep snore on a few occasions, but never quite inhaling enough to calm his rattling lips. I blamed his wheezing for my inability to sleep, but the truth was I couldn't shake the memory of chasing the Honda and that odious crash.

Victor's words had toppled over me like a plunging comet, and I was unable to shake the notion I might someday be judged for that toddler's death. This shook me worse than even the idea of galloping through those pigs in a suicidal race. At least that made sense. A final punishment for my misspent life. That had meaning, while deriving any significance from the crash was futile, especially considering what followed.

How could I justify that? Five additional children killed along with over a dozen adults. It was incomprehensible on its face and that wasn't counting the numerous other lives shattered in the periphery. And through the entire fiasco, I escaped relatively unpunished.

Sure, that dead-eyed bastard knew the score and took my family, so perhaps that was my penalty. Even so, I could never quite square that circle in my head. Every time I raced around that track, attempting to find any meaning, I always ended right where I'd started, only a bit dizzier for the journey. That never stopped me from spending countless hours looping the scenario over and over, trying my best to tell the lies from the half-truths from the absolute bullshit.

I guess the reason for the difficulties was on account that the lies began right away. Hell, I started spinning my story while still pinned inside that cab. My very first thought as the glass settled across the floor-mat was how I would unlink myself from those teenagers. If the police discovered that red Honda, I was screwed.

Not only would that connect me to the drugs and illicit money, but no fib in the world would be enough to explain away how an underage girl ended up alone in my sleeper, not to mention how she'd gotten all bashed apart. The fact they were thieves hardly mattered, since a single glance at that gash across the beauty's forehead and any jury would convict me faster than a bell clapper up a goose's ass.

So even while pinned, I contemplated the possibilities. As long as I didn't mention the Honda; that might give those weasels enough time to disappear. The kids had scored big, so I doubted they were going to get chatty, unless they were stupid enough to get pinched. I couldn't control that, not while stuck in my cab, so I focused on the things under my command.

One troublesome detail did emerge. The girl's gun, the one I'd kicked underneath the seat, was a direct link. If legal, even the most bungling detective would use it to track the girl down. If not, I was in possession of an illegal firearm. Both possibilities would usher in a larger investigation than a simple jackknifed tractor-trailer, especially if ballistics determined the gun had been fired.

So I pushed through the throbbing agony and wedged myself as far as I could reach. I patted across the shattered glass, stretching so far my shoulder felt like it might pop out. After a dozen frantic passes, my hand looked like it'd been through a meat grinder. Worse, I didn't find a single trace of the gun.

Not only was I pinned, but both doors were jammed, so it took over an hour using the jaws-of-life to free me. During the whole ordeal, I thrashed and pounded my arm, both in reaction to the pain and in order to maintain consciousness. By the time I was yanked free, I was rambling sounds more animal than human. The only comprehendible thing I managed was a demand for painkillers, which the EMTs were happy to oblige. However, not before a blood sample was drawn.

By the time I reached the hospital, I was so pumped full of pills, I couldn't remember anything other than a loopy blur. When I did regain my senses, I was handcuffed to a hospital bed. It wasn't long after that when the detectives strolled by for a little chat.

Of course, the toxicology report tested positive for cocaine, which came as no surprise, since by that point I'd been smoking crack almost daily for over a year. The detectives informed me that my CDL had been yanked, but as worries went, my job was low on the list. I hate to admit it, but my primary concern was wondering how I could obtain some crack while being detained. I was still a bit loopy and almost asked the detectives where to score, but my better judgment won out.

I kept my trap shut, but the detectives didn't. They had a whole scoopful of scorn topped with some bullshit sprinkles. They began by explaining how in California, where the accident occurred, they didn't monkey around with firearm violations. I immediately recalled the girl's gun, wondering if they'd located her as well. If so, I was so far up shit creek even a destroyer couldn't tug me free.

The detectives asked if I had anything to say in my defense, but I only smirked and tipped my head back. It was the same tactic I used when dealing with Patti's suspicious questioning. I hoped, similar to her, they'd get frustrated and give up.

Of course, any fool would've know they wouldn't, but that didn't stop this one from trying. I wish I could've blamed it on the painkillers or withdrawing from crack, but really, by that point, my arrogance was so ingrown the only thing I could really see was the shine from my asshole.

That certainly didn't throw the detectives. They explained how my Kansan conceal-carry permit didn't extend across state lines, which was excellent news since that meant they were referring to my .45 rather than the girl's gun. My grin widened, which only infuriated the detectives more, since they wanted to throw that fear of God into me before offering up themselves as my sole salvation.

The whole routine was so predictable that I soon got bored. One of the detectives, the one playing the role of the harsh interrogator bad cop, noticed my dismissive look, and yelled that carrying a loaded weapon was a felony and he could lock me away for decades. I told him to lower his tone and asked for my lawyer, who'd happily hammer out the details. I provided the name of one I'd never met, but had been recommended by the Nigerians in case I ever encountered a pickle exactly like this.

I'd assumed my request for a lawyer would've shut up the detectives, but it had the opposite effect. The mean one said I would sure need a lawyer, especially considering the charges for second-degree murder. For the life of me, I don't know why they didn't lead with that, probably some investigatory technique to throw me off balance.

It worked. I bit at my lip and shook my head in confusion. *Murder*? That hadn't been on my checklist of evil. I asked him to repeat himself. The detective grinned, the only time he displayed any emotion, while relaying how a minivan with a twenty-eight year old woman at the wheel had smashed into my trailer, killing her along with her three year old daughter who was seated in the rear. He repeated their ages a couple of times, ensuring it sunk in.

It didn't end there. They worked me hard with all sorts of talk of butchery, mangled limbs, and dismembered baby toes. By the time my lawyer arrived, I was convinced the next stop on this crazy train was death row, and it took him a good twenty minutes to walk me back. He explained how the detectives were only trying to extract a half-baked confession and as long as I kept my trap shut, justice would be served. I sure didn't believe him at the time.

The first stroke of luck arrived the next day when my lawyer informed me there wasn't a single piece of evidence linking me to the two teenagers. They must've snatched the girl's gun while fleeing with my duffel-bag, since my .45 was the only one discovered in the wreckage. It didn't help that I'd kept it loaded, since they added another felony charge to the laundry list.

My lawyer was peeved at this, but I didn't really care as long as those pesky murder charges were still hanging around my neck like a noose. In my mind, there was no way to avoid being locked inside a cage for many, many years.

So when my lucked turned again, well, I still have trouble believing what happened next. I discovered I wasn't the only one who'd had a blood sample taken at the scene of the accident. The woman who'd been driving the minivan, even though she was a corpse afterwards, tested positive for a blood alcohol level of .084. Go science!

There were some questions over the accuracy of the test, but when the friend she'd visited that night was subpoenaed, she admitted the woman had drank three glasses of wine. Hearing this, my lawyer erupted in joy. Sure, it was only a notch above the legal limit, but over was over, and the prosecutors were forced to drop the murder charges.

Of course, not everyone was ecstatic about this turn of events, and the prosecutors added charges of reckless endangerment and criminal negligence. My lawyer was furious and insisted to the judge these additional charges were out of a personal spite, declaring the law was the law and nothing more. He demanded blind justice, proclaiming he'd reveal the entire truth. I had no idea where the Nigerians mustered up such a fire-breathing fella, but I can't say I was disappointed.

My lawyer scoured through the footage of the highway cams from that evening and it didn't take him long to discover that busted up red Honda. I told him to back off, admitting to everything, but he reassured me all would be fine. I really do believe he convinced himself of that, though I'm sure the money helped grease those levers.

But all was far from fine. Since the accident, I hadn't been able to sleep more than an hour before being jostled awake. The guilt over that toddler's death haunted me worse than a ghost, churning out nightmares as I slept and a throbbing anxiety while awake. Half of me wanted to just fess up to the entire affair, hoping the exposure would alleviate my demons.

My lawyer would have none of it. He demanded I stick to the plan and I relented, even going as far as to engage in his wacky no-sugar vegan diet in order to appear "healthy and vibrant" if the case should go to trial. It did make me feel more positive, though I was hungry a lot of the time.

I hung in there, and lightning struck again when my lawyer discovered the red Honda had been reported stolen. That, along with their big score, ensured those teenagers would never turn themselves in to testify against me. The police did conduct a cursory investigation to determine their identities, but came up short. Only after the dead-eye man's visit did I learned the true fate that befell those kids.

As the police searched for them, my lawyer gathered up statements from anyone else in the area from that night. He got most to confirm the stolen Honda had driven out of control, swerving from one side of the highway to the other in a haphazardly manner.

Out of this, he spun a yarn, declaring the reason I'd chased after this wild driver, who was most likely drunk, and put my life at risk, was in an attempt to force him off the road. From the highway cam evidence, it almost appeared like that was indeed the truth.

He argued I was a hero, while the inept police still hadn't discovered the identity of the wild driver and probably would never find this menace. In order to deflect from their own culpability, they'd pinned all the blame on me. He kept spinning until I was so dizzy I almost forgot the truth myself.

He painted a vision of a world out of control, where maniacs, such as that teenage boy in the Honda, could act unrestrained while decent hard-working citizens, such as yours truly, were attacked. He told how I traversed these dangerous streets, risking my life at every turn, in order to deliver goods to places nobody sane would ever go.

He claimed this was the reason I carried a gun; that it was only for self-protection. That I always kept it locked in my sleeper, but it'd flown loose during the collision. He even found an expert in physics or such, to draw a diagram of the gun's movement across my cab. My lawyer stressed how it was legal in Kansas, how I'd never once shot it, and that it was only crime-loving coastal elitists who demanded drivers go unprotected.

As for the cocaine, (he always used the word cocaine, never crack) he argued that I was far from the first truck driver who'd fallen into the sticky trap of speed and uppers needed to maintain a hectic schedule. According to him, I was a victim of a crippling addiction and needed help in rehab, not punishment inside a cell.

After this performance, and boy was it one, my lawyer was convinced the judge would be forced to drop all the charges. As long as I dummied up and followed the script, I might even get my CDL back after a bit and return to the road sometime the following year.

I was far less enthused. Being shuffled from hospital to hospital, and then to a jail cell, had not only sobered me up, but got me thinking a lot about that three-year-old girl. She'd been just a few months shy of Tyler's age and this proximity was just too close to avoid seeing a connection. Call it God, or karma, or whatnot, but I'd been around far too long to ignore a sign like that.

So when the prosecutors offered a plea for one year, over my lawyer's spirited objections, I took it. The entire process lasted 107 days, cost three times as much as my house, and ate whatever savings I earned from dealing and hadn't smoked away. The 107, a combo of my time in the hospital and the local lockup, was subtracted from the year, leaving 258 days on my sentence. Since I'd pleaded to a first-time non-violent offense, I received probation after 129 days.

So, all in all, for smoking crack with an under-aged minor, beating her to a pulp, engaging in a reckless high-speed chase, and killing a young mother and her child, I spent a little over four months in prison. Justice served!

Little did I know, my punishment was yet to begin.

Monday 3:26 A.M.

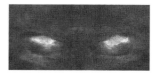 Victor died a minute ago. He wheezed one final time and his head slumped. Then silence. I staggered over, waiting for that puttering snore to return. When it didn't, I muttered his name twice. No reply. I tapped his shoulder with a sharp peck. Again, nothing. I grabbed his wrist. No pulse. When I released my grasp, his hand dropped onto the deck with a frigid *thunk*.

"No, Victor, come on," I pleaded. It was futile. Dead was dead.

My hands shook as I positioned him flat across the deck. As I inched back, his body drooped, sinking unnaturally deep into the rigid bars. I thought about our conversation from only a few hours ago. There was just something eerie about the way he'd predicted his death, but again, he'd also convinced himself there was an imaginary pig up here, so I tried not to read too deeply into it.

"No," I whined. "I can't do this alone. I can't."

I didn't have a choice. I yelled his name as if I did. Loud. Louder. The only reply came from the whispering night breeze.

I poked at his neck, searching for a pulse. Similar to his wrist, I found none. I opened his eyelids, knowing if any life remained, he'd squint them back closed. He didn't. I tapped his eyeball for one final morbid confirmation. It felt like a tiny bouncy ball that had been placed in a freezer.

No doubt, he was dead. Even so, my mind couldn't wrap itself around this truth. I blamed it on his vacant stare. It reminded me of the dead-eyed man, and that bastard had been quite alive. I made a promise. If Victor would sit up right now and grumble in that same hoarse voice, I'd confess everything.

Victor didn't move. He'd never move again. That curtain for the confession booth had slid shut. *A thing done was a done thing.* The dead-eyed man's words never seemed more appropriate. I hadn't understood them at the time, but sometimes the truth worked like that, mystifying and obscured, but similar to a trudging cancer, eventually it always clawed free.

I closed Victor's eyelids and sat beside him. I took his limp hand, gripping it so his chilled fingers drooped between my own. I bowed my head and inhaled. The air tasted muggy and sour. I squeezed my hand and a sweaty jolt slid across my palm. A spark of life? Was he in one of those dreaded blackouts? The lie smothered over me like a mother's embrace. Too often lies lined the sole path leading to the truth.

"You asked about the dead-eyed man," I began. "We weren't properly introduced until the day I got my walking papers."

I recalled my first night back outside in the free world, holed up in that cheap motel. A scraggly man with a long red beard had knocked on my door, informing me I had a call, so I'd assumed it was Patti. The first thing I did after getting out was to leave a message on her voicemail with the motel's name and number. Nobody else had it, so I was surprised when a deep raspy voice spoke on the other end.

"A thing done was a done thing. I've got my boots laced and I'm coming for you," he'd said before hanging up.

As threats went, it was a bit too vague to be taken seriously. Nor was it unexpected, since in my newfound sobriety, I was aware of the scores of lives I'd ruined with my havoc. Plus, any real threats came in the form of action, rather than words. More than anything, I lacked the will to be scared. I was so low at that point, I wouldn't have resisted anyone who came to settle the score. Hell, I might've offered a helping hand.

The doc later clarified this was only another part of my addiction, the desire for self-punishment, which could be just as powerful as any drug. Even that didn't exactly ring true, since my only overriding emotion was disappointment. I'd really wanted that call to be Patti. I'd missed her so much during our time apart, and this was only amplified now that I was sober.

I'd called her throughout my legal troubles, but she'd stopped answering after I took the plea and was transferred to a state facility. Unlike federal prisons, mine didn't allow email, so a phone call was my only option. Worse, if she didn't answer, I couldn't leave a message. Up to then, I'd figured the reason she'd dodged my calls was because she didn't want to pony up for the collect charges, but after my release, she still failed to answer. At least I could leave a voicemail now that I was out, but it became apparent she was evading those as well.

Salvaging my marriage became my top priority, so I called day after day to no avail. I kept leaving genial messages, but I wanted to speak to her directly and warn about the threats. The dead-eyed man's had been the first, but they kept coming like a tidal wave of rancorous revenge. I didn't care what happened to me, but I didn't want either her or Tyler to be harmed for my stupid blunders.

When my calls continued to go unanswered, even after I purchased a burner phone with an area code from Missouri, I realized she was never going to pick up. I argued with my parole officer, demanding I be allowed to travel back to Kansas. I promised I'd check in with whoever he wanted, take any drug test, and even spend my nights in a local jail, but my every request was denied.

As I waited out the parole, I began my court-ordered job hanging billboards. The work was tolerable enough, but in the boredom, I kept mulling over the situation. I came to the realization Patti was dodging my calls because of another man. I despised the idea, which only cemented it further, and envisioned all sorts of wicked things. To tone down my anger, I pretended the reason was purely financial, since the trial had bled away all my funds, but that was like putting a tissue over a vat of boiling tar and hoping it'd be enough to prevent a spill.

I might've been able to excuse her, especially considering my own failings when it came to desire, but Tyler was another matter. Even though I'd never met this stranger who'd taken over my place, or knew for certain if he existed, I grew to detest him. Stealing a woman was despicable, but again, I'd done the same with Patti, however, denying a man from seeing his son was downright unforgivable.

So I made a promise. I'd allow those evil hankerings one final chance to tear free. I vowed to the darkness once I met this malicious fella, I'd be the last person he'd ever see.

The day I received approval to leave the state, I bought a bus ticket, and by that evening, I was plunked down in a lumpy seat, inhaling the stench of diesel, urine, and greasy B.O. The fragrance of my liberation. I wish my newfound freedom was accompanied with high-minded thoughts, but I switched black.

So when Patti opened our front door, before any hellos, hugs, or honeyed words, I yelled, "Where is he?" She gasped, unable to muster a single word. Thankfully this paralysis allowed me to storm inside, otherwise I'm certain she would've slammed the door in my face. As I marched from room to room, searching for any sign of this interloper and finding none, I heard Patti stumble and collapse onto the floor.

I rushed downstairs and found her in the kitchen, sobbing and curled into a fetal position. Instead of helping her up, I demanded she reveal where he was hiding. She only shook her head, turning up the waterworks until eyeliner spilled down her cheeks like cold coffee. I slammed my fist against the counter. She screamed. Then I collapsed beside her.

We held each other for a long time, silent except for our collective tears. I was shaking, so she wrapped around me, tugging close. For the first time in years, I felt safe, comforted, and more than anything, special. I realized I'd forgotten how good felt. I'll never know why I decided to open my stupid mouth, but I did. I guess the doc was right about self-destruction being another form of addiction.

I asked again who he was, and she shoved me away. I scrambled back, though I kept pressing with the questions, needing to know why she'd failed to return my calls. Through the tears, she told me it was because she never wanted to see me again. Not after what I'd done.

I lunged up and snapped she had no right to do that. I hollered I was Tyler's dad, so even if she didn't want no more of me, I had a right to see my son. That no outsider could stop me. That denying this was a form of child abuse. Patti flicked away her tears and screamed that I, of all people, had no right to say anything about child abuse. That I hadn't been much of a father before, so there was no reason to start now.

Her words stung. Out of a blind rage, I kicked, rocketing the kitchen table onto its side. The glass mantelpiece, the one her grandma had bequeathed to us on our wedding day shattered across the linoleum. That hadn't been my intention, but it was what happened. I demanded she answer my question about this other man, yelling I was owed the truth.

Patti shook her head and stood. She shuffled away from the overturned table, careful to avoid the glass spread across the floor. She stopped at the door, turned back toward me, sighed, and proceeded down the hallway.

I didn't follow. I swung toward the overturned table, and though heavier than I expected, I managed to pull it back upright. The broom was in the same closet where it'd always been, so I began to sweep up the glass shards.

My outburst had even shocked me, so I couldn't blame Patti for the rapid retreat, but I was surprised when she returned less than a minute later. She glanced at the table, which was back in place, nodded, and dropped an oversized manila folder onto the wooden surface. She motioned for me to sit, so I leaned the broom against the counter and pulled up a chair. She did likewise and slid the folder across to me.

I looked inside. The folder was filled with photographs, those massive prints they sometimes showed in movies, but I'd never seen in real life. Who even had actual photos these days? Patti had a digital camera, but had never shown any interest in photography, so I wondered if her new man was one of those hippie-dippy artistic types. The thought repulsed me, but when I peered down at the photos, a far worse reality emerged.

My heart pounded like a grenade was lodged in my chest as I shuffled through them. The first print was of a truck-stop and it took me a moment to recognize it. I believe it was outside of Atlanta, but before I could confirm, I noticed my rig parked in the corner. I stared closer, and though blurry, I was in the photo too, bent against the truck. And I was smoking crack.

The next one was worse. The framing was closer, so I couldn't tell the location, but my smirking face was unmistakable. I had my arm around a trixie who was kissing my neck while seated in my lap. My other hand was thrust underneath her blouse, groping in an indisputable act.

I shuffled to the following photo, then the one after that. In some, I was buck naked, while in others, I was clothed, but quite clearly selling drugs. There were girls of every type, some older, some clearly younger, and some I didn't remember at all, but there was no arguing the point. It was me.

I opened my mouth to speak, but it felt like a blazing piece of charcoal was lodged over my tongue. I jammed the photos back into the manila folder as if making them disappear would erase the vile history.

Patti asked what I had to say for myself. Lying was out of the question, so I pleaded, begging for her forgiveness. I repeated what my lawyer had said about being an addict, how it was a disease, how this wasn't me, not my true self. How I was now sober and would never do anything to hurt her ever again. How I loved her and only her. Forever.

Patti only sighed, not believing a single word. She leaned her head down and said she could perhaps forgive a single dalliance, but not seventeen. She must've stared at those photos plenty of times to know the exact number right off the top of her head like that. I didn't dare mention there'd been many more.

She pitched her neck back and hollered that some of the girls looked like they hadn't even reached puberty. I just sat there as she yelled, cried, and yelled some more. I waited until she puttered out and could only whimper the same dreadful points in a broken repetition. Then I muttered I was sorry.

Hearing me must've rekindled that spark, since she added how furious she was that I'd accused her of being with another man on consideration of my own misdeeds. She hollered the word "projection" over and over like a barrage of missiles. She said she'd sworn off men altogether, and Tyler's main male influence was a daycare worker whom he sometimes called "Daddy" by accident. Out of everything, that hurt the most.

After that, she leaned back in her chair and spoke in a slow and serious tone that signaled only one thing. I'd used this same voice while breaking up with all sorts of girls in my youth. She said I was no longer welcome and I couldn't see Tyler anymore on account of my immoral character. She mentioned how she'd consulted a lawyer and with my felony conviction, along with those photos, she could easily win custody. The only result of taking her to court would be to publicize those rotten images. Best I skedaddle and never look back.

I didn't need a second peek in that manila folder to know she was a hundred percent correct. I rose, said I understood, and slunk out the door.

Before I returned to California, she contacted me once more at the friend's house where I was staying. Unlike that initial explosion of emotions, she kept to that matter-of-fact tone, never once yelling, crying, or even spitting a single insult. Perhaps it was on account of my friend being there, but I doubted it. She'd moved on. Damn, she'd moved on.

She had another manila folder, this time it was normal sized, but the contents were just as disturbing. Inside were the divorce papers, along with a document giving her sole custody over Tyler. I promised to sign if I could see him one final time. She agreed, but only if I said my goodbyes at her parents' house under her mother's watchful eye. I agreed and we shook hands like this was some fucking business transaction. That was the last time I saw Patti in person.

Her mom was just as expected, lizard cold and twitchy as if she were guarding the nuclear launch codes. The entire time she stood in front of the door like I might just grab Tyler and make a final dash for it. The way she scowled with her arms crossed made me want to do exactly that, but I handed her the signed legal papers and said my goodbyes. Tyler told me once he thought he remembered that visit, but I doubt it. He was just too young and appeared far more interested in his toy truck.

It wasn't until I was plopped back on that dingy bus, breathing in the urine-soaked air, when I had to chance to muddle through the entire affair. I wondered how the photos had ended up with Patti, since she sure as shit hadn't taken them. But then, who had?

My first thought was that somewhere in my transgressions, I'd hooked up with some fella's sweetheart and this was part of his revenge. However, the photos had been from all over the country, so he'd have to be one well-traveled cuckold, which meant time and money. None of the girls I knew had either.

Perhaps this was the Nigerians' final insurance policy, a reminder if I didn't keep my mouth zipped, those photos could end up with the law. I hadn't been in prison long, but one hour was enough to know cho-mos were considered subhuman and treated as such. Had this been their play after I took that plea bargain over my lawyer's objections? My goodbye retirement package from the drug business?

I recalled that peculiar call on my first night out, his deep raspy voice, and that silly warning over lacing his boots. Did that have a connection to the photos? As I rode west, question after question peppered through me, and I wished to discover any answers. Even a single one might lead me toward redemption, to my family, to Tyler.

God, what a stupid wish. If only that dead-eyed bastard had kept the entire affair to himself. But he couldn't. Wouldn't. I was floating on the healing power of redemption, but that was like a mosquito compared to the soaring hawk-like strength of revenge.

I usually ignored any phone numbers I didn't recognize, but for some reason I didn't that day. I'd spent the entire afternoon hanging billboards in the scorching summer heat, so my head wasn't a hundred percent on par, and I decided to answer. The call registered as *restricted*, but Tyler had grown into a little tech genius, so I'd hoped it was him.

I didn't recognize the hoarse voice at first. Only later, after our meeting, did I connect it with that cryptic one from my first day out. The voice sounded so odd that I pegged him for a foreign telemarketer and almost hung up before listening to what he had to say. Then he told me he was the one who'd given Patti the photos.

I almost dropped the phone. I steadied enough to listen as the peculiar voice continued. He said he knew everything about me; that I'd piqued his interest for years; that he wanted to tell me more but couldn't over the phone. He told me to meet him outside Quik Kluk, a fast-food joint a block away from the shabby studio apartment where I lived. Before I could agree, he hung up. Not that it mattered. Both of us knew I'd be there.

Before rushing out the door, I grabbed a boning knife, and tucked it underneath my shirt. As I arrived at the Quik Kluk, the first thing I noticed was a gray Buick parked on the far side of the lot. All those paranoid thoughts raced back as I rounded the corner out front. The outdoor tables were free of customers. All but one.

As I approached, my hand hovered over the spot where I'd hidden the boning knife, the bald man seated at the table stared up at me. He had a bushy black mustache and was a bit overweight for his snug attire. Though, what caught my attention was his eyes. They were listless, unmoving, dead.

"Hello, Russ," he said in that raspy tone. "Lucky I ain't wearing my boots today."

Hearing this peculiar comment, I couldn't help from peeking at his feet. Indeed, he wasn't wearing boots, but rather a pair of shining black loafers. Boots would've been a better fit for his outfit, which consisted of a wrinkled button-down cowboy shirt and faded navy-blue slacks. I nodded anyhow and took a seat across from him.

"I've been watching you for a long, long time."

He grinned, while staring at me with those deep inset eyes. I was spooked, so I gripped the handle of the boning knife. The dead-eyed man slammed a gun onto the table and spun it around with his index finger. I released the knife and placed both my palms onto the metallic grill of the tabletop. He stopped twirling the gun.

"Do you think you're clever?" he asked.

I shook my head. I'd been called many things throughout the years, but clever wasn't one of them.

"Look me in the eye." He said this as if I had any choice in the matter. Staring away from those pitch-black orbs would've been next to impossible. They were dead, but entrancing. Strange how that worked.

"I need you to know it was me. I was the one who destroyed your life. I was the one who had you fired. I was the one who took your family. I brought your annihilation, you monster."

"I don't know what-"

"Don't insult me," he interrupted. He slammed a thin wallet next to his gun and flipped it open. His credentials flashed for only a moment, before he snapped it closed. It wasn't enough time to catch the dead-eyed man's name, I think he might've had his thumb over it, but I did catch one word. It read FBI.

"I don't have nothing to say to you." I stood.

"That's fine by me." The dead-eyed man grabbed his gun. "But I have something to say to you."

I paused. Shit, the feds. Shit. Shit.

He motioned to take a seat. I did. His hand remained on gun as he reached into a leather satchel at his side. He removed a large manila folder, similar to the one Patti had. No doubt, he was the source of those incriminating photos. Damn, what other evidence did he have against me? This was a set up.

"Look inside," the dead-eyed man ordered.

I opened the folder, same as I'd done with Patti. This time the photos were worse, far more gruesome. There were pictures of all sorts of gore, everything from graphic bullet wounds, to brutal beatings, to corpses that were too disgusting for even a zombie movie.

I felt like vomiting while looking at them, but I flipped through with careful deliberation, taking my time. My mind raced, puzzling it all out. The sole good thing was that I had nothing to do with these crimes, so at least that was something. No underage girls, no dealing illegal drugs, no me at all.

I figured this was his opening in order to demonstrate the brutality of the Nigerians. A feeble attempt to play on what remained of my consciousness. He wanted to flip me. Turn me into a snitch. If so, it wouldn't work. If those photos were any indication of the fury of my former employers, getting shot by the dead-eyed man was a far better option.

"Recognize those two?"

The dead-eyed man slid one of the photos out from the others. I shook my head, though I knew the teenagers. They were the boy and girl who'd robbed me. The ones in that red Honda. In the photo, they were pulverized, having endured a vicious beating. The boy was missing part of his jaw and bone stuck out from the pulpy stump. The gash on the girl's forehead where I'd beaten her was larger while her eyes were also gouged out. The empty sockets reminded me of the man seated across the table.

"You know them. Both of us know you know. But I don't need to hear you admit that. I also know you gave the order to have them executed. We monitored your every communication while you were in the hospital."

He was baiting me. I didn't have those kids killed. He wanted to hear me deny it. I refused to play his fucking game.

"So you're here to arrest me," I said.

"I thought you had nothing to say."

"I don't."

"Then zip your ball washer and let me finish."

It took me a moment to realize by ball washer, he meant my mouth. When it did click, I almost chuckled, but when he slid over the next photo, any humor evaporated. In it, a young girl had a bullet hole lodged in the center of her forehead.

"How old do you think she is?"

"I wouldn't dare to guess."

"Nor did you the night you slept with her." The dead-eyed man slammed his fist against the tabletop. It thrummed a reverberating rattle as he continued. "She was going to testify against you, but before she could, she committed suicide. Or was "suicided." The local boys mucked up the forensics so much we can never be certain."

"I have to leave." I attempted to shove my chair back, but realized it was bolted to the ground.

"Her name was Sydney Byrd. Just so you know. She wasn't just a fuck toy. She was a child. You killed a child."

I didn't recognize her. Not at all. I would've, I told myself. I would've remembered that face.

I might not have.

The dead-eyed man flicked the gun so the barrel was aimed at me. Christ, he didn't want to flip me. He thought I was responsible for all this. I'd always assumed the Nigerians, or whoever ran things, just had a talent for bribing the right people. I never realized this was how they cleaned up the messes. I thought about all those warnings I'd given about suspicious vehicles. If this was the result, no wonder they'd grown sick of my whining.

But the Nigerians weren't my concern. If the dead-eyed man hadn't come to get me to snitch, he had another plan. This was the warning. His boots were laced and he intended to kill me.

"Peculiar how my every witness against you ended up disappeared or dead. Guess you must be one lucky fella," the dead-eyed man continued.

"I'm, I'm not feeling good," I stammered.

That much was true. My stomach wrenched staring at a photo of a tommy I'd known quite well; one I considered a good pal. The Nigerians must've felt differently, since his mouth was slashed from ear to ear in a Glasgow smile. That way, with every scream, the

251

wound had torn wider. Damn, I knew I'd asked the questions, but staring down at those grisly photos, I wish the answers hadn't found me.

"Trust me. They feel worse." The dead-eyed man grabbed the nape of my neck and forced my head down. "Eighteen in total. Look, damn it. Look! Five are children for Christ's sake."

I closed my eyes. He shoved me away. I toppled onto the sidewalk. The boning knife slipped out, dinging as it slid across the concrete. Both of us stared at it.

"Go fetch," he dared. "Just give me an excuse, monster."

"Don't kill me." I remained still, arms locked to my side.

"I don't need your soul weighing on mine," he replied, turning away. "You fucks never think about that, do you?"

I motioned to stand when he whirled back around. I flinched, believing he held the gun in his outstretched arm. Instead, he tossed the manila folder at me. The photos flopped in the breeze, scattering all around. I held motionless, not even inching enough to move the one clinging to my shirt. In it, a girl's severed head was lying in a drainage pipe.

"You remember them," the dead-eyed man continued. "Because they'll remember you. Have fun in hell, you fuck."

I remained frozen in that precarious position until the dead-eyed man stomped away. Only then did I brush off that photo of the girl's severed head. I wish I could say I stuck around long enough to gather up the photos before any families happened to stroll by for a quick bite, but I didn't.

I ran. And I ran fast.

I didn't stop running until I was back safely nestled inside my studio apartment. Even there, I couldn't stop pacing. I feared the dead-eyed man was on his way to finish the job he failed to do at the Quik Kluck.

He never arrived. That was the last time I ever stared into those dead eyes. Nor did I ever spot his gray Buick again. I believe that was his punishment for me. He was correct. I remember. I can't forget. Every single day, I remember.

Even tonight, as I waited for those creeps to return, the memory haunted me. As I finished my confession, I relaxed my grasp on

Victor's limp hand. His soft fingers wobbled in my palm like jelly. Christ. Jelly. *Jelly*!

I licked my lips. He'd given his permission. Said it'd be fine. Not only that, he'd said it was his wish. His dying wish. So how wrong could it be? Just a nibble. One little nibble to get me through the night. Through this demon bitch of a night.

"No!" I hollered.

The noise roused a couple pigs and they began to trample below. Something about that grunting stampede knocked my head back into reality. I dropped Victor's hand. I stepped back.

The truth was I was going to join him tomorrow. My only choice was how I wanted to die.

I closed my eyes and counted down. That would hold off the evil hankerings for one final night. That had to do the trick. Right, Doc? Right?

I made it to zero, but the temptation remained. I was so damn hungry. So fucking hungry. I began to count up.

How many seconds remained until sunrise?

Too many to count, just too many.

Monday 7:04 A.M.

 A buzz blared. I bolted up. To say I awoke would be a lie, instead, I returned. I swung around, attempting to discover the source. I recognized the sound. It was the alarm on my wristwatch. I'd set the silly thing as a reminder of my scheduled arrival in Kansas. Fuck. Before all this, my greatest fear had been falling asleep on the bus and missing my exit, but those worries now seemed as silly as a bull modeling a tutu. I slapped my wrist, silencing it.

Victor's limp arm rested in my lap. I didn't recall sleeping a single wink the entire night, but neither did I remember placing his arm there. I craned over to peek at him, wondering if I'd been mistaken over his passing. His puckered gray skin, sunken chest, and putrid odor confirmed he was dead. No doubt about it.

I winced. Had I, the thought repulsed me, but had I? Unlike setting the alarm on my watch, one wasn't liable to forget eating another human being. Right? The thought caused my stomach to churn, erupting a searing agony all the way to my wilted mouth. I spat, but nothing emerged. Outside of counting, I couldn't recollect much of the night. How could that be?

I raised Victor's arm, but rather than searching for a pulse, I flipped it over, examining for any bite marks. None. That much was good. I tossed it onto his huddled corpse. My stomach groaned, flipping from a charring boil to a rolling vacuum. I licked my lips as images of cake, donuts, and pie flickered in my mind. I hadn't eaten any of that sugary crap in years, not since I'd decided to change my life, but I couldn't stop thinking about them. They sounded like bliss.

But I didn't have any of that shit. What I did have was a corpse. I muttered Victor's name as if he might lurch up as an undead ghoul, relieving me from this ghastly decision. My voice barely emerged from between sticky gums, sounding foreign and separate. Victor offered no reply. No, he'd never utter a single sound ever again.

I pawed at his body, jerking it toward me. I pretended I was searching for any abrasions while patting across his mushy skin. Any evidence of my evil hankerings. Then I spotted it. My salvation. I dove in.

My tongue swiped, lapping up a sticky layer. It was true. This was no hallucination. The liquid danced through my mouth and pirouetted down my throat. I licked a second time. There was more. It coated the entire deck. The sun sparkled in the tiny droplets of morning dew.

I shoved Victor's body to the side and pressed to the deck as if embracing a lover for the final time. I lapped up the dew, sliding across one beam as far as my neck could reach before moving to the next. A metallic splinter lodged into my tongue, but I didn't slow any. Nor did I hesitate when reaching a spot coated with bird droppings. I wish I could say this filth caused me to gag, but I savored the moisture, only spitting the crusted portions after I'd soaked up every last droplet.

A bird chirped to my left, perhaps cheering on my humiliation. I flung up my arm, shooing it away. At that moment, I detested it even more than the pigs. What type of beast could shit everywhere without giving a second thought to the world around them? I cursed God for bestowing the stupendous gift of flight on such selfish and uncaring creatures.

As the vile bird fluttered off, I spotted dust in the distant pastures. It tracked in a straight line, moving parallel to a field of wheat, before curving onto the service road. A vehicle. I stood. The cloud raced closer. I raised my hand to shield the sun from my eyes. The shining front grill sparkled as the vehicle approached. No mistaking it. The cutaway van was returning.

Behind it, another half-dozen vehicles followed in a convoy. If I had any doubts concerning their identity or intentions, they evaporated as a volley of gunfire exploded out. They were too distant to be a threat, but I doubted that was the point. No, this was their twisted version of a wake-up call.

As a second barrage crackled, I looked over at Victor, almost needing his confirmation I should proceed. I chewed my lip and broke off a tough piece of skin, no longer tasting any remnants of the dew. I rubbed my hands together and nodded. It was time.

"Sorry it turned out like this," I muttered.

I tugged at Victor's safety harness. Unlike his floppy cadaver, the restraints clung like cement. They felt just about as heavy as I dragged him toward the ladder. I clipped into the safety line and attached Victor's carabineer to mine. I wondered if the rope could support our combined weight and chuckled. Not as if it mattered now. In a minute, I'd most likely be as dead as the corpse dangling from my harness.

My one real choice was how I wanted to go and I would not die up on this fucking billboard.

I did have one final scheme, though. I shoved. Victor toppled over the edge, whacking his head against one of the ladder's rungs before settling into a suspended mid-air pose. I'd planned on shooting off one final prayer before climbing, but his weight overtook me and I swooped off the side.

The safety catch reeled, hissing a dreadful grind, but held. I hovered a couple feet below the upper-deck, Victor's corpse tugging beneath me. I swung upright and wrapped my legs around the rope like a fireman's pole. With one hand I steadied Victor, with the other I clutched the safety catch. The rope nestled against the heel of my bare foot. I hit the catch, dropping us another couple feet.

As we descended, the rope snaked across my foot, biting a deep gash. A coating of blood dribbled out, but compared to the other sensations racking my body, I hardly noticed it. In fact, the blood worked as a lubrication, allowing me to zip faster down the rope. The descent grew quicker as I passed the lower deck. Then even faster. Half-way down. Flying. I hit the catch. I plowed to a stop just above the bottommost rung.

The pigs glared up. They squealed and stomped. Their slimy mouths chomped the air, eager for this breakfast treat. My hand shook, pawing the clasp linking my harness to Victor's. As soon as I clicked it, I'd have merely a second for the distraction. Not much of a head start, perhaps none at all, but it was what I had.

"If this works, you'll have my eternal gratitude," I said, leaning closer to Victor's dangling corpse. "If not, I'll see you soon. Good knowing you, amigo."

I grabbed Victor's wrist in a final parting handshake. I hit the release. He sagged in my clutch, dangling unrestrained. I held him as long as I could, only a couple seconds, before the weight grew too unwieldy. If I had the strength, I would've held on forever, but the decision slipped from my fingers.

He appeared to float for a moment. His arms swung up as if reaching back toward me. A pig rocketed up and bashed into his torso, flinging them both to the side. He crashed with a watery plop. The pigs swarmed. I steadied against the lowest rung, winding my toes around the metal. It was hot from the morning sun. I unclipped my carabineer. I inhaled a stale breath.

"Time to soar."

Then I leapt into the horde.

Monday 7:17 A.M.

 A wisp of dust puffed out as my feet hit the earth. I attempted to stand, but my knees buckled and I toppled over. Whatever momentary distraction Victor's corpse had provided wasn't enough. The pigs were everywhere. As I tumbled, I slid nose to nose with one.

It wheezed a squelching sound, giving me the impression it was as shocked to see me as I was to see it. I rolled to the side, hoping to dodge, but knocked into another pig. I collapsed. As I peered, all I could see was a blur of swinging snouts and huffing jaws. I shielded my face and awaited for the inevitable.

One pig trampled across my stomach, knocking out my wind. Another bashed against my side. The toasty breath of a third trickled across my outstretched toes. I wiggled them, not trying to avoid the bite, but rather to be doing anything other than just lying there.

The animal sniffed my foot twice and shuffled away. The one at my side likewise pranced back. None of the swine attacked. I lowered my arms and peeked. The pigs were circled around me, but only a few glanced in my direction. Even those appeared barely intrigued and soon lost interest. I didn't dare move, fearing I might rekindle their rage.

A pig to my right coughed, showering my shoulder with the neon-green snot, but staggered past. I glared in the direction where it was heading, fearing the cutaway van had arrived, but the lot was empty. Nor was the pig heading toward Victor's corpse, or what little remained of it. Instead, the silly creature plopped onto the dirt for a nap. I inched up, fearing any sudden movement might spark their attention, but the creatures continued to ignore me.

So I stood. Again, nothing. I spotted the cargo van. It appeared like a mirage, close enough to touch, but always a few steps out of reach. A pig galloped past my side toward an unremarkable spot on the far end of the lot. Not once did it turn in my direction as it ran. It was like I was invisible.

Or was I dead?

It didn't matter if I was a ghost. All that metaphysical shit could be worked out later. Right now, my sole desire was to get as far from these beasts as possible. I sprinted toward the van.

With my first couple steps, I feared being attacked, but when nothing happened, I increased my pace. As I drew within ten feet of the van, I even stopped trying to dodge and instead galloped straight into a group of pigs sleeping in a pile. They squealed and bucked as I stomped past their pudgy bodies, but none launched up to stop me.

Thank goodness, since it took three attempts to wedge the door open, mostly because my hand was shaking so hard. By the time I plopped onto the seat safely inside, I was convulsing so much it could've been mistaken for a seizure. I tapped my chest, but had trouble swallowing any more than a splinter of air. If I was dead, my ghost sure had the same pains as I had in life.

Idiot! In my mad dash, I'd gone to the vehicle without keys. I felt so foolish, especially after being so hard on Slake for making the exact same mistake. It'd all seemed so simple as a bystander, but swamped by those vicious creatures, every thought other than escape had vanished. The van had been closest, so that was where I'd gone.

I told myself to take a breather and think. I couldn't afford to repeat Slake's mistake and just jump out again. I peered into the rear of the van and remembered the cooler. I whirled it open and downed an entire bottle of water in a single gasp. About half of that reemerged with the next breath as I spewed. No matter, I felt fantastic and shocked the water remained cool this entire time.

The cutaway van would soon be here, and if I was anywhere nearby, they'd swoop me up. I had to leave, but not before grabbing my cell phone. I found Harley's vintage hat with its jumble of electronics and added a couple of waters along with a half-eaten granola bar I found on the dash.

After a rapid scan for anything else useful, I kicked open the rear door. A couple pigs peered up, but when I turned in the direction of the service road and spotted the approaching dust, I knew I didn't have time for their interest to wane elsewhere. I clutched the hat to my chest and jumped.

One bottle fell out as I landed, but I didn't even look at it. My eyes locked onto the pickup truck. A pig grunted as I knocked into it beginning to sprint. It didn't chase, nor did the others. That didn't stop me from racing as fast as my legs would allow.

I reached the truck in next to no time, amazed I had even that much gas remaining in my tank. This time, my hand was rock steady while opening the truck's door. The keys were in the ignition. I plopped into the driver's seat and cranked the engine. Unlike its typical grinding putter, the engine turned over on the very first try.

I spun around, hit the gas, and gunned across the lot. A group of swine scurried from my path. I wheeled onto the service road with a couple chasing right behind. After ignoring me for the entire time, I was kind of surprised any decided to pursue, but even they soon gave up as I accelerated across the gravel. By the time I passed the first intersection and peered into the rearview mirror, the dirt road was empty. No sign of the cutaway van either.

I rounded a bend and headed south. I hollered an ear-splitting whoop. I don't think I'd ever cheered as loudly in my entire life. Not when Patti agreed to marry me. Not when Tyler was born. Not even after my first hit of crack. This was a brand new high and I was loving it.

I passed three intersections, but didn't dare stop in case the convoy was hot on my heels. Every few seconds I'd peer behind me, half expecting to see the blazing grill of the cutaway van. I was doing this so much I almost drove smack dab into a roadblock.

I veered just in time to avoid colliding with a pair of wooden sawhorses spread across the road. Painted in a light, police-blue the words *DO NOT ENTER* were printed in block letters. I spun onto the shoulder, passing with room to spare.

To be safe, I drove for another ten minutes before spotting a dilapidated barn situated a ways down another dirt road. I turned at the intersection and slowed while approaching. The decaying barn looked abandoned decades ago, panels hanging like wet toilet paper and the shingles peppered with gaping holes. No vehicles parked anywhere, nor was there a house or any other sign of human life. Perfect.

I pulled up the driveway and passed a concrete foundation that likely served as a farmhouse once. Nothing remained now as I crept past the weedy lot and approached the barn. Most of the red paint along with some illegible graffiti had withered into nothing. One side was crooked, appearing moments away from collapsing. I parked in front of a tattered sliding door.

I exited the pickup and approached with caution, but to my surprise, when I yanked the sliding door, it churned open with no resistance. Inside, a dead owl littered the floor, but outside of that, the barn was empty. I kicked the creepy thing out of the way and cranked the door all the way open.

I ensured the service road was empty before reversing into the barn, sliding the door shut behind me and taking a moment to revel in the darkness. I didn't pause for long because I had to make a call. I shuffled through the hat and found my phone, but when I hit the power, I discovered it was dead. Ditto for the others.

I cursed and punched the steering wheel. I gobbled down the granola bar along with another water, hoping to clear my head. It worked, since I recalled how Slake always stored spare phone chargers in the glove compartment. He'd kept them for any guys who wanted to use the excuse of low juice to avoid his calls. I doubt anyone ever used them, since when I opened it, a puff of dust popped out along with a heaping tangle of wires.

For once, I praised Slake's anal nature, discovering a charger that fit my phone. When I plugged it into the slot for the cigarette lighter, my phone buzzed and glowed dimly. It was about half of its typical illumination, but none of that mattered as I dialed.

"Hello?" I said, as the connection clicked.

"Russ?" I instantly recognized the swaying pitch and throaty sound of Tyler's voice.

"Thank God, you picked up. I couldn't make it to Kansas, but hearing your voice is just as good." I grinned, leaning back against the headrest.

"I know, you missed the bus."

"Oh, it's so much more than that. We were attacked by pigs."

"Pigs? Come on, Russ." Tyler added a nervous laugh.

"I'm serious. Turn on the news. They've quarantined a portion of farmland around Highway 99 here in California."

"Hold on," he muttered. I heard the distinctive patter of typing on the other end.

"We were hanging a sign when this drift of pigs ran up and attacked one of our crew. Ate him all up. I'd never seen nothing like it before in my entire life."

"Drift?" Tyler asked, continuing to type.

"It don't matter. I've wanted to talk to you all weekend. You mean so much-"

"Just stop." The typing ceased, ushering an uneasy silence as I waited for him to continue. He sighed and grumbled something I couldn't quite hear.

"What's that?" I asked.

"What are you on this time?"

"I'm sober, I swear. I vowed to change and I have. This is real. Believe me."

"Man-eating pigs just happened upon you right before your trip. You want me to believe that? Is that what you need?"

"I need you to listen. I'm not lying or on drugs. We were attacked. Men are still out hunting for me."

"Okay, sure. Is there anything else, Russ?"

"I'm your pa. Can you call me that instead of Russ?"

"Really? That's what you care about? You're lucky I don't call you a wasted turd who binged away the weekend instead of coming here as you promised. And that's not to mention all the other shit you've pulled."

"Watch your language."

"Fuck off." Tyler paused, waiting for me to react, but I was at a loss for words.

"That's right," he continued. "Fuck you, *Russ*."

"Please, I'm sorry, but I'm telling the truth."

"That's why there's not a single mention of this quarantine on the internet."

"There's a cover-up. I saw a policeman killed. They took his car."

"Who killed this policeman?"

"The pigs did. Then these men came, but instead of rescuing us, they-" I paused, not wanting to sound even kookier while describing the SHARK races.

"Monster pigs, corrupt police, conspiracy theories. Why can't you just tell me the truth?"

"I'm not making this up!" I replied. "Do another search and I'm certain you'll find the truth."

"I don't need a search to know the truth. The truth is I barely know you. You're a stranger to me. Genetics, that's all our relationship is. And that's not enough to call yourself my father."

"It should be."

"It isn't."

The phone clicked off. Fucking teenagers. I started to countdown before redialing. When I reached fourteen, an itch climbed up the base of my nose. The sneeze was so powerful I almost lost my grip on the phone. I was about to count again when a second tickle forced an even larger explosion from my nostrils.

I wiped my face, noticing a long trail of snot. This time, I did drop the phone. Snot was everywhere, coating the dashboard like a spilled can of paint.

Worse, it was a bright neon-green.

About the Author

Drake Vaughn's *crinkled fiction* is a blend of horror, dark fantasy, and speculative fiction with a heavy psychological bent. His tales appear deceptively simple, but transform into a wild spree of suspense, madness, and trauma. He lives in Santa Monica, California with his wife and a black cat named Shadow (who he is certain has come back from the dead on a number of occasions).

More from Moon Lily Press

If you liked this book, you may like...

What would you die for?

   Samantha Danroe doesn't believe in magic. Her ex-husband cured her of happily-ever-after when he cheated on her three days after saying I-do.

   She doesn't believe in ghosts. Until her mother's ghost rises from a Halloween bonfire with a warning of death from beyond the grave.

   And she certainly doesn't believe in witchcraft. Until she becomes the prey in an ancient war waged between good and evil. A war whose rules she must scramble to learn to stay alive.

   In need of protection, Samantha turns to the mysterious Nicholas Orenda, a sixth-generation witch on the trail of a creature who is systematically killing off his family. According to his family's prophecy, three will be sacrificed to the dark. His mother and grandmother are already dead, and Nicholas doesn't have time to play by the rules.

   Samantha finds herself in the center of a deadly hunt for a mysterious foe. Can she find the strength to defeat a supernatural killer and prevent the third sacrifice? Or will she be the catalyst that opens the gates to the Underworld?

   Song of the Ancients is the debut book in the Ancient Magic series.

For more releases by Cactus Moon Publications, visit:
www.cactusmoonpublications.com

Made in the USA
Lexington, KY
20 November 2015